Hannah Dennison was born in Britain and originally moved to Los Angeles to pursue screenwriting. She has been an obituary reporter, antiques dealer, private-jet flight attendant and Hollywood story analyst. After twenty-five years living on the West Coast, Hannah returned to the UK, where she shares her life with two high-spirited Hungarian Vizslas in the West Country.

Hannah writes the *Honeychurch Hall Mysteries* and the *Vicky Hill Mysteries*, both set in Devon, as well as the *Island Sisters Mysteries*, set on the fictional island of Tregarrick in the Isles of Scilly.

www.hannahdennison.com
www.facebook.com/hannahdennisonbooks
www.instagram.com/hannahdennisonbooks
www.twitter.com/hannahldennison

Also by Hannah Dennison

Murder at Honeychurch Hall
Deadly Desires at Honeychurch Hall
A Killer Ball at Honeychurch Hall
Murderous Mayhem at Honeychurch Hall
Dangerous Deception at Honeychurch Hall
Tidings of Death at Honeychurch Hall
Death of a Diva at Honeychurch Hall
Murder in Miniature at Honeychurch Hall

The Island Sisters Mystery series

Death at High Tide
Danger at the Cove

The Vicky Hill Mystery series

Exclusive!
Scoop!
Exposé!
Thieves!
Accused!
Trapped!

A Killer Christmas at Honeychurch Hall

Hannah Dennison

CONSTABLE

CONSTABLE

First published in Great Britain in 2022 by Constable

A CIP catalogue record for this book is
available from the British Library.

ISBN: 978-1-40871-590-1

Typeset in Janson MT Std by SX Composing DTP, Rayleigh, Essex
Printed and bound in Great Britain by Clays Ltd, Elcograf S.p.A.

Papers used by Constable are from well-managed forests
and other responsible sources.

Constable
An imprint of
Little, Brown Book Group
Carmelite House
50 Victoria Embankment
London EC4Y 0DZ

An Hachette UK Company
www.hachette.co.uk

www.littlebrown.co.uk

For Lizzie Sirett
Editor of Mystery People *and much-loved friend*

Chapter One

Where on earth was Shawn? I'd dashed outside into freezing weather without a coat or my mobile. The message a friendly female police officer had given to me was that Shawn would swing by in ten minutes with a surprise just for me.

That was twenty minutes ago and I was getting cold and cross. Not only that, with Christmas just under a week away, today was one of the busiest days at Dartmouth Antique Emporium where I rented a space for Kat's Collectibles and Mobile Valuation Services.

When a biting rain mixed with snow began to fall, I gave up and headed back to the main entrance as a tide of carol singers in Victorian dress spilled out into the car park. Two were helping the elderly homeless woman we all knew as Annie to a bench. Dressed in a grubby pink Puffa and pink beanie hat, Annie looked bewildered.

I stopped the trio. 'What's happened?'

'She fainted,' said the woman. 'I asked Annie if she wanted an ambulance but she says she'll be fine. It gets very hot inside. Sorry,' gesturing to the troupe who were piling into a minibus with 'Dartmouth Carollers' written on the side, 'got to go. We're off to Kingsbridge now.'

When I turned to check on Annie, she'd disappeared.

Glad that she must be okay, I went back inside, wondering what had happened to my boyfriend.

The Emporium during the festive season was a magical fairyland and I loved working there. Heavily decorated with garlands of holly, fake snow, fairy lights and a plethora of Christmas trees, piped music was only silenced for daily performances from the local harpist, an a cappella choir, and wassailing carollers in Victorian dress in that order. The smell of mulled wine, roasting chestnuts and mince pies, handed out by seasonal staff dressed as elves, added the finishing touch.

My friend and colleague Di Wilkins rushed towards me. Her face was ashen. 'I've already called the police. They're on their way.'

'Annie doesn't want an ambulance— What?' I stopped. The look on Di's face made my stomach drop. 'What's happened?'

'Barbie's been stolen,' she blurted out. 'It must have happened when the carol singers came through. There was so much chaos! Annie fainted and—'

I didn't wait for Di to finish her sentence and pushed her aside in my haste to prove she was wrong. She had to be wrong.

When I'd run outside to meet Shawn, Di had promised to hold the fort.

My three-sided enclosure was close to the main entrance and kitty-corner to Di's where she sold vintage jewellery. Both had counters that fronted onto one of the many arteries that zigzagged through the converted barn. Access to mine was through a space just wide enough for one person to pass through.

I stared at the empty glass display box and felt sick. Someone had stolen a doll worth thousands and thousands of pounds not just in broad daylight but under Di's nose.

'I'm sorry,' Di whispered. 'You're insured, though, right?'

Of course I was, but that wasn't the point.

Emerald Barbie was headlining the Christmas Gala and Silent Auction at Honeychurch Hall in exactly five days' time. Worse, the doll wasn't even mine having been generously donated by Cathy White, a former colleague and fellow TV celebrity from my *Fakes & Treasures* days.

Barbie was not just an 'original' Barbie doll from 1959, she was called Emerald Barbie because the elaborate choker she wore around her neck contained a real emerald.

I had been so worried about the doll being stolen that every night, instead of trusting the Emporium's excellent security system, I'd taken Barbie home and locked her in my own safe. As well as CCTV cameras inside and outside the building, I had my own nanny-cam app on my mobile – I resolved to look at it as soon as I could – and was hopeful that at least one had captured the theft.

I'd known that publicising the doll had been asking for trouble. It had been the brainchild of the new power couple who had moved into Peggy Cropper's old cottage, on the Honeychurch Hall estate, to have Emerald Barbie as the star of the silent auction. After the cook's retirement, Ryan and Marion Cartwright had become the estate manager and head of house respectively. My mother called them Ken and Barbie

– not nicknames I could handle in the present circumstances – because they were so perfect and polished. The Cartwrights had worked for Hollywood celebrities, managed super-yachts and vast estates for the über-rich, and organised high-profile galas, festivals, week-long retreats and conferences.

Although Ryan was from California, Marion had been born in Devon and, according to my mother, who had her finger on all the gossip, wanted to come home because her mother was terminally ill. None of us thought they would stay for long – Ryan hated the cold – but the Cartwrights were certainly making their presence felt. The dowager countess, Lady Edith Honeychurch, loathed everything they stood for, and the couple's ostentatious marketing campaigns were putting many noses out of joint, including mine.

I'd had serious doubts about broadcasting the location of the doll before the gala, but Marion had insisted that the chance for people to see her close up would boost ticket sales. At a staggering £250 per ticket, I assumed they needed all the publicity they could get but I was wrong. With the promise of an appearance by a mystery celebrity, tickets quickly sold out, as did local accommodation in Airbnbs, pubs and hotels for those travelling from afar.

I whipped out my mobile and checked the nanny-cam. Unfortunately, I'd angled the lens towards the counter, which held small and easily pocketed items, like Steiff keyrings and miniature bears.

I looked at the narrow entryway that Di had promised to guard. 'How could anyone get past you?' I said.

'I don't know how it happened,' Di said. 'I was standing

right where you are now.' She reddened. 'Apart from when Annie fainted. It must have happened then – I moved but just for a minute.'

I gazed at her pale, elfin face. She looked thinner than ever in black skinny jeans, her red-and-green tartan holiday jumper embroidered with sleigh bells.

A mobile chirp interrupted my thoughts. It was Di's phone, but she let it ring. It stopped, rang again, then stopped and rang yet again.

'Aren't you going to answer that?' I said.

'It's just a sales call,' she said quickly. 'Don't you have sales calls?'

'But it might be the police,' I pointed out.

'It's not the police,' Di retorted. 'I told you. They're on their way.'

But when the phone rang again and she switched off the ringer, I wondered what was going on. Di seemed jumpy, too.

'Have you told Fiona Reynolds yet?' Just the thought of telling the owner and manager of the Emporium filled me with dread.

'Jesus, Kat,' Di snapped. 'It's just happened. Give me a chance.'

'All right. I'll go and tell her,' I said. 'Please stay here.'

I caught Fiona as she was coming out of her office. I had liked her the moment I'd met her. Mum said she reminded her of a military wife – efficient and brusque. She was friendly with everyone but close friends with none. Like me, she had not been keen to have such a well-publicised and valuable doll in the Emporium at the busiest time of the year.

Fiona wasted no time in enlisting her husband Reggie and some of the temporary workers – dressed as elves – to conduct a bag search of all shoppers leaving the building. 'I'm afraid it's a case of the stable door being bolted after the horse has gone,' she said. 'We'll have the footage to the CCTV cameras this evening. Any luck with your nanny-cam?'

I shook my head. 'Nothing.'

Fiona gave me a comforting smile. 'I'm sure Barbie will turn up. It's not the sort of thing you can sell on the street.'

I wasn't so sure. Unlike Sindy, Barbie's counterpart, original Barbie dolls had exploded in value. There would be plenty of takers on the black market.

Di left her post the moment she saw me coming back. 'Excuse me. I don't trust those girls,' she said. 'I wouldn't be surprised if one of them took it.'

Two girls in their late teens wearing jeans and long cardigans, their naked midriffs exposed, were sifting through a tray of earrings on Di's counter. They carried cloth bags large enough to hide a doll, but would anyone be that obvious? I didn't recognise them but when a third joined them, I relaxed. It was Willow Mutters, dressed in a sensible padded coat, her strawberry-blonde hair swept up in a high ponytail. Home from uni where she was studying criminology, Willow had been working for me. Her grandparents, Stan and Doreen Mutters, ran the Hare and Hounds in Little Dipperton. Willow's parents had died in a car accident when she was ten and she had lived with Stan and Doreen ever since. The trio shared a private joke, did the hugging and kissing thing, then Willow came over with her big smile.

With a nod to the two girls, she said, 'Kylie and Teresa want me to join them tonight but I'm working in the bar at the pub.' Willow put down a hessian shopping bag emblazoned with the image of Emerald Barbie – another marketing idea of the Cartwrights – and tucked her coat out of sight behind the Japanese tri-fold screen.

'How was the dentist?' I said. If Willow hadn't had the morning off, none of this would have happened.

She pulled a face. 'A filling and it hurt.' Spying the empty glass display case, she raised an eyebrow. 'Where's Barbie?'

I hesitated. Willow would know when the police came but there was no point in announcing it to the world quite yet. 'Having a facial.'

Willow grinned. 'Shall I make up a sign saying just that?'

'That would be helpful,' I said.

Willow pulled a notebook out of her shopping bag and set to creating a sign. I regarded her with admiration. She was smart and savvy. I didn't remember being like that at nineteen.

I kept an eye on Di, but she studiously avoided me. When I saw her grab her mobile and dart out of the Emporium without her coat or her handbag, I decided to find out what was going on. Telling Willow I'd be back in ten minutes, I went after her.

I tracked Di to the car park where she was smoking a cigarette by the skip. It was the end game for broken furniture and stood at the far end of the building next to a fire exit opposite a bank of trees.

'There you are!' I exclaimed. 'Jeez. Aren't you cold? And I didn't know you smoked.'

Di bristled. 'There's a lot you don't know about me.'

I was taken aback by her tone. 'I just wanted to know if you were okay.'

'No, I'm not,' Di shot back. 'I'm devastated by the theft and the fact that you blame me. It's written all over your face.'

I gazed at my friend with dismay. 'Di, please, what's going on?'

'Your gorgeous policeman is here.' She flicked the half-smoked cigarette into a pile of snow.

I turned to see Detective Inspector Greg Mallory get out of an unmarked car. In plain clothes, he towered above everyone else.

'Yes, he's gorgeous and single,' I said to Di, in an effort to lighten the atmosphere between us. 'But, as you know, I already have my own gorgeous policeman.'

At this comment, Di would usually have made a joke about Shawn's fascination for trains and bad ties but all she said was, 'Let's go and get this sorted out.' She walked off, leaving me to trail after her.

My phone rang. It was Shawn. 'What happened to you?' I demanded, more sharply than I intended.

'What do you mean, what happened?' He sounded distracted. I could hear paper rustling and the buzz of voices in the background.

'I got a message telling me to meet you in the car park at one.'

'A message?' Shawn said slowly. 'Who gave it to you? It certainly didn't come from me.'

My heart skipped a beat. 'It was someone in your office saying you had a surprise for me.'

'Kat. You know how my life is.' There was a hint of weariness in Shawn's tone. 'I'm thirty miles away and I don't have time for lunch or surprises.'

Shawn had often used one of his staff to contact me when he was running late or wasn't able to come to the phone and I told him so.

'Who gave you the message?' he asked me again.

I started to feel light-headed. Surely someone hadn't deliberately lured me to the car park. And then there was that weird stuff with Annie, who, I remembered, was not allowed inside the Emporium.

When I didn't answer, Shawn said, 'Why? What's wrong?'

'Emerald Barbie has been stolen,' I said.

'Emerald what? Hold on.' The phone was muted and when Shawn came back on the line he said, 'Sorry. Is that the doll?'

'Yes,' I whispered.

'Is Mallory there?'

'Yes.' He and Di were engaged in earnest conversation outside the entrance.

'Good. Look, I can't talk now,' said Shawn. 'If anyone can help it'll be him. I'll call you later.'

I had no chance to say goodbye before the line went dead.

Chapter Two

'Di's filled me in,' said Mallory, as I joined them and a crowd of shoppers, some trying to leave the building after their bags were searched, and others trying to get in. It was chaos.

My mother had written Mallory into her last Krystalle Storm romance novel as the hero and it was easy to see why. At six foot three, Mallory was handsome with a strong square jaw, cropped dark hair and grey-green eyes. He was also a very good policeman.

He gave me a sympathetic smile. 'Try not to worry.'

I felt the usual twinge of something I didn't want to acknowledge. True to his promise to his colleague and my boyfriend, Mallory had checked in on me from time to time while Shawn finished his London assignment.

Mallory and I had even enjoyed an evening drink together. He had made me laugh but I'd felt guilty too. We'd shared what my mother would term a 'moment' when he had seen me back to my car and I had tripped up the kerb. To quote my mother again, I'd felt a frisson of excitement as he caught me. I knew he'd felt it too because we'd jumped apart like scalded cats. We didn't meet alone again.

Shawn and his twin boys were now back in their Edwardian semi-detached house on the outskirts of Little Dipperton, but Shawn hadn't returned to his old policing job. To everyone's surprise, Mallory had opted to stay in Devon, and when Shawn was offered more responsibility at Devon and Cornwall Police Headquarters in Exeter, he'd accepted.

I'd be lying if I said that Shawn's promotion hadn't put a strain on our relationship. I was doing my best to be understanding and supportive. I wished I could have spoken to Helen, his late wife, and asked her what it was like to be married to a policeman, but if she had still been alive, I wouldn't have had this problem.

'Let's go and talk somewhere private,' Mallory suggested.

'The café,' Di said. 'We should be able to get an outside table in the courtyard where it will be quiet.'

We made our way to the café entrance along a corridor opposite the Gents and Ladies toilets and the fire exit.

A woman in her late forties with sharp, angular features and long dyed-black hair was setting up a cleaning sign. She wore a dark brown caretaker's uniform and yellow Marigold gloves. A trolley holding supplies of loo rolls, paper towels, boxes of tissues and cleaning fluids was parked in front of the fire exit. Looped on the rear was a black plastic rubbish bag. Her movements were slow, as if she was just too weary to be alive. I had never seen her before.

'I'm afraid you'll have to move that trolley,' said Mallory.

'The fire exit needs to be clear at all times, especially when the Emporium is at full capacity like today.'

The woman glared. 'I doubt there's going to be a fire in the next five minutes.'

'But if there is …' He smiled. 'I'm a police officer.'

The caretaker gave a grunt and manoeuvred the trolley away from the door. 'Satisfied?'

'You're new here, aren't you?' I said.

'Elaine's gone to New Zealand to see her son for Christmas,' Di put in. 'She left on Friday. This is Pam Price, who's filling in.'

'And you're Kat Stanford,' said Pam. 'I recognise your hair. Rapunzel. I've been wanting to talk to you about my son.'

'Perhaps a little later today.' I looked at Mallory, who seemed to guess what I was thinking.

'Where were you when the carol singers came through, Miss Price?' Mallory asked.

'Where I am right now,' Pam replied. 'And it's Mrs if you don't mind.'

'What time would that have been?' Mallory asked.

'I get here at eight in the morning and I leave at four,' said Pam. 'I do a toilet check every hour.'

'On the hour?' Mallory said.

Pam's eyes narrowed. 'What's all this about? I heard someone fainted. Probably from the singing. I've heard better caterwauling from the cats in the alley behind my house.'

'I'm afraid something's gone missing,' said Mallory. 'I'm going to have to search your trolley.'

'Everyone is being searched,' Di said quickly.

'What's missing?' Pam looked at Mallory, then back at me.

'We're not releasing that information at present,' said Mallory.

'It's the doll, isn't it?' Pam said suddenly. 'Emerald Barbie.'

I felt a rush of hope. 'If you saw anything suspicious—'

'Why?' A peculiar expression crossed Pam's features. 'Is there going to be a reward?'

Mallory caught my eye and shook his head. It didn't go unnoticed.

'You think I nicked it?' Pam gestured to her trolley. 'And what? Hid a doll among the toilet rolls?'

'No one is suspecting you, Pam,' said Di.

Pam scowled. 'I want him to look. Go ahead. Be my guest.'

Mallory hesitated and then, decision made, politely asked her to move aside. He swiftly checked the contents of the trolley and inspected the black plastic rubbish bag. It was empty.

'And let's not forget our pockets, shall we?' Pam turned them out and set down her mobile phone in a leopard-spotted case, a business card saying Glitz Cleaning Services, and a small key on top of the trolley. 'Locker number five. Knock yourself out.'

'It's just routine.' Di seemed unusually concerned for Pam's welfare. 'We're looking at everyone.'

Mallory picked up the key. 'Thank you. Who else has a locker?'

'Shoppers can leave their bags,' I said. 'Fiona Reynolds has the master key.'

'I'll go and talk to her,' said Mallory. 'Order me a black coffee. I'll be there shortly.' He left.

'Thanks, Pam,' said Di, warmly.

Pam ignored her. She put a hand on my arm. 'My son is very talented. Lance wants to be a film director. You must know the right people who can give him a job.'

I stifled a groan. This happened to me all the time. The industry just didn't work like that but it was hard to explain unless you were a part of it. 'I'm very happy to chat to him after the holidays.'

'Lance is the photographer of those amazing wildlife Christmas cards,' Di chimed in.

I was impressed. 'They're your son's photos?' I'd seen them for sale in the community shop in the village and in the Emporium. 'They're incredible. It sounds like he doesn't need any help.'

Pam thrust out her jaw. 'Yes, he does. He's got big dreams. Here.' She picked up a business card. 'My mobile number's on the back. You could say I'm his manager. But I suspect you'll meet him soon enough because—'

'Oh, no!' wailed a young woman, holding her little girl's hand. 'How long are the loos going to be closed?'

'Ten minutes,' Pam said. 'Use the Gents.'

The woman recoiled, obviously repulsed by the idea. 'Oh, no, thank you. I couldn't.'

'We'll leave you to it.' I grabbed Di. 'Let's go and get a table.'

The café was still packed but there were a few empty tables in the outside courtyard under heat lamps. Fake snow coated half a dozen miniature Christmas trees and topiary reindeers. A teenage waitress dressed as an elf, bearing the nametag Daisy, came over to take our orders and checked the heat lamp was working.

The moment she left I turned to Di. 'How well do you know Pam Price?'

Di bristled. 'What are you trying to say?'

I was surprised by Di's reaction. 'I wasn't trying to say anything. I've not met Pam before, and you clearly know her. It was just a question.'

'I was the person who recommended Pam for the job here,' said Di. 'Elaine told me she was going away and asked if I knew of anyone who could take her place for six weeks. Pam cleans at Sunny Hill Lodge—'

'Sunny Hill Lodge?'

'My mother is in care there and Pam is one of the cleaners,' said Di. 'She's always asking for extra work because she wants to get Lance into film school and I wanted to help her out.'

'So she's working two jobs?'

'And needs the money, yes, Kat.' Di rolled her eyes. 'She's had a sad life. Pam used to live in a cottage on one of the big country estates until Earl whatever his name was said they didn't need her or her husband any more. Her husband was one of the gamekeepers and she used to handle all the shooting parties and run the social side.'

'What happened?' I asked.

'The earl turned them out after twenty-five years.'

'Not Honeychurch Hall, surely?' I seriously hoped it wasn't.

'No,' said Di. 'Somewhere else. How can someone do that? Her husband drank himself to death and left her homeless with a load of debts. Lance is her pride and joy.'

I felt a rush of compassion. It went a long way to explain Pam's attitude. 'That's a terrible thing to do. Poor woman.'

'She was wrongly accused of theft before,' Di said, 'so you can see why she doesn't exactly like the police. Ah, here comes Mallory. And our coffees.'

Daisy returned and set down a tray. Mallory pulled out a chair. I searched his face for any sign of hope. 'No luck. They're continuing to do a bag search of everyone leaving the premises but it's not looking good.'

I picked up my mug but set it down again. 'I think it's a professional job.' I went on to tell them about Shawn's non-existent message to meet him outside at one o'clock. 'The carol singers come through every day around that time—'

'And Annie fainted,' Di exclaimed. 'Everyone rushed to help her and in that split second, the doll was snatched.'

'It means that the thief must have been waiting for the right time to strike.' Mallory took out his notebook again. 'Tell me about this woman called Annie.'

'She's been around for ever,' said Di. 'Ask anyone. You'll easily find her down by the harbour, although I was surprised that she'd dared come inside the Emporium.'

'Why?' said Mallory.

'Fiona discourages it,' said Di. 'Apart from the fact that

Annie smells, Fiona feels that she makes the customers uncomfortable.'

Mallory nodded. 'So it was out of character for Annie to be here at all. I'll want to talk to her.' He turned to me. 'When did Emerald Barbie first appear in your space?'

'Mid-November,' I said.

'What we should be looking at is anyone who has been acting suspiciously these past few weeks,' said Mallory. 'Whoever took her had to have been studying the comings and goings at the Emporium.'

I felt depressed. 'If this is a professional job the chance of getting Emerald Barbie back is zero.'

'Why don't you tell me about the doll?' said Mallory.

As I filled him in and answered a barrage of questions, my heart sank even lower.

Di said nothing. She just dipped her spoon into the sugar bowl and drew crop circles.

'Twenty thousand pounds for a *doll*.' Mallory sounded incredulous. 'And you think she would have fetched that sum at the silent auction?'

'More than that,' I said. 'Twenty grand is just for an original Barbie doll. The emerald pushes the price much higher.'

Mallory continued to scribble in his notebook. 'What's the auction in aid of?'

'The Happy Meadows Donkey Sanctuary,' I said. 'One of Lady Lavinia's favourite charities.'

'I heard it was to pay for the guttering outside the north wing of the Hall,' Di put in, with a tinge of malice. Judging by her comments on Pam Price's domestic situation, I guessed she didn't care much for the ruling classes.

'Well, that's true too,' I agreed. 'But Marion – she's the new head of house for Honeychurch – said the word "guttering" wouldn't attract the right clientele.'

Di sniggered. 'That's true.'

'Marion maintains that people dig deep in their pockets when it comes to children and animals,' I said. 'The Cartwrights are very well connected and have organised a gazillion big events like this. People are coming from all over the country and a few from Europe. At least, that's what she's told me.'

'As long as we don't get that snowstorm,' said Di. 'Then no one will get here at all.'

'It's supposed to turn mild this weekend,' I said. 'Many of the guests are staying in the area overnight. A couple of hotels have laid on minibuses and Marion has organised vouchers for taxis.'

'Which means you don't get a tip,' Di put in, adding hastily, 'If you're a taxi driver, I mean.'

'They've got a catering company lined up with waiting staff,' I said. 'An eight-piece live band. Party bags with high-end goodies that must have cost a fortune. The main draw is the mystery guest, who will be the after-dinner speaker and announce the winners of the auction and the raffle. If everyone shows up you're looking at two hundred guests.'

'And how much are the tickets?' Mallory asked.

'Two hundred and fifty apiece,' I said.

Di gave a snort of disgust. 'Fifty thousand quid in tickets and there's a raffle.'

'Raffle tickets are twenty-five pounds each,' I said, then felt a need to defend the extravagance. 'The prizes are amazing.'

Mallory raised his eyebrows. 'I'm impressed. And where do you fit in?'

'I'm the MC and the auctioneer.'

'The silent auction goes live so if you're interested in bidding, Officer,' said Di, 'you'll have to pay seventy-five quid to access the link.'

'It sounds like there are going to be some very happy donkeys at the end of the evening.' Mallory sat back in his chair and frowned. 'Why Little Dipperton? It sounds like this power couple could work anywhere.'

'Lavinia's brother, the Earl of Denby, introduced them.' I thought of my romantic brush with her playboy jet-setting brother, Piers Carew. Charming, handsome and wealthy, but as mad as a hatter with an equally crazy ex-girlfriend, I hadn't run into him for a long time. 'Apparently many of Piers's friends have used the Cartwrights' services over the years, organising balls, festivals, plays all over the world,' I said. 'Ryan's an American and used to be an actor but Marion grew up in Devon.'

Daisy drifted over with a pot of coffee. 'Would anyone like a top-up?'

Mallory and Di held out their cups. I realised I had hardly touched mine.

'What about Willow and her two friends?' Di said suddenly. 'I wouldn't put it past them to shoplift a few things.'

I was astonished. 'Willow? Absolutely not!'

'Don't look at me like that,' said Di. 'We were all young once.'

'Well, I never shoplifted,' I retorted. 'And, besides, to sell a Barbie doll on the black market you'd have to have connections. They'd be caught straight away. Isn't that right, Mallory?'

To my surprise, Mallory hesitated. 'Yes and no. But it's something to consider. Perhaps it was a dare or a prank. If those three girls are involved, it's highly likely you'd get the doll back for the gala. Where are they now?'

'Willow is working for me. I don't know about the other two,' I said. 'You'd have to ask her.' I thought of how Willow had reacted when I mentioned Barbie was having a facial. The idea was ridiculous. She was conscientious to a fault and I trusted her implicitly. But I wasn't so sure about her friends.

'I'd like to talk to them,' said Mallory.

I had a sudden thought. 'Whoever snatched Barbie could have slipped out through the fire exit. It leads straight to the car park.' It was also next to the skip where I had seen Di smoking earlier.

'But wouldn't we all have heard the alarm go off?' Di pointed out.

'Not if it was disabled,' said Mallory. 'I'll check but usually when the alarm is disabled, the fire exit is too. Who has the alarm code?'

'All the vendors,' I said. 'I've never had to use it because I've never come when the Emporium's been closed. Have you, Di?'

'Sometimes,' said Di.

I had an idea. 'We need to talk to Nigel.'

'And Nigel is?'

'The car-park attendant. He might have seen someone leaving that way,' I said. 'He's ex-military and has a mind like a steel trap.'

'Good,' said Mallory. 'And if our thief did come in by car, we might even get a number plate, which means we can—'

'Trace the owner,' we chorused. I felt that odd twinge again and felt compelled to add, 'And I know Shawn will help too.'

'Let's leave Shawn out of it for the time being,' said Mallory. 'His workload is pretty heavy, with the new job.'

'Is it?' I said. 'He doesn't talk about his new job much to me.'

'He can't,' said Mallory. 'But you can take it from me that Shawn's under a lot of pressure.'

Mallory's comment went a long way to quelling my increasing frustration at Shawn's unavailability. He rarely called me first, and if I called him it almost always went to voicemail. He had also started cancelling our dates at the last minute, promising he would make it up to me 'when things ease up' but, so far, it didn't look like that was going to happen any time soon.

Daisy reappeared with the bill. Mallory took it. 'My treat,' he said, pulled out his wallet and paid.

'I hope you can claim that on expenses,' I said.

Di's phone chirped. She glanced down and her expression hardened. 'Excuse me. I must take this.'

And she left, knocking over a chair in her haste.

'Your friend is obviously upset,' said Mallory.

'Not as upset as me – or as Cathy will be when she finds out,' I said.

'Cathy is?'

'Cathy White. The sponsor,' I said. 'She collects Barbie dolls. I dread telling her. She's back from a skiing trip on Thursday so I have a reprieve.'

'Horrible situation for you.' Mallory met my eyes. I saw compassion there.

I felt a lump in my throat. 'You have no idea.'

'You know I'll do everything I can, don't you?' He reached over and gently squeezed my arm. 'Let's go and talk to Nigel.'

Chapter Three

Mallory and I tramped through the icy slush to the wooden hut to see Nigel. As usual he was dressed in a Parka, sheepskin gloves and a deerstalker hat with the flaps down.

Following the death of his wife, Nigel liked to earn extra pin money. In his late seventies, he was remarkably spry and took his job very seriously, noting down the number plates and tallying up the cash. Fortunately, we exhibitors didn't need to pay. Dartmouth was notoriously challenging for parking, and although the first hour was free at the Emporium, Fiona had endorsed a charge after that.

The car park had a one-way system with a barrier next to Nigel's hut. It was packed.

While we waited for a lull, I pointed out the location of the fire exit behind the skip and next to the bank of trees.

'What's behind those trees?' Mallory asked.

'Open fields, a lane. God knows.' A handful of pedestrians strolled by. My heart sank again. 'Foot traffic doesn't need to check in with Nigel. It's hopeless, isn't it?'

'Let's not give up yet.'

'Sorry about that. Busy day.' Nigel brandished his clip-board and answered Mallory's questions. 'I write every number plate down. Cash only. No cards.'

'That's quite a job you've got there, Nigel,' said Mallory.

'Excuse me a moment.' A car pulled up to the barrier. Nigel duly checked his list and waved him on through. 'He came in fifty-five minutes ago. Taking advantage of the one-hour free parking. Now, how can I help you, Officer?'

'It's a long shot,' said Mallory, 'but would you happen to have seen anyone leave by the fire exit between one and one thirty today?'

'Yes,' Nigel said.

I gasped at the unexpected stroke of luck. 'You did? A man? A woman? How many people?'

'I can do better than that,' Nigel said, with a hint of pride. 'I can tell you the car he got into.'

'A man!' I exclaimed.

Nigel scanned his clipboard. 'Yes. Here we are. It was a peppermint-green Mark 1 Ford Fiesta. The number plate was TDV 31Y. A 1978 model.'

'You are amazing!' I leaped forward and gave Nigel a hug. He turned pink with pleasure.

'The man had wavy grey hair, a moustache and heavy-rimmed glasses,' said Nigel. 'I'd guess he was in his sixties. Tall. Long navy coat. What's happened? Or is it on a need-to-know basis?'

Mallory cracked a wry smile. 'On a need-to-know for now.'

'Understood,' he said. 'I'll keep an eye open for that car.'

'Have you seen it here before?' I asked.

Nigel nodded. 'Yes. And I can tell you which days he came in and how long he stayed.' Because of all the interruptions, with cars coming and going, it took a while for Nigel to give us the information. But it sounded as if the man had spent just under the hour 'to qualify for the free parking' in the Emporium three or four times a week. The visits began in mid-November around the same time that Emerald Barbie appeared in my space.

'Our first lead!' I was beside myself with excitement. This was proof that the thief had been casing the joint for weeks.

'Thanks, Nigel,' said Mallory.

As we were about to leave, Nigel said, 'There is one more thing. It's about a silver Polo. Number plate WP63 EKK. It's always here before I am – I start at eight thirty. The Emporium doesn't open until nine. It belongs to a woman with long dark hair. She *will* lift the barrier to drive her car in. The barrier is there for a reason!'

'That must be the caretaker, Pam Price.' I turned to Mallory. 'Didn't she tell us that she started work at eight?'

'She refuses to park in the exhibitors' car park, too,' Nigel grumbled.

'I'll talk to her,' said Mallory. 'Thanks again for your time.'

'I'll notify you the moment I see the Ford Fiesta again,' Nigel said.

'Somehow I doubt you will,' I said miserably.

Mallory and I returned to the Emporium. 'I'll run the number plate tomorrow. If you can give me Willow's phone number, I'll call her tomorrow as well and have a word with her friends.'

'I'll text it to your mobile,' I said, and did so on the spot. 'I really appreciate this.'

'It's my job,' said Mallory. 'I'm glad I was here. Try not to worry. You know I'll do everything I can.'

His eyes met mine and held my gaze for just a second too long. I looked away. 'Thank you,' I said.

'I'll let you know if I see anything in the CCTV footage,' he went on, all business. 'Let's hope there was a camera outside the fire exit.'

'What about Pam Price?' I said. 'Now we think the thief left that way and we have a description, perhaps it will jog her memory.'

'Or our thief timed it for when he knew she wouldn't be around,' said Mallory. 'Leave her to me. Don't question her. In fact, let's keep this quiet until I've tracked down that Ford Fiesta.'

'I definitely want to keep it quiet,' I agreed. 'But can't I at least ask if anyone noticed a man behaving suspiciously? Judging by what Nigel says, he's been around a lot. You never know.'

'All right,' said Mallory. 'But be discreet.'

Mallory left just as my mobile rang. It was my mother. 'Are you still in Dartmouth?' she demanded. When I told her I was, she added, 'I'm glad I caught you. On your way home, can you stop at the community shop and check your PO box? You haven't been there for a while, and I always get so much fan mail at Christmas.'

'Will do,' I said.

'Will do?' my mother echoed slowly. 'Just, will *do*? Is something wrong?'

I didn't want to explain what had happened standing outside in the cold and, besides, it was too complicated. 'Everything is fine. Honestly.'

'Fine. Honestly,' Mum echoed again. 'What's happened? Something has, hasn't it? I can tell by the tone of your voice.'

Why did mothers have an uncanny way of knowing when something was wrong?

'Is it over between you and Shawn?' she went on.

'No, Mum!' I didn't like the way she jumped to the conclusion that Shawn had something to do with the tone of my voice. 'I'll tell you when I see you.'

'Aha! So there is something wrong!' she crowed. 'I knew it! When are you going to get here? I can't wait.'

'You'll just have to,' I said, and disconnected the line, accidentally cutting off whatever she had been going to say next.

I didn't see Mallory again or have a chance to talk to Di, or any of the other vendors, for the rest of the afternoon because we were all busy. When there was a lull, I went in search of Pam only to discover that she had left for the day.

In the end it was Willow who turned out to be the most helpful when I finally had to tell her that, far from enjoying a facial, Emerald Barbie had been stolen.

'Tall, wavy grey hair, long coat, heavy-rimmed glasses and a moustache,' Willow declared. 'I was in the Ladies when he walked in, apologised for his mistake and left.'

I felt a twinge of suspicion. 'But weren't you at the dentist this morning?'

'Yes,' said Willow. 'But I told you what time I'd be in, remember? I don't often get a chance to look around the Emporium because I'm always working. Why?'

'Nothing,' I said. 'And you think it was one, one fifteen?'

'Positive,' said Willow. 'I didn't connect the messy trolley at the time but you're right. He must have gone out of the fire exit.'

'The messy trolley,' I repeated. 'Pam Price's trolley?'

'She was cleaning the Gents – maybe that was why he came in to use the Ladies.' She shrugged. 'But yeah. All the cleaning supplies had fallen over and one of the bottles hadn't got the top screwed on properly so there was liquid everywhere.'

So, although Pam Price had been in the vicinity, with her trolley parked across the fire exit, neither she nor Willow had seen our mystery man escape.

Nigel's comment sprang to mind. The thief had spent just under an hour in the Emporium. What was he doing? Hardly prowling the aisles.

'Did you ever notice him in the café?' I said.

'No, but maybe ask the waitresses if they did.' Willow looked worried. 'Do you think you'll find the doll in time for the gala?'

'Let's hope so,' I said. 'Detective Inspector Mallory is on the case. I gave him your mobile and he asked for your friends' numbers too. Will you forward them to him, please?'

'Kylie and Teresa?' Willow sounded surprised. 'Why? What would they know?'

'He's talking to everyone,' I said.

Willow helped me cash up for the day. I looked at the empty display box with her handwritten sign. I felt sick. I was reluctant to ring Cathy – I didn't want to spoil her holiday – but I'd certainly have to call the insurance company. And then there were the Cartwrights and what this would mean for the gala.

I felt a light touch on my shoulder. 'Don't worry, Kat,' said Willow. 'I'm sure she can't be far.'

I wished I had the confidence of youth. 'How are you getting home?'

'Bus,' said Willow.

'That'll take for ever,' I said. 'Let's go.'

As we set off, I thought of Willow's comment about Barbie not being far away. 'Do you think your friends might have taken Emerald Barbie for a joke?'

Willow seemed shocked. 'Of course not. Is that why the police officer wants to talk to them? Does he think they stole her? Do *you* think they stole her?'

'Honestly,' I said. 'I just don't know.'

I gave Willow a sideways glance. She was looking out of the window. Her hands were clenched tightly on her lap.

'That emerald is worth thousands of pounds,' I said quietly. 'I'm just saying that whoever took it will be in a lot of trouble and it won't just be a shoplifting charge.'

Willow gave a heavy sigh. 'Ever since I went to uni things have been different between Kylie and Teresa and me. We used to be so close, but they didn't want to leave Devon and I did. We may all have changed but I know they would never steal anything.'

'Yes, people change,' I agreed. 'And sometimes people we thought we knew are people we didn't really know at all.' I was thinking of my mother and her shocking alter ego Krystalle Storm. Not only had she deceived me as to what she was doing in her bedroom – writing – throughout my teenage years, but she'd deceived my father too. I didn't think I'd ever understand Mum's need for secrecy. True, her romance novels were not for the pure and unsullied, but I was proud of what she had accomplished. Unfortunately, her secret life and subsequent eye-boggling earnings had gone beyond the point of no return. Her unveiling might well bring forth a chorus of adulation but it would almost certainly end in a prison sentence for tax evasion.

'Why do you suspect my friends?' Willow broke into my thoughts. 'You just told me you thought it could be the man who left by the fire exit.'

'I suppose I was hoping it was a prank and the doll would be back tomorrow,' I said sheepishly. 'That's all.'

It was getting dark when we turned off the main two-lane road and began the descent into the village of Little Dipperton. The lane had been cleared of snow, but the tyre tracks were still hard-packed ice. Even though the council salted the roads, I had learned my lesson last winter and had snow chains put on my Golf.

As I cautiously approached the steep hill to Bridge Cottage, my chest tightened. There had been a car accident at the bottom. Two vehicles: a familiar hunter-green Land Rover and a black Kia. The Kia had mounted the low bank above the fast-running stream and was pitched forward, ready to topple in at any time. The lane had skid marks and it looked as if the Kia had gone out of control and struck the Land Rover at the bottom of the hill.

'Quickly,' I said. 'Let's hope no one's hurt.'

Chapter Four

We needn't have worried.

An irate figure dressed in a red tweed wool coat and matching cloche hat – presumably the driver of the Kia – was slamming her handbag against the windscreen and screaming obscenities at the driver of the Land Rover, who was reading a magazine.

At first, I thought it was Lady Lavinia Honeychurch at the wheel, but, as we drew closer, I realised it was the dowager countess.

Willow gave a cry of shock. 'That's . . . Surely not . . . Is that Lady Edith?'

'Yes,' I said grimly.

'But she's not supposed to be driving!'

'I know,' I said.

Not only had Edith's driving licence expired, Rupert, the current Earl of Grenville, had banned his octogenarian mother from driving following an accident in the village where she'd hit the accelerator instead of the brake and struck a delivery van that was double-parked outside the community shop. No real harm had been done but it had caused a huge scandal in the village.

Edith didn't seem to care. Many a time I'd seen her steal away in her battered old car. Once, in a rare moment of honesty when we were out riding together, she told me her freedom to ride and drive was the only thing that kept her alive. Her biggest nightmare was being bedridden and a 'burden' to others or, the ultimate punishment, being 'incarcerated', as she put it, in a care home.

This was not going to be an easy conversation.

I pulled onto the apron of the burned-out building. I'd never liked Bridge Cottage. It was a fly-tipper's paradise and always seemed to have a new addition to the ever-growing collection of abandoned refrigerators and broken furniture despite the numerous penalty warning signs.

Willow brandished her mobile. 'I'll call the police and an ambulance.'

'Let's not do that yet,' I said quickly, knowing that it would cause problems for Edith if the incident was officially reported – especially to Shawn, who had kept the delivery-van incident out of the local newspapers and magistrate's court. He had warned the family he would never bail her out again.

Fortunately, reception was rubbish down there, which Willow soon discovered.

'Ugh. No signal. This place gives me the creeps. Isn't it where you and your mum almost died in that fire?'

I didn't answer. It was something I preferred to forget.

We got out of the car and remarked on how low the temperature had dropped in the dip. I could hear the rushing water: a gentle stream in summer but a roaring river at this time of year. It was going to be another freezing night.

I took in the scene. Edith's Land Rover was parked in a turning, which meant she'd either stopped after the accident or had not been moving at all. I desperately hoped it was the latter.

I had to make this go away.

I caught myself. Had I *really* just thought that?

When Mum and I had first moved to live on the Honeychurch Hall estate, we regarded the loyalty that the locals felt for the Honeychurch family as archaic and amusing. But over time my respect and affection for the family had grown and made me loyal too.

The driver of the Kia spotted us but, rather than stop her attack on Edith's windscreen, she redoubled her efforts with her handbag. Even from a few yards away I could see that her flushed face was twisted in fury. Edith continued to read her magazine. It looked like *Horse & Hound*.

'That woman looks mad,' Willow whispered. 'I think we should film it.'

'Don't you dare!' I exclaimed. 'I don't want to see this on your Instagram page.'

Willow grinned. 'I hadn't thought of that. What a good idea!' Seeing my expression of dismay, she rolled her eyes. 'Of course I won't. My grandmother would never forgive me.'

The woman stopped her attack. She waved and started towards us but slipped and fell down hard with a cry of pain.

I hurried over. 'Are you okay?'

'No, I'm not,' she snapped, as she batted away my helping hand. 'That stupid old bag shouldn't be driving!'

Willow's jaw dropped and even I felt a tremor of horror. No one, absolutely no one, ever insulted the dowager countess. It was like insulting the Queen.

'Look at her, reading her la-di-da magazine. I could have been killed. I know she can hear me.' The woman turned back to the Land Rover and screamed, 'I'm going to report you to the police!'

Edith's face was white, making her trademark scarlet lipstick seem garish.

'Let's all take a breath,' I said. 'Are you hurt?'

'I don't know yet,' said the woman. 'I might be. I might wake up tomorrow morning with whiplash. She'd better be insured! I could have drowned.' She pointed to the Kia. 'And what about my car?'

I spied an orange banner with the logo SIXT Rentals on the rear window, which confirmed my suspicion that she wasn't a local. Since the car was beached on the ridge, I was confident it could easily be pulled back onto the lane. Eric Pugsley, Rupert's right-hand man and jack-of-all-trades, was the community's go-to person for getting cars out of snow-drifts or flooded rivers with his tractor.

'I'm sure we can get your car back on the road,' I said.

'But probably not tonight,' added Willow.

'That's unacceptable,' the woman exclaimed. 'And not my fault.' She jabbed a finger at the Land Rover. 'She shouldn't be driving. She's got to be over a hundred years old!'

'But the Land Rover is parked in the turning,' Willow said firmly. 'It's clear that the skid marks belong to your car – they're too narrow for a Land Rover – so if there is fault, it could be yours since you slid into a stationary vehicle.'

'Oh.' The woman's expression darkened. 'I see how it is. You're going to blame me, aren't you?'

'Not at all,' said Willow, smoothly, and gestured to the hill behind us. 'The police will be assigning blame once they have measured the skid marks. I assume your hire car is fully insured?'

'It's insured all right,' she went on and, shooting another venomous look at Edith, who continued to read her magazine, added, 'But I bet *she* isn't. Hold on a minute.' The woman studied my face. 'Are you on the telly?'

Before I had a chance to answer her face broke into a smile. 'Kat Stanford! You're Kat Stanford! Well, I'll be blowed! I loved *Fakes & Treasures*. Of course, I recognise that mane of hair! I can see why everyone called you Rapunzel! I read in *Star Stalkers* that you'd moved to the West Country and opened a shop.'

I repressed a shudder of revulsion at hearing the name of that awful celebrity-gossip tabloid. I certainly didn't miss being in the spotlight. And then, with a pang, I remembered I could well be back in the spotlight if word got out that Emerald Barbie had been stolen.

'That was a while ago now.' I pressed my advantage. 'I'm sure we can sort all this out, Mrs . . .?'

'Bone, Harriet Bone,' said Harriet.

The name seemed to suit her.

'Well I never. I loved reading about your wardrobe malfunctions.' Harriet laughed. 'Pity you gave all that fame up.'

'We'll take you to the village and find someone to retrieve your car,' I said, ignoring the jibe. 'It looks like there isn't any real damage. No one was hurt.'

'That still doesn't excuse the fact that the old bag shouldn't be driving and that tomorrow I might wake up with whiplash.'

'Then let's exchange phone numbers,' I suggested.

Harriet fumbled with her handbag and brought out a scrap of paper with a pen. 'Why are you giving me your number rather than hers?' She shot Edith a filthy look.

'Because I'm a friend of the family and easier to get hold of,' I said, thinking I'd regret this in the morning. 'Do you have anything in your car? Just in case it's stuck here all night.' If that was the case, I didn't dare to ask where she planned on staying, and I noticed that Willow didn't mention that the Hare and Hounds might have a spare room.

'You know . . .' Harriet hesitated '. . . bit of a cheeky ask but I'd love you to have a look at my pearl and diamond necklace. My husband bought it for our thirtieth wedding anniversary and you'd settle a family argument.'

'Oh, er, yes.' If this was what it would take for Harriet to go quietly, so be it.

Suddenly the Land Rover engine burst into life and, with a graunch of gears, moved into the lane, reversed onto the apron, clipping the bumper of my car, and sped away.

'Oh. My. God!' Harriet shrieked. 'Did you see that! She

hit your car! That's a hit-and-run, that is.' She looked at me with dismay. 'Don't you care?'

'You get used to not caring about your car when you live around here. We call them country cars,' I said. 'Speaking of which, where are you trying to get to?'

'Honeychurch Hall.'

Willow's snigger turned into a cough.

I knew that the Cartwrights had taken on extra staff for the gala and prayed Harriet wasn't one of them.

'For the gala?' I asked.

Harriet frowned. 'No. I'm having a mini-break. I found a shepherd's hut in an . . . How did they describe it? An idyllic, isolated location in the grounds of a stately home.'

'Are you positive?' I was surprised that Lavinia was renting it out in the depths of winter although, as my mother often said, the aristocracy don't feel the cold like normal people. Probably due to living in draughty mausoleums with ancient radiators and no double-glazing.

'It was all I could get,' said Harriet. 'Apparently there's a big function, and all the other places are fully booked.'

'Couldn't you have gone somewhere else altogether?' Willow asked.

'No,' Harriet declared. 'It has to be around here.'

'You do know that the loo and the shower are outside,' I said.

'It said adjoining in the description.'

I wasn't about to clarify that adjoining meant the shower was outside behind a screen of woven hazel and that the compost loo was housed in a wooden shed. There was a small wood burner inside the shepherd's hut so at least Harriet would have some form of heating.

I couldn't press her further, because we all heard an approaching car downshift gears to tackle the steep hill. Thank God. Help was at hand.

A metallic-grey Land Cruiser came into view and stopped alongside us. Marion Cartwright was at the wheel.

She opened the window and pointed to the beached Kia. 'Is everything okay?'

As always, I was struck by how beautiful Marion was, with her high cheekbones, taut, porcelain skin and deep blue eyes. It was hard to pinpoint her age because she bore the tell-tale sheen of Botox, but I guessed she had to be somewhere in her early forties. The only feature that marred her perfection was an over-wide mouth. My mother said it was like a letter-box, that you could post the whole African continent and still have room for China.

Today, Marion's blonde hair was tucked under a stylish red trilby with a sprig of holly in the band.

'No. I was run off the road by an old bag in a Land Rover,' Harriet said bluntly. 'But, as you can see, she has left the scene of the crime.'

'A Land Rover, you say? Oh dear!' Marion met my eye and knew intuitively who had been driving.

'Do you have a tow-bar?' Harriet demanded.

'I do, but no ropes, I'm afraid,' said Marion.

'I'm going to ask Eric if he can help with his tractor,' I said.

'Eric is busy keeping the drives clear, Kat,' said Marion, in the patronising tone that I'd started to find irritating. 'I'm sure we can find someone else. Perhaps in the village.'

I noticed that Harriet was staring at Marion. 'You look familiar to me. It's your big mouth.'

Marion didn't flinch but Willow sniggered and coughed again. I was taken aback by Harriet's lack of tact, until she blushed.

'No!' Harriet said hastily, and laughed. 'I didn't mean it like it came out. I meant Hollywood actresses would pay a fortune to have a big mouth like yours. Are you an actress? I'm sure I've seen you on the telly.'

Marion smiled. 'That was in another life.'

'You were an actress!' Willow seemed impressed.

'I recognised Kat Stanford, didn't I?' Harriet gabbled on. 'If you give me a minute, I'll remember where I saw you.' She frowned. 'Maybe it wasn't on the telly. But I know I've seen you before.'

'I'd be very interested to know where,' Marion said, and smiled again. 'It's usually my husband who gets recognised.' She turned her attention back to me. 'Kat, take— I'm sorry. I don't know your name.'

'Harriet Bone,' said Harriet.

'Take Harriet to the village and organise a tow,' said Marion. 'But, as I mentioned, Eric is unavailable. Good luck!' With that parting comment Marion drove away.

'Let's all go to the village before we freeze to death,' I said.

Harriet retrieved a small suitcase covered with travel stickers of cruise ships. She handed it to Willow. 'Make yourself useful and put that in the boot.'

I could sense that Willow was about to say something derogatory and shot her a warning look. She forced a smile. 'Wow. It looks like you've done a lot of travelling, Mrs Bone.'

Moments later Harriet was sitting in the front passenger seat with Willow in the rear.

'I know where I've seen that woman before!' Harriet said suddenly. 'It wasn't on the telly. It was on a cruise around the Med. My husband and I are great cruisers.'

Willow leaned forward. 'Where's your husband now? Is he going to join you later?'

'Goodness, you're an inquisitive little madam, aren't you?' Harriet said. 'In my day children should be seen and not heard.'

I caught Willow's eye in the rear-view mirror and winked.

The next ten minutes were spent listening to Harriet trying to remember on which cruise she had seen Marion. 'And she wasn't a tourist,' Harriet mused. 'That's it. She was crew. Worked in one of the shops. Or maybe she was a croupier in the casino.'

The 'Welcome to Little Dipperton' signpost couldn't have come soon enough.

It was a typical chocolate-box Devonshire village consisting of whitewashed, thatched and slate-roofed cottages with a handful of shops and a seventeenth-century pub. A narrow road snaked around the green and past the Norman church of St Mary's. At one time the Honeychurch estate had owned the entire village of Little Dipperton, but now only a handful of cottages were tenant-occupied, their doors and window frames painted a distinctive dark blue. In the fading light the village looked enchanting, lit by fairy lights and with Christmas trees standing in every window.

Harriet gave a cry of delight. 'It's wonderful! How pretty! How quaint! Oh! And it's all lit up for Christmas.'

It was nearly five o'clock and the village was practically empty. I pulled up in the only parking space outside the community shop. 'I have to make a quick stop here and I'll also see if we can get some help for your car.'

Willow and I got out. 'Thanks for the lift,' Willow said. 'I can walk from here. I'll see you tomorrow.'

I smiled. 'You're going to make a very good lawyer.'

Willow grinned. 'After today, I think prosecution is more my thing than having to defend someone like Harriet Bone in court.'

Chapter Five

Like many post offices and village shops that were forced to close throughout the UK, some had managed to turn into community-run enterprises and Little Dipperton's was one such.

Twenty-something Bethany Davis and her partner Simon Payne had done a great job of keeping the spirit of the traditional shop alive, hanging on to the old-fashioned cash register and brass bell, and keeping the rows of large glass jars filled with sweets along the back wall. I often wondered just how hygienic those jars really were since no one seemed to buy any of their contents.

Volunteers from the village gave up an hour or two of their time to help. In return the shop carried a vast array of homemade wares from honey to jewellery and knitted scarves. Lance Price's stunning Christmas cards of wildlife were for sale there, too.

Bethany was proud to support local vendors and sold wine and the most amazing cheeses from the Sharpham estate nearby. Since it was Christmas, they also sold my mother's Honeychurch gin and, given that it was 57 per cent proof, it was highly popular. All of Mum's Krystalle Storm books were displayed on a carousel near the door although no one knew the author lived in their midst.

This year Bethany was promoting another local photographer. Copies of Nicola de Pulford's annual Naked Farmer Calendar were displayed alongside my mother's latest release, aptly titled *Exposed*, which attracted much hilarity.

My mother claimed to use her calendar for 'reference and research'. Tongue-in-cheek, she'd also suggested that Marion's husband Ryan throw his name into the hat for the following year, and he got the wrong idea. Now, whenever Mum cornered Ryan in conversation, he always made a point of saying how much he loved Marion and that he would never leave her.

Ryan might well be handsome, but we soon discovered that he had no sense of humour and, as my mother liked to say, instead of all mouth and no trousers, Ryan was all trousers and no mouth but Marion made up for that with hers.

Bethany appeared from the depths of the shop, holding a mug of tea in her hands. With her large Bambi eyes and cloud of blonde hair, she was a dead ringer for Blondie, the 1980s pop icon. She knew it too and only wore 1980s clothing.

'Oh, good!' she exclaimed. 'I was about to call you about your post. I'll go and get it.' She glanced over my shoulder and smiled. 'I'll be right with you.'

I turned to see that Harriet had followed me into the

shop. She wore a massive smile and couldn't stop beaming. 'Isn't this incredible?'

Bethany set her mug on the counter and disappeared behind a door, which led to the post-sorting room.

I waited at the Plexiglas window that encased a small cubbyhole with the sign *Post Office*. An adjacent notice board was peppered with the usual classified advertisements. A large poster of the upcoming Christmas Gala, featuring Emerald Barbie, made me want to cry.

'Oh, *Star Stalkers*,' said Harriet, as she picked up the dreaded trashy tabloid that had given me so much heartache during my television days. 'I preferred *Paparazzi Razzle*, but they went out of business when they got sued for libel.'

I had never heard of *Paparazzi Razzle* and, judging by its name, I was glad I hadn't.

'*Star Stalkers* only offers fifty pounds a tip but thousands for a proper exclusive.' Harriet put it back on the rack next to the local newspapers – the *Dipperton Deal*, the *Dartmouth Packet* and the *Western Times*. 'Don't you miss being in the spotlight?'

'Happily, no.'

'I sold something once to *Paparazzi Razzle*.' She gave a secret smile. 'Do you want to know what it was?'

'Not really.' I was hit by a wave of nausea. Little did Harriet know that she had an exclusive standing right in front of her. I swiftly changed the topic. 'You might want to buy some groceries for your stay.'

'There's a hamper laid on,' said Harriet. 'Do you live around here? You never said.'

Luckily Simon appeared, mobile in hand. He was built like an American-football player and had to walk with a permanent stoop because of the low ceiling. He also ran the Totnes Sea Scouts of which young Harry Honeychurch – the future sixteenth Earl of Grenville – was an enthusiastic member. I was looking forward to seeing Harry again. He was due back from a school skiing trip the day before the gala. It seemed that everyone was going skiing. Right now I'd have done anything to be on a mountain top, far away from here.

'You must be Harriet Bone,' said Simon. 'I hear your car went off the road.'

Harriet scowled. 'That's one way of putting it, I suppose.'

Unfortunately it had been Simon's delivery van that Edith had struck with her Land Rover. Like Shawn, he was obsessed with rules and public safety.

'And I wouldn't have gone off the road if that old bag in the Land Rover had moved out of the way,' Harriet went on. 'She shouldn't be driving.'

'Don't tell me it was Edith,' Simon said, deliberately not using the dowager countess's title.

'Who?' said Harriet.

'It's okay,' I said quickly. 'There was no harm done. No one was hurt.'

'Whiplash takes a day or two to settle in,' Simon pointed out, 'so don't speak too soon.'

Harriet nodded vehemently. 'That's what I told Kat.'

'Write down what you remember as soon as you can,' Simon went on. 'That's what I tell my boys. That way, if there are any questions, you have it all logged. Memory is a funny thing.'

'Thank you, Simon,' I said pointedly.

'Yes, thank you,' Harriet echoed. 'I will.'

Simon regarded Harriet with curiosity. 'You're not here for the gala, are you?'

'I didn't know anything about it until now,' said Harriet. 'But I'm staying on the Honeychurch estate so perhaps I can gatecrash.'

'You'll be lucky,' said Simon. 'From what I hear, the place is going to be heaving with celebrities and security. Maybe Kat can treat you to a two-hundred-and-fifty-pound ticket.'

Harriet's eyes bugged out. 'Good grief! That's so expensive!'

'I wish someone would throw me a party and get my guests to pay for my guttering.' Simon said it in a light-hearted way, but I knew he was one of the few locals who did not hold the Honeychurch dynasty in awe. 'Where are you staying?'

'I'm in the shepherd's hut,' said Harriet.

Simon laughed. 'Rather you than me, but if you get too cold, I'm sure Kat's got a spare bedroom.'

I could have throttled him.

Harriet's eyes widened. 'Really?'

'I was joking,' Simon said hastily, obviously seeing the horror on my face. 'We'll find someone to bring back your car. Don't worry. May I have the keys?'

Harriet delved into her handbag and gave them to him. 'That's very kind.'

Bethany emerged with some letters kept together with an elastic band. There were also four packages. All were wrapped in brown paper and heavily taped but two were decorated with festive reindeer and snowmen stickers.

'Well, goodness me!' Harriet said. 'Someone gets a lot of post. Is that all for you?'

'Kat has lots of fans,' said Bethany. 'That's why she has a PO box.'

In reality, the PO box was solely for my mother's use.

'It's not all for me.' I pulled a foldable nylon bag from my tote and loaded it up.

Harriet and I returned to my car. I put my tote and the bag of packages in the footwell behind my seat.

We set off for the Hall and Harriet bombarded me with questions on the drive over. Who used to run the post office? Were the cottages in the village part of the estate? How many people lived in the grounds of the estate? How big was it? How old was Honeychurch Hall? What were the gardens like? Was there a lake? Were there a grotto and a stumpery? I answered as best I could and found her excitement and interest rather touching. Finally, I was able to ask Harriet why she had chosen Little Dipperton for her mini-break and so close to Christmas, too. 'Have you been to this area before?'

'No,' Harriet replied. 'I need to get my head straight. My husband retired a few months ago and he's driving me to distraction.'

'Oh dear,' I said. 'What does he do?'

'For starters, it's the way he stirs his tea,' she said. 'He stirs it at least ten times – I lose count – then taps the spoon on the rim of the cup three times before putting it onto the saucer. Timothy thinks everything is muck. It's his favourite word.'

I laughed. 'That wasn't quite what I meant. What did your husband do before he retired?'

'He worked for the post office,' she said. 'Nothing like your adorable little post office in the village. A big one. You know, where the numbers flash up and a computerised voice says, "Customer number four, please."'

I smiled. 'Where was that?'

'Basingstoke,' said Harriet. 'One of those awful nineteen-seventies town-centre experiments made of concrete. Timothy promised we'd move to the country but now we can't afford to. You're not married, are you?'

'Not yet.'

'Well, if I were you, I'd think twice about it,' she said ruefully. 'My husband asks me what I'm doing all the time. I had a life when he went to work, but now he's under my feet all day.'

'Oh dear,' I said again.

'It was all right when I was working,' Harriet added.

'What did you do?'

'I was a chemist for years – we didn't have kids – but I got fed up with people talking about their health problems and then I was laid off.'

'Oh dear,' I said yet again.

'Timothy expects me to cook him lunch every day,' she grumbled on. 'Well, he'll have to learn how to make his own sandwiches while I'm gone but, as usual, the neighbours will take pity on him and invite him over.'

'I'm sure he'll miss you,' I said lamely.

'I thought, if I'm not going to strangle him over Christmas I need to get away,' Harriet carried on, oblivious. 'Always make sure you have your own mad money to do what you like with, Kat. Do you know what my husband's nickname is?'

I said I didn't.

'Tightwad Tim.' She laughed. 'Well, not for much longer. I've got a plan.'

'Ah. It's always good to have a plan,' I said.

'Yes,' she said quietly. 'It's a very good plan. I'm going to be rich and then we'll see who wears the trousers.'

We turned into Cavalier Lane, which was flanked by the towering hedgerows that Devon was famed for, coated with snow. Eric had cleared the road that morning but, with more snow forecast for tonight, he'd be doing it all over again tomorrow. Harriet remarked on how narrow the lane was, but my thoughts turned to Friday's gala. Perhaps there would be a blizzard and then it would have to be cancelled because no one could get there.

'I hear that Krystalle Storm lives in the area,' Harriet suddenly declared. 'Have you met her?'

My stomach did a funny flip-flop. Only Shawn knew that my mother was Krystalle Storm. We'd had a couple of close calls but, as far as I knew, my mother's true identity was still a secret.

'Who?' I said lightly.

'You know, the romance writer,' said Harriet. 'I saw all her books in the community shop.'

'Oh, those,' I said. 'The former postmistress was a huge fan. When her niece – that's Bethany – took the shop over, she just kept the stock.'

'Kept, and added to it,' Harriet said firmly. '*Exposed* is Krystalle Storm's latest. It's not as good as her others, mind.'

'Isn't it?'

'Hah,' Harriet grunted. 'I suppose you locals protect her. You know, like when Kate Middleton was living with Prince William in Anglesey.'

'Did they?' I kept my eyes firmly on the road and quickly changed the subject. 'Did you call ahead to make sure the shepherd's hut is ready?'

'I got an email from the team telling me where I can find the key.'

'The team?'

'The email was signed "the team",' said Harriet. 'I heard that the Duchess of Rutland always welcomes her paying guests. I was hoping to meet the earl. Perhaps they've already left for Balmoral to see the Queen. Or is it Sandringham for Christmas?'

'I wouldn't know.' But I did know that Lavinia was only too happy to pass on the meet-and-greet responsibility to the Cartwrights. It was another step towards making the estate more of a commercial enterprise and that saddened me. I'd even heard talk of converting the outbuildings and glass-houses in the walled garden into Airbnbs. And – horror of horrors – glamping in the park.

We sailed by the impressive main entrance to Honeychurch Hall, with the matching eighteenth-century gatehouses and soaring granite pillars where stone hawks sat with out-stretched wings.

'Isn't that where we're going?' Harriet asked.

I explained that the estate was very large and that we had to take the next entrance.

'Ah, yes.' She nodded. 'Of course.'

We followed the boundary wall for quite a distance before turning into the service drive marked 'Tradesmen'.

As we passed a sign marked 'Carriage House', Harriet said, 'Who lives there?'

'My mother,' I said.

'And what's her name?' said Harriet.

'Iris Stanford,' I said. 'She's the Honeychurch historian.'

'And over there?' Harriet pointed to a pair of unsightly corrugated-iron gates that were partially covered with ivy.

'It's Eric Pugsley's scrapyard,' I said. 'He's been hard at work clearing the drives of snow.'

'A scrapyard!' Harriet pulled a face. 'How horrible. Wait. Is he the man who's going to get my car?'

'Simon's sorting that out,' I said. 'You met him in the post office.'

Harriet didn't speak again until we pulled up outside Honeychurch Cottages next to the walled garden. The terrace of three had been built towards the end of the nineteenth century for the gardeners when the Hall was in its heyday. All the windows were lit up with Christmas lights and holly wreaths hung from each front door.

'Who lives there?' she asked.

'The Cartwrights – he's the estate manager and she's the

head of house – Delia Evans, the housekeeper, and Eric Pugsley.'

'Eric from the scrapyard?' said Harriet. 'Is he also the gamekeeper?'

I frowned. 'There hasn't been a gamekeeper on the estate for years. No, Eric does most of the manual labour the earl requires.'

I cut the engine and we both got out. It was deathly quiet. There didn't seem to be a soul around, but a faint yellow glow was visible through the open gates to the walled garden.

Harriet walked on ahead, leaving me to retrieve her suitcase from the boot. When I caught up with her she was standing still in what I could only describe as awe.

'It's . . . it's like Narnia.'

I thought that was pushing it, but I could see what she meant.

Snow had transformed a wasteland of derelict glasshouses and abandoned potting sheds into a winter wonderland.

The Cartwrights had installed a series of Victorian-style streetlamps along the gravel path to a screen of twelve-foot-high woven hazel panels that shielded the shepherd's hut. The fence was draped with twinkling fairy lights and, in the darkness against the snow, seemed almost magical.

Harriet was in raptures.

I followed her to the shepherd's hut, thinking she was going to be disappointed, but I was wrong. She turned to me, eyes shining, and whispered, 'It's a gypsy caravan!'

To a lay person, the shepherd's hut looked nothing like a gypsy caravan despite its bow-topped roof. Wooden steps led up to a stable half-door that opened into the living space, with the wood burner, a tiny cooker and stone sink. A two-seater sofa in a cheerful yellow print stood opposite a small fold-out table and two chairs. At the end, spanning the width of the hut, a raised bed was framed with carved wood and painted with primroses and violets. The shepherd's hut even had a small Christmas tree.

It was lovely and warm and had been prepared for Harriet's arrival. A hamper of expensive basics sat on the table, with a decent bottle of wine. A laminated, beautifully hand-drawn map of the estate, dotted with landmarks and footpaths for exploring the grounds, lay on the table, with a small binder embossed with the Earl of Grenville's coat of arms. Presumably it contained instructions on how to use the facilities.

Marion had thought of everything.

'I love it! It's amazing! Like a dream!' Harriet was ecstatic. 'I'm so sorry about today. I know I was rude. It's just that the old bag reminded me of my mother-in-law.'

I couldn't help but laugh. There was something about Harriet that I liked and, besides, hadn't we all had bad days? Today for me had been a nightmare.

'I'll leave you to settle in,' I said.

'And Simon will leave my car outside the walled garden?' she asked. 'What about the keys?'

'I expect they'll be left inside the car,' I said, adding, 'They'll be perfectly safe.'

Harriet took off her coat and flung it onto the bed. She was neatly dressed in a wool skirt and polo-neck jumper and was wearing a pearl and diamond necklace.

'Is that the necklace you wanted me to look at?'

'Yes, please. Now is as good a time as any.' Harriet thrust her chest forward, holding up the strand of pearls interspersed with five small diamonds. 'Pearls for thirty years. I can tell you that year five wasn't that exciting. It stands for wood and Timothy gave me a stick. I said, "What do you think I am? A dog?"'

'They're very pretty.' I leaned in to take a closer look.

'Majorica pearls and real diamonds,' Harriet said proudly. 'It was on our cruise. I made Timothy take me to this beautiful pearl shop in Mallorca. This necklace is a limited edition because of the diamonds, you see.'

I did see. I also had a sinking feeling that although the pearls were what Harriet said they were – Majorica pearls were excellent and affordable – the diamonds were almost certainly zircons.

'Yes,' Harriet went on. 'This necklace set Timothy back several thousand pounds!'

'Did it come with a certificate of authentication?'

'Oh, yes.' Harriet nodded again. 'But my mother-in-law told me the diamonds aren't real and that's why I want you to settle this family argument once and for all.'

Given everything that had happened today, I couldn't face telling Harriet that her diamonds were fake and, besides, maybe I was wrong.

'The light isn't very good in here,' I said. 'Why don't you come to my showroom tomorrow at nine thirty? We passed it on our way. It's one of the gatehouses at the main entrance to the Hall. Bring the certificate of authentication with you as well.'

'Oh, I don't have that here,' Harriet said. 'I didn't expect to meet you. It's very kind of you to offer to do this.'

I assumed that meant I was doing the valuation for free. Saying I'd see her in the morning, I paused at the door. 'I hope you won't be lonely.'

'I won't,' said Harriet. 'I'm just happy to be alone and read without Timothy watching football all evening and demanding snacks. Oh, and don't forget to play postman.'

Seeing my puzzled look she added, 'The packages you picked up in the village?'

I had forgotten. 'Thank you.'

I left Harriet turning on the kettle and exploring the tiny kitchen space, relieved that someone was happy.

I returned to my car and went to see my mother.

Chapter Six

'Oh dear,' said Mum, as she poured us a gin and tonic. 'I always knew that Di Wilkins was a flake.'

Mum's reaction was exactly as I'd feared. It wasn't that she didn't like my friend, she just claimed it was one of her 'feelings' that urged caution.

'And the nanny-cam?' Mum went on. 'Did you see anything on that?'

'Useless,' I moaned. 'The Christmas decorations were obstructing the view and, besides, I'd angled the lens at the counter and not at the doll on the shelf. Mallory is hoping he'll have better luck with the CCTV.'

'Ah, the gorgeous Mallory,' Mum mused. 'Working on a Sunday evening? Doesn't he ever stop?'

'It's very kind of him,' I said. 'And it is his job.'

'Kind? Not kind, dear.' Mum gave a knowing nod. 'He'd do anything for you.'

I wasn't in the mood to discuss my love life and couldn't

help but go on the defensive. 'Well, he's going to be disappointed because I'm with Shawn and we're very happy.'

Mum smirked. 'Of course, dear. Anything you say.' She adjusted a silk scarf around her neck. It was a distinctive green and coordinated perfectly with her dark brown cashmere jumper. 'Gosh, is it hot in here or just me?'

'It's you,' I said. 'I feel terrible. I'll have to call the insurance company first thing.'

'At least the doll was insured,' Mum said.

'I know Cathy will be upset. I dread telling her, let alone the Cartwrights, that the biggest auction item is missing.'

'Not missing,' Mum reminded me. 'Stolen. Frankly, I've always thought Barbie was a tart. Flat-chested Sindy had more class. Don't you still have yours? You could make the switch.'

'She's in my storage unit in Exeter,' I said.

'I could give her some breast implants and run up a ballgown,' said Mum.

'Be serious for once.'

'I was. I thought it was a good idea.' She waved a hand dismissively. 'I don't know what all the fuss is about. Before the Cartwrights came, things were always going wrong at local events, and everyone had a good laugh. Do you remember the panto last year?'

I managed a small smile. '*Jack and the Beanstalk*.'

'That's right.' Mum grinned. 'The giant fell off his stilts and brought down all the scenery. Did anyone care? Of course not! But with the Cartwrights in charge, everything is so serious. Delia thinks they want Honeychurch to become the new Longleat.'

I pulled a face of disgust. 'I can't see that happening. I also can't see them staying. It couldn't be more different than their international jet-setting life.'

'I think the minute Marion's mother dies, they'll be gone,' Mum said. 'Apparently Ryan doesn't like the English weather.'

'How can the Honeychurch family afford to pay them?'

'Delia told me his lordship sold a painting,' said Mum.

I was appalled. 'To sell a painting for something so – so superficial. Do you know which one?'

'No idea.' Mum took a long drink and gave a shudder of satisfaction. 'Although I say it myself, this year's Honeychurch gin is a really good batch.'

'And what does Edith think about it all?'

'Delia says she hardly sees her,' said Mum. 'Her ladyship either keeps to her room or is at the stables.'

'Or in her Land Rover,' I said. 'I caught her out driving today.'

'She is naughty.' Mum chuckled.

'Unfortunately, she had an accident,' I said, and told Mum how Willow and I had come upon Harriet attacking the Land Rover with her handbag.

'What on earth was her ladyship doing down by Bridge Cottage reading a magazine?'

'No idea.' I shrugged.

Mum chuckled again. 'And you say that this Harriet Bone is staying in the shepherd's hut? What on earth possessed her at this time of year? She'll freeze to death.'

'It's surprisingly warm and cosy inside,' I said. 'Harriet's husband has just retired, and she needs some time away.'

'Did you stop at the post office?' Mum said suddenly.

'Yes. You have some parcels. They're in the car,' I said. 'While I get them you can top up my drink.'

When I returned with the nylon bag of parcels, I noticed that my mother had discarded her scarf and was exploring her neck with tentative fingers. 'I think I've come up in a rash. Can you see anything?'

'Let me look,' I said.

It was true. Her neck was covered with ugly red blotches. It looked like one or two might blister.

'You must have eaten something you're allergic to, Mum.'

'I doubt it. Anything alien in my body would be instantly killed off by the gin.' She pointed to the bag. 'Let's look at what my adoring readers have sent me for Christmas.'

'Modesty was never your strong point.' I tipped the contents onto the kitchen table. 'Fan mail for Krystalle Storm.'

Mum pushed the stack of letters and cards to one side, grabbed some scissors and undid the parcel with the festive stickers. Inside, a gift was wrapped in sparkly tissue paper. Eagerly, she tore it open to reveal a pair of beautiful green kid gloves with tiny buttons at the wrist.

'Oh, look!' Mum enthused. She picked up the discarded scarf. 'They're the same colour as this. And they smell like it too.'

'Let's have a whiff,' I said.

Mum thrust it under my nose. 'Is it garlic?'

I pulled a face. 'A little bit but it's more likely your breath.'

'Thanks,' Mum said drily. 'But don't you think it an unusual shade of green? It's very pretty. How would you describe the colour? Not emerald – oops, sorry, darling. I didn't mean to remind you of your little problem.'

'I don't need reminding,' I replied. 'I can't stop thinking about it. And please don't say anything to anyone. Not yet. Promise?'

'Cross my heart and hope to die,' Mum said solemnly. She turned back to the gloves. 'It's like the iridescent green of a lizard.' She hunted through the tissue paper. 'Ah. Here is the note. It says, "Dear Krystalle, I hope when you wear your scarf with the matching gloves and the little beret, you think of me." It's signed "A Fan".' She turned the note over. 'No name or return address.'

'And no beret,' I pointed out. I counted the parcels on the table. There were just three, not four. One must have fallen out in the car.

Mum pulled on the gloves, but they were far too small. 'Oh, what a pity. My fingers are too long, and yours are too stumpy.'

'I do not have stumpy fingers, thank you very much,' I said. 'Open the others.'

Mum set the gloves and scarf on the oak dresser. She picked up the second package. Inside was a padded envelope addressed to Krystalle Storm, c/o Goldfinch Press along with the publisher's London address on a label. Inside this envelope another gift was wrapped in Christmas paper. It turned out to be a delicate piece of Brussels lace along with a sweet note saying how much someone called Beryl loved the Star-Crossed Lovers series. Mum opened the third and, again, the brown paper covered another package addressed to Krystalle Storm c/o Goldfinch Press. It was a small book of poetry by Elizabeth Barrett Browning inscribed by a reader called Sandra.

'How lovely,' I enthused. 'I assume your publicist writes and thanks your fans on your behalf.'

But Mum didn't answer. She was studying the mound of brown paper with a peculiar look on her face.

'What's the matter?' I asked.

Mum picked up the paper covered with festive stickers. 'This one was sent directly to the PO box. Not the publisher.' She picked up one of the padded envelopes marked Krystalle Storm c/o Goldfinch Press. 'See? It skipped Goldfinch Press.'

'Don't you have the PO box listed on your website?'

'No.' Mum's frown deepened. 'Any correspondence always goes directly to my publisher.'

'Perhaps someone at the publishing house knows your PO box,' I suggested, 'and told a fan by mistake?'

'It's possible.' Mum bit her lip and frowned. 'There was a new intern. Monica something, or was it Mary?'

'What about the scarf?' I asked. 'Did you notice if that was sent directly to the PO box, too?'

'I can't remember, but would you pop into the garage?' she said. 'The blue recycling sack hasn't been collected yet this week. I just want to know.'

But I didn't have a chance.

'It's only me!' Delia Evans strolled into the kitchen dressed for the Arctic in snow boots, coat, scarf and hat. She didn't drive and had to go everywhere on foot or on her bicycle. She was very red in the face from her exertions.

Spying the bottle of Honeychurch gin on the kitchen table, she said, 'I'll have a quick one.'

Mum gestured to the oak dresser. 'You know where the glasses are.'

Delia carefully removed her hat so as not to dislodge her chin-length aubergine wig, then tore off her coat and hung it on the back of a kitchen chair.

I did a double-take. Delia was wearing a black dress with a white peter-pan collar and white cuffs. 'Is that a uniform?'

'Yes. Marion insists I wear one.' Delia scowled. 'I feel like I'm dressed for a funeral.'

'You could brighten it up with a nice scarf.' Mum gave a nod to the green scarf on the dresser.

'What a pretty green,' Delia said, then shook her head. 'Marion wouldn't allow it. She's a tyrant and he's no better. I can only stay fifteen minutes or I'll be in trouble.'

'Why?' Mum said.

Delia pulled a face. 'I'm only here to tell you there's a staff meeting tonight in the ballroom at seven thirty sharp.'

Mum gave a snort. 'A *staff* meeting?'

'Marion said that drinks and nibbles will be provided,' Delia said. 'And we'll all freeze to death because his lordship refuses to turn the heating on in there until Friday morning.'

'So what staff is she talking about?' Mum said. 'I thought you were the staff. We're not staff. We're residents.'

'Don't be difficult, Iris,' said Delia. 'Marion wants to run through everyone's responsibilities for the gala.'

'Is the donkey coming too?' Mum said, with a snigger.

'No.' Delia grinned. 'The donkey has already been booked for the church nativity play this evening.'

'Having a live donkey turn up at the gala is asking for trouble,' Mum went on. 'They're not house-trained.'

'Ah, that's where you come in.' Delia struggled to keep a straight face. 'You're going to be given a bucket and a shovel . . .'

Mum's jaw dropped and then she roared with laughter. 'God! You had me worried for a moment!'

'You're off the hook,' said Delia. 'Alfred already volunteered since he loves playing around in manure. But you'd better volunteer for something or you'll end up being the loo lady.'

'Over my dead body.' Mum picked up the gin bottle to top up our drinks.

I covered my glass with my hand. 'I think I need to pace myself.'

'No more for me either,' Delia said grimly. 'I'm in enough trouble as it is.'

Mum rolled her eyes. 'What have you done this time?'

Delia delved into her handbag, retrieved her mobile, scrolled through her photographs and handed Mum the phone. 'Look at that, Iris.'

'I don't know what I'm supposed to be looking at.'

Delia jabbed a finger at the screen. 'The cushions!'

'Yes,' said Mum. 'I see three cushions – are those owls?'

'Yes. The three cushions are arranged on their corners on the sofa but, oh, no, Marion wants the cushions arranged on their sides.' She flipped to the next photo. 'Like so. I got a real telling-off for it, too. They're just *cushions*!'

'Oh dear,' Mum said.

'And not only that, I have to use a compass divider—'

'A what?' Mum exclaimed.

'You know, one of those things that measures distances,' Delia said. 'I have to make sure the cushions are the same distance apart. It's all got to be perfect.'

'Let me see,' I said, and took a peep. 'Those photographs weren't taken at the Hall.'

'Iris didn't tell you?' Delia said. 'I'm cleaning the Cartwrights' cottage now. Yes. Me. Twice a week. I may as well clean Eric's while I'm at it!' To my surprise, Delia's eyes grew watery. 'I'm sorry. But . . . I feel so pushed out.'

I knew that Delia had been unhappy about being overlooked after Peggy Cropper had retired. She'd thought she would be promoted to Head of House with underlings. Instead she'd been demoted and she didn't like it one bit.

'Go on. Have another gin. A small one won't hurt,' Mum said. 'It must be hard thinking you were going to rule the roost but are nothing more than a glorified maid-of-all-work.'

Much as I wasn't sure how I felt about my mother's on-again-off-again best friend, I did think the Cartwrights were treating Delia badly.

'I mean, who do they think they are?' Delia wailed.

Mum slammed her glass onto the table. 'Exactly! *Who* are they? And now you have access to their cottage, you can jolly well find out. Look around. Rummage through their drawers and, while you're at it, you might discover who the mystery guest is going to be.'

'Mum!' I was horrified. 'You can't ask Delia to do that! That's just wrong!'

'Is it? I always thought there was something odd about them.' Mum warmed to her theme. 'I know Marion's mother is ill but why bother to get a job? They've obviously got money. They've both got new cars. She drives the Land Cruiser and he's got a Shogun. Or is it the other way around?'

Delia's tears had disappeared in a flash. She straightened her shoulders. 'Yes! Who are they really? Other than one snap of the pair of them on holiday, there are no other photographs on display. Nothing at all. I never have to empty their rubbish bins because they have a shredder in the back porch. It's all very sterile. Like a show house. Minimalist. Even the bookshelves are sparse. I mean, where do they have all their real stuff?'

'They must have a storage unit,' I said. 'I still have mine.'

'That must be it,' Delia agreed.

Mum's birdsong clock chimed the half-hour.

Delia leaped to her feet. 'I must go.'

As she donned her coat and hat, Delia glanced at the gloves and scarf on the oak dresser. 'I've never seen such a pretty green.'

'You can have them,' Mum said, in a rush of generosity. 'The gloves are far too small for me. And why don't you wear the scarf with your uniform? I dare you! You work for her ladyship, not Marion Cartwright.'

Delia snatched them up. She wound the scarf around her neck and pulled on the gloves. 'They're so soft!' She beamed. 'You really don't want them?'

'No.' Mum smiled. 'My hands aren't as dainty as yours.'

It was strange that whenever one of them was unhappy, the other was always so kind, yet when both women were on an even keel, their conversations tended to be mostly snipes and barbs. It was a peculiar friendship.

Delia stroked her face with her gloved hand and wrinkled her nose. 'They smell a bit funny.'

'Nonsense,' said Mum. 'It's your breath.'

'Oh.' Delia reddened. 'Marion asked me to taste the dip and I told her she'd put in too much garlic. Are you *sure* you don't want them?'

'Call it an early Christmas present,' said Mum.

'Well, thank you.' Delia beamed again. And, with a wave, her own scarf and gloves abandoned on the kitchen table, she said she'd see us later and left.

My mobile phone rang. The caller ID flashed *Mallory*.

'I need to talk to you,' he said, before I had even said hello.

'You've found something?' I said eagerly. 'The footage? Shall I come to the station?'

Mum pointed to the clock. 'You haven't time. We've got to be at the Hall at seven thirty sharp, remember.'

I ignored her. This was too important.

'I'm parked outside your house,' said Mallory. 'I'm sorry but you won't like what I have to tell you.'

Chapter Seven

Ten minutes later I was unlocking the front door to Jane's Cottage and ushering Mallory ahead. My heart was thumping. It had to be bad news.

He looked so grave that it made me nervous. 'Do you want to sit down?' I asked. 'A cup of tea, perhaps?'

'A quick one.'

I headed for the archway that led to the kitchen. Behind me I heard a loud crack and cry of pain.

'I'm so sorry!' I said. 'Are you okay?'

'When will I learn to duck?' Mallory rubbed his head.

We stayed in the kitchen, perched on the bar stools with our tea.

'I'll get straight to the point. Di lied,' he said bluntly. 'The footage captured the carol singers and Annie fainting – by the way, she seems to have vanished into thin air.'

My heart sank. 'Oh.'

Mallory cleared his throat. 'The CCTV camera picked up Di near the entrance to the café.'

'Okay, but that doesn't—'

'And moments later, our man with the moustache and glasses appeared.'

'Are you suggesting that they were *together*?'

'Your friend moved out of frame. Our suspect pushed Pam's trolley aside and went out of the fire exit.'

'But that doesn't mean Di had anything to do with it,' I protested.

'You heard her say she never left your area, Kat. I'm sorry.'

Di had lied to me.

'When I talked to Fiona Reynolds,' Mallory went on, 'she asked for a word in private. Di Wilkins owes three months in unpaid rent.'

I sat for a moment trying to take it all in. I knew that Di had been struggling financially for a while. She had confided in me about car problems, how expensive interest was on her credit cards and that she had decided to take a second job.

Dad had always driven home 'neither a lender nor a borrower be' and that was a rule I stuck to, having learned my lesson the hard way years ago. It had ended a friendship. For that very reason I had avoided asking Di for details and perhaps I should have done.

'This is horrible.' I ran my hand through my hair. 'I don't know what to think.'

'I'm afraid there's more.' Mallory took a deep breath. 'Someone has been shoplifting.'

I thought of Di's comment about Teresa and Kylie. 'Did you talk to Willow's friends?'

'I left messages for all three,' said Mallory. 'But none have returned my call.'

'Willow is working at the pub tonight,' I said. 'I wouldn't know about her friends.'

'Have you had any instances of shoplifting?'

I shook my head. 'I set up the nanny-cam on my phone for that very reason.'

'Can I take a look?' said Mallory.

I retrieved my phone from my tote bag. It took me a few moments to open the app and locate the time record.

'May I?' he said, and took it from my hand, brushing my fingertips. We both jumped apart. Again, the touch was electric.

'As you can see, the lens is focused on the easily snatched and portable stuff on the counter,' I said.

'Pity the other vendors don't have something like this in place.' He thought for a moment. 'I'd still like to take a closer look on a larger screen. You can make out the display shelf in the background. I can slow the speed right down and zoom in. We might be lucky and see the doll snatch take place.'

It was a crumb of hope but my mind was still coming to terms with the possibility that Di must have seen the thief walk right past her. 'Shall I email the file to you?'

Mallory stepped closer again and spelled out his email address.

I accidentally hit the wrong button. A screensaver of Shawn and me flashed up. He had his arm around my shoulders. I was smiling for the selfie, but Shawn looked serious. I remembered the day that photograph was taken.

I had met him after his lunch with fellow train enthusiasts. He was wearing his favourite tie covered with railway signals under a V-neck sweater. I also remembered teasing him about it but, instead of taking my light-hearted comments in the spirit I had intended, Shawn had seemed offended.

'Ah,' said Mallory. 'The happy couple.' He nodded. 'Shawn's a good man. A good man.'

'Yes,' I agreed firmly. 'Very much so.'

There was an awkward silence.

'You need to talk to your friend before I do,' Mallory said. 'I'll give you until tomorrow lunchtime.'

'Thank you.' I bit my lip. 'But Di knows just how important the gala is to me.'

'People often let us down when we least expect it,' he said. 'But if she is involved, there's a chance you might get the doll back.'

I nodded.

'In your worst-case scenario, can you donate something else instead?'

'I've thought of that.' The problem was that I'd already donated a valuable Steiff bear for the silent auction. Another high-end item would really set me back financially.

Thanking me for the tea, Mallory left, making sure to duck through the front door.

My mobile rang. It was Shawn. 'Right,' he said. 'Sorry I couldn't talk to you earlier but you have my full attention now. What's happened?'

I brought him up to date.

'And Mallory's on it?' said Shawn.

'Yes, he is,' I said. 'But I'm worried about this whole situation with Di. Can we talk about it when you come over this evening,' I went on. 'I've got this stupid meeting at the Hall first.'

'Ah, yes,' said Shawn. 'I was about to tell you about tonight. I've just left Gran in the ballroom.'

'You're at the Hall right now?' I was confused. 'Why? Is Peggy involved in the gala?'

'She's been asked to guard the kitchen,' said Shawn. 'Lady Lavinia's orders. She wanted someone she trusted on site to make sure they don't use the Minton dinnerware.'

'Does that mean you can't stay over?' I was disappointed. 'I thought the twins' grandmother was going to look after them tonight.'

'Change of plan,' said Shawn. 'There's more snow forecast and I must be in Exeter first thing tomorrow morning. I can't risk being stuck.'

'Why don't I come back with you tonight?' I suggested. 'Oh, no, I can't. I have a valuation at the gatehouse at nine thirty but—'

'To be honest,' Shawn cut in, 'I wouldn't be good company. I'm in the middle of a case.'

'Aren't you always?' I teased.

'Don't give me a hard time,' he said wearily. 'You know I'm under a lot of pressure.'

'I was joking, Shawn,' I said. 'But you're still coming to the gala on Friday, aren't you?'

I sensed his hesitation and felt a pang of dismay.

'If I can, I will,' he said. 'But you know I have a lot of work on, and you know I hate that kind of thing anyway. You won't even miss me. You'll be too caught up in being the MC and the auctioneer.'

'I will miss you,' I protested. 'I really need your support – especially now. And, besides, I want to see your train bow-tie.'

There was an intermittent beep in my ear.

'I've got to take this call,' he said. 'We'll talk later. I promise.'

And with that he disconnected, leaving me more than a little bit miffed. And then I saw the time. It was already seven thirty. I was going to be late.

Chapter Eight

I left my car in the rear courtyard next to the service entrance to the Hall kitchens. On the big night, cars would be parked in an adjacent field with matting laid on the grass so that high heels wouldn't get muddy.

I took the path that skirted the main part of the hall. I always liked taking this route and seeing the different architectural periods from the Hall's Tudor beginnings to late Victorian additions.

Directions to the ballroom were displayed on water-resistant placards handwritten in beautiful calligraphy, designed by Marion. She had also done the invitations and the illustrated map of the estate. Marion seemed to be good at everything.

Moments later I had passed through an arched pergola strung with fairy lights and into another courtyard bordered by dilapidated outbuildings that certainly looked better in the dark, as did the row of Portaloos.

I couldn't help thinking how unappealing – and tricky – it

would be going outside for a pee in the freezing cold dressed in a flimsy ballgown.

Topiaries in pots covered with fake snow lined the flag-stone terrace that ran along a range of floor-to-ceiling French windows. The ballroom entrance was through a central double-door framed with boughs of holly, tartan ribbons, baubles and more fairy lights. The whole thing created an ambience of romantic luxury.

A glance through the window showed preparations were well under way. There were twenty circular tables with ten chairs each. The chairs were of the mass catering kind, gold plastic with red velour seats. The tables were of durable plastic too, but once they were laid up with linen, silver, table decorations and flowers, they would look nice. A huge Christmas tree, decorated with no expense spared, stood to the left of the grand fireplace. On the right was the podium where I would act as MC and auctioneer, and where the mystery guest would give the after-dinner speech. Above, and opposite, a minstrels' gallery was accessed by a hidden staircase. This was where the live band would play quietly during the meal. After the speeches, auction and prizes, the tables would be pushed aside for dancing in the centre of the room.

The Cartwrights' staff were huddled in their outdoor coats under the minstrels' gallery. I noticed that Delia wore the green scarf and gloves. Rupert was in his usual attire of tweed jacket and corduroys and Lavinia – bizarrely – was wearing a thin blouse and a long black velvet skirt.

I pushed open the door, struck by how cold it was – so cold inside that my breath came out in misty puffs.

'Ah, Kat,' Marion called. 'Glad you were able to join us.'

'My daughter always likes to cut it fine,' I heard Mum say.

I took in the assembled staff: the stable manager, Mum's stepbrother Alfred Bushman, Delia Evans, Eric Pugsley, Rupert and Lavinia, and Peggy Cropper. Each held an official-looking clipboard. Ryan wasn't there. I didn't expect to see Edith, but I did expect to see Shawn. He must have dropped Peggy off and would come back later.

I made my apologies, which went unacknowledged. Marion handed me a clipboard. It had my name and role in bold type at the top. Even the paper had been custom-made, sporting the Earl of Grenville's coat of arms and motto, *ad perserverate est ad triumphum* – to endure is to triumph – in which I found no comfort in my present predicament.

Marion tapped her clipboard. 'We've run through everyone's assignments except yours and the videographer's. He's late too.'

'Must have got lost,' Lavinia said, in her usual clipped way. 'I'll go—'

'No need, your ladyship. Ryan is doing that right now,' said Marion. 'I just can't understand it.' She seemed irrationally annoyed. 'We have the signage! I hope he can read.'

'Um. I think so.' Lavinia didn't sound so sure.

'But, really, it's just too bad that he can't be here on time,' Marion persisted. 'It's critical that he's familiar with the programme, your ladyship.'

'He's frightfully good.' Lavinia looked downcast. From her reaction, I thought she must have recommended him.

'Can we get on?' Rupert grumbled. 'Not exactly how I would choose to spend my Sunday evening.'

Marion checked her watch again. 'I'll give you a quick recap – sorry to everyone who has heard all this before. From the top. Mrs. Cropper will be in the kitchen, Delia is going to be on coats—'

'The hat-check girl,' Mum said.

'Alfred is taking care of Hannah – that's the donkey. Eric is on car-park attendance along with Master Harry.' Marion pointed to the French windows where I had come in. 'Lord Rupert and Lady Lavinia will be welcoming the guests as they enter over there. Waiting staff will offer Veuve Clicquot champagne and pass round platters of canapés.' Marion consulted her clipboard again. 'I think that's it. Does everyone know what they're doing?'

'Iris doesn't,' Delia said. 'She's not doing anything.'

'I know!' Mum raised her hand. 'Why don't I look after the mystery guest?'

'If you feel you're up to it,' Marion said. 'Our mystery guest will have his or her own suite of rooms but, from experience, celebrities can be quite demanding.'

'Do I have to pick up whoever it is from the airport?' Mum asked eagerly. 'I really hope it's Princess Caroline. Actually, her correct title is Princess of Hanover, Duchess of Brunswick-Lüneburg. Personally, I don't think she made a good choice in marrying Ernst.'

Marion gave a small smile. 'I'm afraid I'm not going to comment. Our mystery guest agreed to come providing their appearance was kept utterly secret until the gala.'

'We had a world-famous opera singer here once,' Lavinia put in. 'And at least we won't have to contend with the bats.'

Marion looked pained. 'The bats?'

'Oh, yes.' Lavinia beamed. 'The Devon horseshoe bat. Very rare. We have them every year! It caused a frightful stir. But don't worry, they're hibernating now.'

'Sorry, we got lost,' came a female voice. We turned to see a young man in his early twenties being ushered in by none other than Pam Price.

The videographer was her son.

I immediately panicked and squirmed my way to the back of the group, glad that Marion was so tall, and desperate that Pam wouldn't see me or, worse, say something about the theft. I knew I had to tell the Cartwrights but I definitely didn't want them to hear about it from the caretaker! I tried to remember what Mallory had said to Pam. Had he specifically mentioned it was Emerald Barbie that had been stolen?

Lance looked nervous and shifted from foot to foot. He was wearing a Northern Face jacket with the price tag still attached, and crisp jeans.

'Hello, Mrs P. Fancy seeing you here,' Lavinia gushed. 'Um. Everyone, this is Lance's mother.'

'Fancy still calling me Mrs P,' said Pam, with a sneer. 'Those days are long gone now, aren't they? Just call me Pam.'

Marion, always polite, stepped forward to offer her hand. 'And I'm Marion Cartwright.'

To my horror, I was completely exposed and slipped quickly behind my mother. But I needn't have worried: Pam seemed far more interested in Marion. 'Have we met? You look familiar.'

Harriet had recognised Marion and now Pam had. I was so glad to be out of that celebrity world.

'Marion was an actress,' Mum put in helpfully. 'Maybe you've seen her in films. But really you need to meet her husband, Ryan. They would have been the modern-day Richard Burton and Elizabeth Taylor.'

'Iris, you're too funny,' Marion said, but she wasn't smiling.

'Hollywood.' Pam nudged Lance. 'Do you know any famous directors?'

'Mum! Please!' Lance seemed mortified. 'You promised.'

'All right, all right.' Pam rolled her eyes. 'I'll wait in the car. How long is this going to take?'

'I don't need you to wait in the car, Mum,' Lance hissed. 'I'll take a taxi home.'

'A taxi! Who can afford a taxi?' Pam barked. 'I'll go to that pub in the village and you can call me when you're ready. I'll come back and pick you up.'

'Eric can drop Lance to the pub, Mrs P – Price. I mean, Pam,' Lavinia said quickly.

Eric nodded. 'No problem, milady.'

'All right,' said Pam. 'I'll leave you all to it, but just so you know, you're in the company of the next Steven Spielberg!'

She headed for the exit. Thank heavens she'd gone. I felt myself relax.

Lance gave a rueful smile. 'I'm sorry about that. Mum wouldn't let me ride my moped because of the snow.'

'Never mind,' said Lavinia, warmly. 'You're here now.'

Marion handed Lance a clipboard but it was obvious to everyone that she wasn't very happy.

'Has anyone seen Lance's beautiful wildlife Christmas cards?' Lavinia said desperately.

'I have,' I said. 'And they're stunning.'

'I'm sure Lance will have a field day photographing the wildlife at the gala,' Mum whispered.

'Right, then,' said Marion. 'Everyone, except the latecomers, can come with me to the kitchen where we'll have some mulled wine and snacks. Kat and Lance can wait here for Ryan.'

Marion swept out of the ballroom with the others trailing behind. Mum waved, and said, 'We'll try to leave you some scraps.'

'I saw some of your work in the community shop,' I said, into the silence that followed. 'The white hare by the snowdrift is one of my favourites. How you captured the light on such an obviously grey day is incredible.'

'Yeah. It took me a long time to get that right.' Lance smiled, and when he did, his passion for his craft lit up his face.

'It sounds like you want to move to California?' I asked.

'No, I don't,' Lance said hotly. 'I want to move to Dartmoor, but Mum won't have it.'

I felt a pang of sympathy. Even though Lance was old enough to stand up for himself, I suspected that Pam was a force to be reckoned with.

'How do you know Lady Lavinia?' I asked.

'Dad was one of the gamekeepers for the Earl of Denby,' said Lance. 'We had a cottage on the estate.'

All too late I remembered Di telling me Pam's sad story about being turned out and her husband's subsequent death. I felt terrible.

'I don't have many contacts in TV,' I said. 'But perhaps we can have coffee sometime and you can tell me what you'd like to do.'

Lance's jaw hardened. 'I already told you what I want to do. It's convincing my mother.'

Ryan bowled into the room all smiles. He wore a huge padded jacket, Russian hat, scarf and sheepskin gloves. 'You both made it!'

It was easy to see why Mum had nicknamed him Ken. He reminded me of a shop-window mannequin, with his polished film-star looks and dazzling veneers. The only thing he didn't have was height.

There didn't seem much point in going through the itinerary because it was listed on the clipboard, but Ryan did so all the same at breakneck speed.

'We have the live band playing in the minstrels' gallery. Guests arrive. Champagne. Canapés. Mingle. Dinner is served. Then comes the mystery guest speaker. Kat picks up the silent auction and we go into live bidding, which will be streamed on Facebook. Raffle will be drawn, prizes announced and the donkey arrives. Then dancing until midnight.'

Lance brightened. 'There's a live donkey?'

'That's right,' said Ryan. 'From the donkey sanctuary.'

Lance grinned. 'Where's Mary and Joseph?'

Ryan frowned. 'Mary and Joseph? What's their last name?'

I caught Lance's eye and winked. 'Perhaps they're the mystery guests.'

'No.' Ryan shook his head slowly. 'There's only one mystery guest.'

'Baby Jesus?' Lance suggested. I laughed.

Ryan shook his head again. 'No kids allowed. Adults only.' And Ryan wasn't joking.

'Okay?' said Ryan. 'Any questions?'

Lance pointed to the minstrels' gallery. 'I'd like to set up there. Can I come back tomorrow?'

'Knock yourself out, buddy. The ballroom is open anytime to you.' Ryan guided us through a pair of double-doors that opened into a pale green octagonal room. Empty trestle tables had been set around the circumference. This was where the silent auction would take place.

'Where are the auction items now?' I asked.

'Marion has it under control,' said Ryan. 'She's creating backdrops to showcase each experience. We've got hot-air ballooning, falconry, fly-fishing on the River Dart, wine tasting – that kind of thing.' He pointed to a table covered with a shimmering dark green cloth. 'And that's for Emerald Barbie.'

My heart began to hammer in my chest. I had to say something, but the words just wouldn't come out.

'We got lucky,' said Ryan. '*Dolls Galore* magazine are running a piece on Emerald Barbie for their digital edition that will come out on Thursday, the day before the gala. All they need is a photograph and five hundred words by Wednesday at the latest.'

I took a deep breath. 'The thing is—'

'Great.' Lance smiled. 'We could photograph her tomorrow if you're available, Kat.'

'Um. Possibly,' I said. 'Can we talk first thing in the morning?'

Lance pulled out his business card, which featured the hare in the snow I had admired. 'And call me. Not my mother.'

'Ryan,' I tried again. 'I need a word in private—'

'Talk to Marion,' said Ryan. 'Let's get to the party!'

As I trailed after them I mentally ran through what I could offer as a substitute for Emerald Barbie but desperately hoped for a miracle.

Instead of going outside and accessing the kitchen through the rear courtyard, Ryan led us through a maze of corridors to the grand two-storey galleried reception area in the main house. This, too, had been elaborately decorated for Christmas with an enormous tree that reached the landing. A huge crystal chandelier hung suspended between two domed-glass atriums.

Full-bodied suits of armour were arranged randomly throughout the hall. Small gilt nameplates identified the family portraits that lined the walls. On the right, below each painting, stood a seventeenth-century Dutch walnut marquetry chair inlaid with flowers, foliage, parrots and urns. Interspersed between other chairs were Victorian pedestal plant stands on top of which sat Christmas poinsettias.

Lance stopped to take it all in. It was an impressive sight, especially with Florian, the stuffed, rearing polar bear standing by the magnificent fireplace. The bear had been brought back from the Arctic by one of the Honeychurch explorers in the late nineteenth century. Harry had begged his grandmother to move Florian from the museum into the reception area so he, too, could be part of the festivities. Needless to say, the bear was decked out in a woolly hat and striped scarf, and was draped with tinsel.

Lance pulled out his camera, but before he could take a single photograph, Ryan said, 'No point doing that, buddy. This area is out of bounds. Understand? No pictures. Ballroom only.'

Lance pointed to the shafts of moonlight that spilled through the domed atriums, casting eerie shadows over the black-and-white marble chessboard floor.

'Come on,' he said. 'Just one quick shot.'

'Sorry,' said Ryan. 'Rules are rules. This way.' He pointed to a corridor that led to the kitchen and servants' quarters.

The doorbell tolled.

'You both go on ahead,' I said quickly. If it was Pam I wanted to get to her first.

I hurried to the inner front porch as the tolling of the bell became more insistent.

But when I flung open the door, it wasn't Pam. It was Harriet Bone and she did not look happy.

Chapter Nine

'What are you doing here?' Harriet demanded, but she didn't wait for the answer and barged past, almost tripping over the nineteenth-century elephant-foot umbrella stand in her haste.

I hurried after her into the entrance hall. 'Is everything all right?'

And it all came tumbling out.

Yes, Harriet's car had been returned as promised and left outside the walled garden with her keys on the dashboard 'for any thief to steal'. But that wasn't the problem.

'The idiot attached the tow rope to the radiator grille!' Harriet fumed. 'Almost pulled it off! Didn't even leave a note! I knocked at those cottages, and no one answered. It'll have to be paid for.'

Marion had made it clear that Eric was off-limits, and it was highly unlikely that Simon would have made such a mistake. Which left Ryan.

'Are you sure that the grille wasn't already damaged when—?'

'Most certainly not!' Harriet squawked. 'My husband is going to be livid— Oh, it's you!'

Marion was heading our way. She did a double-take. 'Ah. You're the lady whose car was stuck on the bank. Is everything okay?'

I let Harriet tell the story and watched as her face got redder by the minute.

'Kat,' said Marion. 'You should have told me that Mrs Bone was staying at the shepherd's hut this afternoon.'

There it was again, the patronising tone she used with me. 'I didn't know she—'

'We really can't have our paying guests treated like that, Kat,' said Marion.

I bit back a retort. I was not a member of her wretched staff!

Harriet seemed slightly comforted to have a sympathetic ear. 'Whoever towed my car is an idiot.'

Marion gave a concerned smile. 'Oh dear.'

'The repairs will cost thousands,' Harriet ran on. 'Yes, I'm insured, but that's not the point, is it?'

Marion kept smiling. She reminded me of a flight attendant, trained to smile even when the plane was going down in flames. 'Surely the damage to the radiator grille must have been caused when your car mounted the bank.'

'I didn't mount the bank on purpose!' Harriet said angrily. 'I told you the old bag wouldn't get out of the way. It was her fault. She should pay for the damage.'

I scanned the entrance hall, dreading the very real possibility that Edith would suddenly appear and overhear Harriet's tirade.

Marion must have thought the same thing because she said, 'Why don't you come and have a drink and we'll sort it out over a glass of mulled wine. It's Christmas!'

Harriet frowned. 'Do you live here?'

'No,' said Marion. 'But I am the head of house.'

'Will I meet the earl? What about the dowager countess?' Harriet said.

I didn't say that she had already met the latter.

'The dowager countess does not come into the kitchen,' said Marion. 'But Lord Rupert and Lady Lavinia are there this evening.'

'And what about the idiot who towed my car?'

'Not one of us, fortunately,' said Marion, quickly.

I looked at Marion in surprise. She was lying. And the only reason she was lying was to protect her husband.

'And how do you like the shepherd's hut?' Marion asked, as she led the way.

'It's lovely and warm,' said Harriet. 'But I feel I'm in *The Blair Witch Project*! All those noises. And then I heard someone get murdered!'

'I expect that was a fox,' Marion said. 'The screams scared me the first time I moved to the country. You'll soon get used to it.'

Harriet seemed to perk up when we crossed the black-and-white marble chessboard floor, and when she saw the polar bear she went into raptures. 'It's just how I imagined it would be! And there are the atriums! And the staircase.' She nodded eagerly. 'Yes. Just as I thought.'

Marion paused. 'Have you been here before?'

'You could say that,' said Harriet, slyly.

We entered the kitchen, which, unlike the ballroom, was warm. Ryan had insisted on the heating being on full blast twenty-four hours a day, which, of course, didn't go down well with the family, who were used to the cold. Michael Bublé crooned from a portable CD player on the windowsill.

Harriet seemed mesmerised by the high-gabled roof and clerestory windows. There was an old-fashioned range flanked by warming cabinets. A large metal vat of mulled wine stood on the hob.

The Cartwrights maintained that presentation was everything: the kitchen table was laden with food and decorated with red candles and more holly – would there be any left on the entire estate? I wondered – which seemed to bear that out. I'd expected a few sausage rolls and some crisps but this was a feast. There was quiche, a cheese board with chilli jam, stuffed red peppers, smoked salmon roulades and tiny vol-au-vents. And for those with a sweet tooth, Delia's homemade mince pies.

Marion introduced Harriet to Ryan but made no mention of her damaged car. Harriet didn't bring up the subject either. She couldn't stop staring at him. Then she snapped her fingers.

'That's it!' She beamed happily. 'You were in that movie with Russell Crowe. *Gladiator*. You were eaten by the lion in the first big forum scene. I'm right, aren't I?'

Ryan seemed thrilled. 'That was my big acting break. I was in a few more movies but—'

'It was over twenty years ago,' Harriet stated. 'Gosh.

What happened? You could have been the next Tom Cruise. He's just as short as you.'

'I could have been his stunt double.' Ryan didn't seem to notice the insult. 'But Tom does all his own stunts.'

Marion offered to take Harriet's coat. 'Oh, what a beautiful necklace. I have one very similar to that.'

'Thank you,' said Harriet. 'It was a thirtieth anniversary present from my husband.'

Marion leaned in. 'Those are Majorica pearls, aren't they? And, gosh, diamonds too?'

'Yes, that's right,' Harriet said proudly. 'We bought it on a cruise around the Mediterranean.'

'So did I!' Marion said. 'In Madrid?'

'No, the factory showroom in Mallorca. Kat is going to value them tomorrow.' Harriet studied Marion intently. 'I wish I could remember where I'd seen you before. Was it on the *Octavia Royale*?'

'All right. Full disclosure.' Marion leaned in and whispered, 'I was in *Gladiator*, too. I was one of Lucilla's handmaidens.'

'She got two lines,' Ryan boasted. 'But, yeah, we've worked on the cruise ships.'

'But not the *Octavia Royale*,' Marion said firmly. 'And mostly super-yachts.'

Harriet seemed satisfied and scanned the kitchen. 'I can't believe I'm here.'

'So this is where the party really is.' Mum had joined us. 'Ryan. You're looking particularly handsome this evening.'

'Excuse me a moment,' he said hastily, and darted away.

Mum turned to Harriet. 'And who is this?'

'Harriet Bone from the shepherd's hut,' I said, giving her a pointed look. I prayed she wasn't going to mention the car accident. 'This is my mother, Iris Stanford.'

'Harriet hasn't got a drink!' Mum said. 'Delia! Over here. Bring another glass of mulled wine!'

Moments later, Delia appeared with a glass of wine in each gloved hand. I noticed she was also wearing the green scarf with her black uniform. 'Who wants the wine?'

'It's for Harriet,' I said, adding, for the umpteenth time, 'Harriet is staying in the shepherd's hut.'

Delia laughed. 'You poor thing! You wouldn't get me staying there. It's like the setting for a horror film.'

I waited for Harriet to repeat her comment about *The Blair Witch Project* but all she said was, 'Your gloves and scarf! What a beautiful green.'

'Thank you,' Delia said happily. 'Aren't they lovely? They were a gift.'

'Now all you need is a hat to go with them,' said Harriet. 'Do you live here?'

'Yes,' said Delia.

'Perhaps you could give me a tour tomorrow,' Harriet ventured. 'I'm very interested in the stumpery.'

'The stumpery?' Mum and Delia exchanged amused looks. 'Whatever for?'

'Would you? I know it's a lot to ask.' Harriet seemed to go coy. It was most peculiar. 'I'd really like that.'

Delia faltered a little but then nodded. 'There's not much to see, just a load of stumps. That's why it's called the stumpery.'

Mum nudged Delia and they laughed.

Harriet leaned in. 'I didn't catch your name. Delia, was it?'

'Delia Evans,' said Delia. 'Happily, free of Mr Evans. Just in case you're interested. As far as I'm concerned, marriage is overrated.'

'I *am* interested!' Harriet enthused. 'I didn't know you had a husband. Does he have a wandering eye like mine? Has he retired?'

'No.' Delia knocked back her mulled wine in one go. 'Mine's in prison.'

Harriet looked shocked. 'In prison? Oh. Goodness. What happened?'

'Do you really want to know?' said Delia.

'Yes. Very much so,' Harriet said eagerly.

'Then let's go and sit down and I'll tell you all about it.' Delia linked her arm through Harriet's and bore her away.

'Delia's found a new best friend,' said Mum.

I grinned. 'Are you jealous?'

'No,' said Mum. 'Green just isn't my colour. Speaking of green,' she lowered her voice, 'have you told the Cartwrights that Emerald Barbie has been kidnapped?'

I bit my lip. 'I haven't had a chance—'

'I can guarantee that Barbie will be back in her little display case at the Emporium first thing tomorrow morning,' Mum said. 'Di will have come to her senses. It was a momentary lapse of judgement. Am I ever wrong?'

'Yes,' I moaned. 'Often. Here comes Ryan again.'

Ryan appeared and blatantly ignored my mother.

'A message from Marion,' he said to me. 'Are you guys set for the photoshoot tomorrow?'

'Allow me to say that Lance is nowhere near as good-looking as you, Ryan,' Mum cut in. 'Don't worry. I'm not expecting you to leave your wife for me. I just want to say that, as an admirer of the male physique for reasons I can never disclose, yours is spectacular.'

Ryan wore a look of sheer panic.

'And I am more than happy to introduce you to Nicola de Pulford,' Mum went on, with relish. 'As you know, she is the photographer and creator of the Naked Farmer Calendar. It's a huge success and all the money goes to a good cause.'

'Will you excuse me?' Ryan darted away again.

'Mum!' I scolded. 'Stop teasing the poor man. It's not appropriate, these days.'

'I can't help it,' said Mum. 'He takes himself so seriously.'

Suddenly everyone stopped talking. At first, I thought it was because the Michael Bublé CD had come to an end – which it had – but then I saw the real reason for the silence.

The dowager countess had entered the kitchen, with Shawn close behind. She was dressed in a mid-calf tweed skirt, twinset and pearls, and seemed upset. Shawn's eyes met mine.

'What is all this?' she demanded. 'Mrs Cropper? What is going on? I have been waiting in the dining room for dinner to be served for the last thirty minutes.'

Mrs Cropper looked stricken. 'Milady!' she said quickly. 'Would you like some scrambled eggs?'

'And who are these people?' Edith pointed to the Cartwrights. 'Why are they here?'

'Oh, good grief,' muttered Mum. 'Her ladyship's lost the plot.'

Lavinia and Rupert hurried to Edith's side and we heard a rush of whispers. I caught snatches of 'We told you' and 'Staff party' and 'We only have eggs on Sundays'.

Unfortunately, Harriet – who had been closeted with Delia – gave a cry of recognition. 'There's that old bag who nearly killed me in her car!'

'Mother!' Rupert exclaimed. 'For God's sake! You're not supposed to be driving!'

'Driving?' Shawn said sharply. 'I thought we'd all agreed!'

'Aha! I knew it!' Harriet was exultant. 'I knew she shouldn't be behind the wheel! I'll sue!'

Lavinia seemed distraught. 'Not in front of the servants – I mean, the staff!' She desperately tried to pull Edith towards the kitchen door, but Edith shook her off and strode towards Harriet instead.

'What did you say?' Edith said icily.

'You heard me,' Harriet retorted. 'You're a danger on the road!'

'Harriet Bone is a paying guest. She's staying in the shepherd's hut, milady,' Marion said, stepping in. 'There's obviously been a misunderstanding—'

'Shepherd's hut? What shepherd's hut?' Edith pointed to Eric. 'Make sure she's out first thing tomorrow morning.'

Harriet, arms akimbo, stood her ground. 'I'm not going anywhere. I've paid for my stay and you should be careful. I've got connections at *Star Stalkers*. I demand an apology.'

'Rupert, do something!' Lavinia begged.

'Come along, Mother,' Rupert said cheerfully. 'Let's go and have some scrambled eggs.'

'Is it Sunday?' was the last thing I heard Edith say, as she was bundled out of the kitchen.

I appealed to Shawn to intervene, but he seemed to misunderstand my intention. 'What you are implying is very serious, Mrs Bone. Was the dowager countess driving?'

'Who are you?' Harriet demanded.

'This is Kat's boyfriend,' said Mum. 'Detective Inspector Cropper.'

'A policeman! Good. I want to make a formal complaint.' Harriet jabbed a finger at me. 'She was there. She saw the accident. Go on. Tell him.'

Shawn's eyes widened. 'Are you saying that her ladyship caused another accident?'

'*Another!*' Harriet shrieked.

'Oh, who cares?' Mum trilled. 'No one got hurt. Let's all forget about it. Don't you agree, Delia?'

'Definitely.' Delia nodded. 'It's Christmas!'

To my surprise, Harriet hesitated. 'Do you think I should forget about it, Delia?'

'Definitely,' Delia said again. 'Don't you think Harriet should forget about it, Marion?'

'Oh, yes!' said Marion, eagerly.

'But what about the grille?' Harriet said.

'Eric can mend it,' Delia said. 'He's good with metal, isn't he, Iris?'

'Very good,' Mum agreed.

Shawn rubbed his chin. 'Well . . . it's up to, er, Mrs . . . ?'

'Just call me Harriet,' said Harriet. 'If Delia thinks I should drop it, then I will.'

'Duly noted.' Shawn brought out a business card and handed it to Harriet. 'If you change your mind about filing the report, here is my contact information.'

Marion pulled Delia aside and whispered something in her ear. Delia rejoined us with a spring in her step. 'I have been dismissed for the evening! No clearing up for me. Marion said she'd do it and I am to escort Harriet back to the shepherd's hut. Isn't that nice of her?'

After confirming that I'd meet Harriet at nine thirty in the showroom the following morning, Harriet and Delia left together.

I turned to Shawn. 'I didn't want to get into it in front of Harriet,' I said, and told him what had transpired at Bridge Cottage. 'I'm positive that Harriet lost control of her car. Edith's Land Rover wasn't even moving.'

Shawn looked grave. 'That's not the point, I'm afraid. Lady Edith's driving licence expired a year ago.'

'Come along, Shawn,' Mum said. 'Where's your Christmas spirit?'

'It's not only that,' said Shawn. 'Lady Edith thought that Gran still worked here. You heard her. She's getting confused, which means she's a danger to herself and everyone around her.'

The awful thing was that I knew he was right. 'Poor Edith,' I whispered.

'What did the Cartwrights say about the stolen doll?' he said, changing the subject.

'I haven't told them yet,' I said. 'I have to pick my moment.'

'And what about Di?' Shawn demanded. 'What did she say?'

I felt my hackles go up. 'I haven't had a chance, Shawn.'

'I think the party is over,' Mum said, coming to my rescue. She pointed to Peggy Cropper, who was standing by the kitchen door. 'It looks like your grandmother is fit to drop.'

'I'll call you later,' said Shawn, and gave me a chaste peck on the cheek. 'I'm sorry about tonight. I'll make it up to you.'

'I've heard that before.' It came out harsher than I meant, but before I could apologise, Shawn had vanished.

I walked to the car with Mum and we went our separate ways.

As I drove past the walled garden I slowed down to look at Harriet's car. The grille was twisted away from the bumper. No wonder she was angry! My suspicion grew that Ryan had done it.

I spent the next two hours trying to reach Di. Each time the call went straight to voicemail. I suspected she had the phone on charge. Mallory had said he'd talk to her tomorrow but I was desperate to get hold of her first. At this point I didn't care if Di was involved in the theft, so long as I got Emerald Barbie back in time for the gala.

Tomorrow couldn't come soon enough.

Chapter Ten

The following morning, I rang Di again but, again, it still went straight to voicemail. I tried to squash my feeling of annoyance. Surely she wasn't avoiding me. When Harriet didn't appear at my showroom at nine thirty or return my calls, I set out for the shepherd's hut.

Snow had fallen heavily during the night and even though Eric had been up early clearing the drives, I suspected that Harriet might have had second thoughts about driving in her damaged car. The path through the walled garden had fresh footprints. This was promising but, to my surprise, no telltale smoke was curling out of the chimney from the wood burner.

As I mounted the steps, the sense that something was horribly wrong grew by the second.

I tapped on the door but there was no answering reply to my cheerful hello.

All was silent.

I tried the door. It wasn't locked. Cautiously, I went in.

The wood burner had gone out and it was cold inside. Harriet's bed had not been slept in and yet her handbag was still on the table along with a copy of *Forbidden*, one of my mother's books. A Post-it note with the word 'stumpery' was stuck on the cover. A bottle of Honeychurch gin and two empty glass tumblers stood on the draining-board. Judging by what was left in the bottle, it looked as if Harriet and Delia had continued the party.

I pulled out my mobile and called Harriet again.

The answering ring came from her handbag, which seemed a little odd. I hesitated. Should I check her phone? What if she suddenly appeared and caught me going through her things? Perhaps she had stayed in Delia's spare bedroom and left her handbag behind.

Five minutes later I was knocking on Delia's door. There was no answer. I peered through the letterbox and caught the lingering smell of toast, but no sign of life.

I stifled a wave of annoyance. I didn't have time for this today!

I called the Hall. After what seemed like an age, Delia answered the phone.

'Good morning,' she said, adding, in an ostentatious voice, 'the Earl of Grenville's residence.'

'Delia? Is that you?'

'Yes,' she said. 'I've been promoted to answering the phone. I have to say, "The Earl of Grenville's residence." If you want Marion, she's at her mother's house.'

When I told Delia that it was Harriet I was looking for Delia burst out, 'That woman is barking mad. She wanted me to give her a tour of the grounds in the dark! And it had started to snow. Mad, I tell you.'

'Do you know where she is now?' I asked.

'No. Thank God,' said Delia. 'But isn't she with you? She told me you were going to value her necklace this morning.'

'She didn't turn up,' I said. 'Did she stay in your cottage last night?'

'Of course not!' Delia said. 'But, trust me, it wasn't for lack of trying. She told me she felt scared sleeping in the shepherd's hut and asked if she could stay in my spare room.'

I thought of the gin and two tumblers. 'But you did go back to the shepherd's hut with her, yes?'

'Only because Marion insisted,' said Delia. 'I was under strict instructions to give her a drink and soften her up a bit.'

'Soften her up?' I mused. 'Because of what she'd said about suing the dowager countess?'

'I suppose so,' Delia said. 'I was just following orders. But Marion needn't have worried. Harriet didn't mention her ladyship once. She wanted to talk about how much naughty stuff should go into romance books.'

'Naughty stuff? What do you mean? Oh—'

'Sex,' Delia declared. 'Apparently in romance novels there are heat levels that range from zero to five. Zero is clean and wholesome, and five is explicit naughty stuff. I had no idea what Harriet was talking about, and when I told her so, she got all bolshy!'

I was barely listening. Harriet's car was still outside and her mobile and handbag were in the shepherd's hut. Her bed had not been slept in and she'd said she was afraid of the dark.

'What time did you leave her?' I asked.

'Around eleven thirty,' said Delia. 'But come midnight, there was a god-awful racket outside my front door. It was Harriet, shouting and demanding to be let in! There was no way I was going to let her in. Oh!' There was a gasp. 'I've got to go. The gladiator's just walked into the arena.'

And with that, Delia disconnected.

I got back into my car, determined to shrug it off. Harriet was a grown woman and surely could look after herself. She must have had too much to drink, gone to see Delia and decided to go for a walk in the grounds on her own. In the dark.

But what if she'd had a fall? The temperature last night had been well below freezing. She could die of hypothermia. Unless, of course, she set off on foot this morning to see me. I dismissed that idea as quickly as it came. Would Harriet have left her handbag and mobile phone behind?

I called my mother.

'Haven't seen her,' said Mum, in answer to my question. 'But …' She paused. 'Call it my gypsy blood—'

'Mum, you weren't a real gypsy,' I reminded her. 'You were part of a travelling fair and boxing ring.'

'Exactly and, trust me, we Travellers are highly intuitive,' Mum said. 'I think you're right to be worried. Was there anything telling in the shepherd's hut?'

'Telling, as in a copy of your book on the table?'

'Which one?' Mum said.

'*Forbidden*,' I replied. 'With a Post-it that had "stumpery" written on it.'

'Really?' Mum paused again. 'I didn't think the stumpery featured in that book. I can't remember. Can you?'

'I can't,' I said. 'But, if you recall, Harriet asked Delia to show her the stumpery.'

'How strange,' said Mum. 'But there's your answer. I bet she's gone to the stumpery.'

'Maybe.' I hesitated. 'But her bed wasn't slept in, and the wood burner had gone out.'

'Where are you now?'

I told her I was sitting in my car outside Honeychurch Cottages.

'The stumpery isn't far,' said Mum. 'Just cut through the stableyard. It shouldn't take you more than fifteen minutes and at least it will set your mind at rest.'

Mum suggested I call Marion just in case she had seen her, so I did. Marion was driving and put me on speakerphone.

'I'm just leaving my mother's house now,' said Marion. 'I can go via Little Dipperton and see if Harriet is there. Perhaps the accident shook her up more than she thought, and she didn't want to drive on these roads.'

'But why would she have left her handbag and mobile phone behind?' I said.

'I have no idea.'

'Did you hear Harriet shouting outside your cottage last night?'

'I didn't hear anything,' said Marion. 'I was exhausted. I might lose you in a minute. Going into a bad area. Oh, I had an email from *Dolls Galore* this morning. They're expecting the photographs and copy—'

And we were promptly cut off.

I sat there in a dilemma. Mum was right. It wouldn't take long to check on the stumpery.

I got back out of my car and headed for the archway that opened into the stableyard. Built around a stone courtyard, three sides of the quadrant housed four loose boxes each, the fourth side divided by a second archway topped with the dovecote and clock. Horses peered over green-painted stable doors. As always, I felt an overwhelming sense of peace among these noble creatures.

Edith emerged from the tack room dressed as usual, in her side-saddle habit. She waved a greeting. 'Thank heavens. A normal person at last,' she said. 'I don't think I can stand another minute in that household. Where shall we ride out this morning?'

I gestured to my tailored trousers, black wool coat and leather boots. 'I can't today.'

Alfred led out Tinkerbell, Edith's chestnut mare, tacked up and ready for mounting. I always thought him a peculiar little man with his thatch of white hair and wire-rimmed spectacles but Edith loved him.

'Come and say hello to Mr Manners, Kat,' said Edith. 'Doesn't he look well this morning?'

I caught a flicker of alarm in Alfred's eye. Mr Manners was buried in the equine cemetery and had died in 1970.

'Mr Manners is looking forward to his ride, milady,' said Alfred, without flinching. 'If you go to the mounting block, I'll bring him over.'

Edith turned away and headed for the stone mounting block.

'Alfred,' I said in a low voice. 'Edith called Tinkerbell Mr Manners—'

'I know. Her ladyship has been getting very muddled these past few weeks.'

'Is she losing her memory?' I was worried. 'Do the family know? Have they noticed?'

Alfred looked at me steadily. 'She's just getting old like all of us.'

There was getting old and getting confused. I thought of the incident at Bridge Cottage and what had happened in the kitchen last night. Perhaps Edith really shouldn't be driving.

'She's not riding out alone, is she?' I said anxiously.

'No. Lady Lavinia is joining her,' said Alfred.

I was about to leave when I thought I'd ask: 'You haven't seen Harriet anywhere, have you?'

'Not since last night,' said Alfred. 'Excuse me. Her ladyship is waiting.'

I left him helping Edith into the saddle and exited the yard, taking a right-hand path through an avenue of horse-chestnuts that skirted the wood. Tracks of deer and rabbits peppered the fresh snow.

At the end of the avenue, the path narrowed and descended steeply between two stone walls covered with ferns and moss. It dead-ended at a wooden door.

A rush of goosebumps crawled over my skin.

The door was closed but the ground had been disturbed and there was a jumble of footprints.

I pushed open the door and stepped into another Narnia, only this one didn't feel magical at all. It was creepy.

By its very nature, a stumpery thrives in shadow and damp, but the snow had coated the gnarled, twisted stumps and root wads into grotesque shapes. Ferns poked their tips through snow-packed pockets and lined the narrow, uneven path that curved out of sight.

I called Harriet's name but there was no answering reply.

It was deathly quiet. My heart began to pound. Every fibre of my being told me something was wrong.

The path sloped gently down, flanked by banks of snow and felled trees. I turned a sharp corner and stopped at the base of an oak. Nestled among the roots was a fairy ring: a cluster of buttons, stick-on silver stars, loose glass beads and marbles. It looked as if someone had created it not too long ago but I couldn't think who might have done it.

Above, carved into the trunk, were the barely legible initials VH and RC inside a heart. They were old and unfamiliar.

Just behind the tree, a dozen or so short wooden treads protruded from the bank and zigzagged steeply up to an overhanging granite slab.

Curiosity trumped fear and, besides, it might give me a good view of the stumpery.

I began to climb and stepped out onto the rock.

Cautiously, I edged my way to the lip and took in the 360-degree view, feeling marginally disappointed that the stumpery was bounded by dense trees on all sides. There were no views of distant Dartmoor here. Presumably, when the stumpery had been created in the late nineteenth century much of the surrounding woodland would have been no more than saplings and acorns.

It was only when I turned back to tackle the treads that I caught sight of a splash of red partially covered by the snow. Harriet lay face down, draped over a cluster of stumps.

I scrambled to her side but I already knew it was too late.

Harriet Bone was dead.

Chapter Eleven

'Drink this,' said Mum and handed me a large balloon of brandy.

It wasn't just the shock of finding Harriet's body; I had waited in the cold for the best part of an hour for the Cruickshank brothers – Little Dipperton's paramedics – and Mallory to arrive. After I'd shown them where Harriet's body lay, I headed straight to the Carriage House and promptly burst into tears.

'Oh dear,' Mum said, patting my shoulder. 'You do seem to have bad luck when it comes to finding bodies.'

'Thanks, Mum,' I said, and blew my nose.

'A fall, you say?' Mum mused.

'I think she went up to the lookout and just fell over the edge and broke her neck.' I gave a shudder of revulsion. 'Why would she go there in the dark?'

There was a knock and Marion stepped into the kitchen. She was as white as a sheet. 'Are you all right, Kat? What a terrible shock. What on earth was Harriet doing in the stumpery?'

'We have no idea,' Mum said, answering for both of us. 'Do you want a brandy?'

Marion nodded. She took off her trilby hat and Barbour coat and pulled out a chair while Mum found her a balloon and poured a hefty slug.

For a few moments, no one spoke. Marion took a dainty sip of brandy. 'What a PR nightmare this is. I'm counting on everyone to keep this horrible accident quiet until after the gala.'

I caught Mum's eye. She looked as surprised as I was.

'Don't look like that.' Marion blushed. 'Delia told me that Harriet had drunk quite a bit when she went back to the shepherd's hut last night. I don't see why her accident should impact the gala, but it certainly will if it gets into the newspapers.'

Mum and I exchanged more looks of surprise.

'But don't you see?' Marion said, exasperated. 'Once the Hall is officially open to the public, we'll have to deal with health and safety and, trust me, they're difficult at the best of times. I have a friend who volunteers for the National Trust. Do you know that birthday celebrations for the volunteers cannot involve cakes with candles? It's a fire hazard, you see.'

'No one is celebrating a birthday,' Mum pointed out.

'What if Harriet's husband wants to sue the estate for not having the correct safety railings in place?' Marion went on.

'Oh, for Heaven's sake!' Mum exclaimed. 'This isn't America!'

'Well, we all heard Harriet threaten to sue the dowager countess for her driving.' Two bright pink spots bloomed on Marion's cheeks. 'And what if health and safety run checks on the ballroom? Sprinklers? Fire doors? There aren't any! I told his lordship to get the sprinklers sorted out weeks ago but he dismissed the idea.' Marion's flush deepened. 'Ryan is livid. The stumpery should have had a sign saying "Private" or "Danger". Or something!'

Fortunately, the phone rang. Mum answered. 'Ah, Inspector.' She covered the mouthpiece with her hand and whispered, 'It's Mallory.'

Marion and I waited as Mum listened then ended the call with 'Yes. We'll see you there.'

'What does he want?' Marion asked anxiously. 'Health and safety, I bet. He's going to ask questions.'

Mum shrugged. 'We're all to go to the Hall this afternoon at four o'clock.'

'The Hall?' I said sharply. This did not bode well.

Marion looked worried. 'Why do we all have to go to the Hall? What else did he say?'

'Bring a bottle, it's a party?' said Mum.

'I'm sorry. It's just so upsetting.' Marion stood up. 'I've never been in this situation before.'

'Well, Kat's an old hand,' said Mum. 'I'm sure she'll be only too happy to show you the ropes.'

'The ropes?' Marion looked blank. 'Oh, I see. I'm sorry. I must go. And please don't mention the brandy to Ryan.'

As Marion put on her coat and left, a text from Willow popped up on my mobile.

I read it with sheer disbelief and intense joy. *Emerald Barbie is back in her cage!* I zipped a quick reply telling Willow I'd be at the Emporium within the hour.

'Are you all right?' Mum demanded. 'You look like you've won the lottery.'

'I feel like I have.' I was stunned.

Mum regarded me with astonishment. 'For someone who found a dead body this morning, you look remarkably cheerful.'

'Emerald Barbie is back!' I shrieked. 'She's back!'

'I told you so,' Mum responded. 'I knew Di would come to her senses. I hope you're going to demand an explanation.'

'You have no idea how relieved I am,' I said. 'I could cry! I'm heading over there right now.'

En route, I called Lance and we arranged to meet at my gatehouse at five to take Barbie's photograph.

I zipped off two more messages. One to Shawn and the other to Mallory to let them know that Emerald Barbie had been returned and all was well.

I made it to Dartmouth in record time. I was anxious to get to the Emporium and extremely anxious to talk to Di, who had still not returned my calls.

I crested the brow of the hill where the magnificent building, home to the Britannia Royal Naval College, afforded a spectacular view of the fishing port below.

Nigel was at his usual post, but since I had a few vehicles behind me as I queued to enter the car park, I made a mental note to tell him later that yesterday's problem had been solved and that it had had nothing to do with the Ford Fiesta.

I left my Golf at my usual spot in the exhibitors' parking area and felt a sudden rush of nerves. I wasn't sure how to approach the matter with Di but then I noticed her Ford Focus wasn't there.

In fact, Di wasn't in the Emporium, and as my calls continued to go unanswered – a sign of guilt if ever there was one – I began to feel tetchy.

When I got to my space, Willow was entertaining a handful of Barbie fans and seemed to be enjoying herself.

'Yes, the first Barbie doll was issued on March the ninth 1959,' she said. 'My birthday, in fact, although obviously the wrong year.' There was a ripple of laughter. 'Three hundred and fifty thousand dolls were made in the first edition. The original Barbie had very unattractive holes under the soles of her feet so she could be displayed on a stand. Original Barbie had golden hair, blue eyeshadow and a white bathing suit. Does anyone know the value of the most expensive Barbie doll ever made?'

There were a few shouts of 'A thousand,' and 'A hundred thousand,' which got a lot of jeers and taunts.

'Wrong!' Willow said triumphantly. 'The most expensive Barbie doll in history is the Stefani Canturi Barbie valued at just over three hundred thousand dollars – that's two hundred and thirty thousand pounds.'

There were gasps of disbelief all round.

'She was manufactured in 2010 with all the traditional Barbie features but there are two things that make the Stefani Barbie special. The jewellery was designed by Stefani Canturi – hence the name. She wore a necklace of emerald-cut Australian pink diamonds. Each diamond is a carat and the stones are encircled with an additional three carats of white diamonds. But . . .' she gave a dramatic pause '. . . the best thing of all about Stefani Barbie was that she was created to raise funds for the Breast Cancer Research Foundation.'

There was a round of applause. Willow held up her hand. The crowd fell quiet. 'And this is why we're so lucky to have Emerald Barbie donated for the upcoming charity gala in aid of the Happy Meadows Donkey Sanctuary.' She picked up one of Marion's custom-made clipboards and waved it. 'And what's more, you don't have to attend the gala to place your bid. You can do it right here. The auction will be live streamed on Friday night on Facebook and callers will be on hand should you want to up your bid. Once you register – for a fee naturally – details and links to the event will be sent to your email address. Thank you for your time, everyone. Merry Christmas!'

Most of the crowd dispersed but quite a few lined up to register.

Willow saw me watching. I gave her the thumbs-up. She would go far in her chosen career. I thought of the first time I'd met her when she'd been helping in the village tea shop. Willow had seemed so unsure of herself and had been a little nervous. University had brought out her confidence. It was good to see.

I made a beeline for Emerald Barbie, took her out of the display case and gave her the once over. She looked perfect.

'And you're positive she was here when you came in this morning?' I said to Willow. The Emporium was alarmed at night and only the vendors had the code. 'Did you see Di?'

'Not yet,' said Willow. 'Why?'

'I just wondered,' I said. 'Let's hope the CCTV cameras show us who returned the doll.'

'Speaking of CCTV cameras . . .' Willow hesitated.

'What?'

She motioned for me to come closer, scrolled through her mobile and showed me the screen. 'It's all over social media.'

There was an establishing shot of the exterior at Honeychurch Hall and then Harriet's face filled the screen. She looked drunk.

'I could have drowned in that stream,' she slurred. 'And she just sat there laughing. I didn't know it was the Dowager Countess Lady Edith Honeychurch at the time but then I found out she'd been banned from driving. Look what she did!' The camera cut unsteadily to Harriet's car and attempted to focus on the warped front grille as her voice went on, 'But she's not the only one being protected at Honeychurch Hall. I'm close to a major discovery – or should I say exposé?'

The clip ended with a series of emojis and hashtags: #oldbagdriving, #hotsecrets, #expose, #starstalkers.

I thought of Harriet lying dead in the stumpery and felt sick. Accident or not, this would not look good for the family. Harriet must have filmed this after Delia had left her. Then, for some reason, she had set off for the stumpery.

'I don't think I'd want to be in her shoes when the dowager countess finds out,' said Willow.

'Great news about Emerald Barbie,' came a familiar voice. Fiona Reynolds was all smiles. 'Do we know what happened?'

'She was back in the display case when Willow arrived this morning,' I said.

'Perhaps we can talk about what our next steps should be in private,' Fiona suggested. 'Have you spoken to Di yet?'

'No,' I said. 'I expected to find her here this morning.'

'She rang me from the nursing home to say that her mother had a fall last night,' said Fiona.

'Oh dear!' I exclaimed. 'I've been trying to call her.'

'Apparently her phone isn't working.' Fiona pulled a face. 'More likely she didn't pay her bill.'

My mobile rang. I prayed it was Di.

Fiona pointed in the direction of her office. Presumably I was to find her after my call. But it wasn't Di, it was Shawn.

'Are you all right?' he said.

'Yes,' I said. 'Just relieved that the doll is back.'

There was a sharp intake of breath. 'I'm not talking about the doll. I'm talking about Harriet Bone.'

How could I have forgotten Harriet Bone?

'I had to find out from Mallory that my girlfriend discovered a dead body this morning.' Shawn sounded angry. 'How do you think that made me feel?'

'I didn't intentionally not tell you,' I said. 'It was a horrible accident.'

There was a silence. 'We'll talk later. I'm coming to the Hall this afternoon.'

This was highly unusual. 'Whatever for?'

'You don't know?' said Shawn. When I didn't answer he added, 'Harriet Bone was murdered.'

Chapter Twelve

For a moment I was lost for words. Someone turned up the Christmas music. 'Hold on a moment, Shawn,' I said. 'I can't hear you.'

I gestured to Willow that I had to take the call and headed for the quiet of the Ladies.

'Are you still there?' I said.

'Where are you?' Shawn asked.

'At the Emporium,' I said. 'But there was nothing to indicate that Harriet had been murdered, nothing at all.'

'Mallory believes she was pushed off the lookout,' said Shawn.

'But that would mean someone persuaded her to go to the stumpery and climb the steps in the dark. It makes no sense.'

'Have you any idea what made her go there alone?' Shawn asked.

'No,' I said. 'But she was asking about it earlier. Why?'

Shawn didn't answer.

'Why?' I said again.

'Keep this to yourself for now,' said Shawn, 'but I just wanted to give you a warning.'

My mouth went dry. 'A warning about what?'

Shawn hesitated. 'I wouldn't normally be involved in this, but the reason Mallory called me was twofold. First, he wants to talk to everyone who was at the Hall last night, and second . . .' he paused '. . . Mallory asked about Krystalle Storm.'

I felt faint.

'I know Harriet had one of Mum's – I mean Krystalle Storm's books in the shepherd's hut,' I said. 'I saw it. I'm sure Mallory's just asking a general question.'

There was a pause. 'If your mother is involved in any way . . .'

'Why would you say that?' I said quickly.

'Because it wouldn't be the first time!'

It was true. My mother seemed to find herself in the centre of whatever the drama of the hour might be.

I tried to keep the fear out of my voice. 'Harriet told me she was a great reader. She's also savvy when it comes to actors on the telly or in movies. Mum barely spoke two words to her. You should be asking Delia. She was the one who went back to the shepherd's hut for a nightcap.'

'Calm down,' said Shawn, quietly. 'I'm just asking. As it is, I shouldn't be discussing any of this with you, but you know how much I care about you.'

'I do, Shawn.' I felt miserable because, knowing my mother, she might have been involved. We'd gone our separate ways after the staff party. Maybe she'd joined Delia in the shepherd's hut later. But since I'd only spotted two glasses in the little kitchen area, it seemed unlikely.

'Was there anything,' said Shawn, 'anything at all, that would give cause for harm to come to Harriet Bone?'

I filled him in on Harriet's social media post and suddenly felt very tired. 'It was really aimed at Edith.' But then I recalled Harriet's choice of hashtags, especially #expose and #starstalkers, which took on a more sinister air.

'Were you with Iris last night?'

'No, Shawn,' I said crossly. 'I wasn't.'

'You don't need to be so defensive,' said Shawn. 'I'm only trying to help— Wait.' There was a click and then another. Shawn came back on the line. 'I'll see you later. We'll talk more then.'

And, finally, Di called from her mobile.

'How is your mum?' I said. 'I've been trying to reach you for hours.'

'I don't have any transport,' said Di, neatly avoiding both questions. 'My car is still in the garage. It needs a new alternator.'

I was puzzled. If that were true, how did Di return Emerald Barbie to the Emporium this morning? 'Fiona tells me you're at Sunny Hill Lodge. How did you get there?'

'My neighbour dropped me off,' said Di. 'I was hoping you could pick me up and bring me back to the Emporium.'

'No problem,' I said. 'I'm on my way.'

I left the loo and bumped straight into Pam putting out the 'Toilets Closed for Cleaning' sign. She seemed worried. 'I got a call from that policeman this morning asking Lance and me to come to the Hall this afternoon. Do you know what it's about?'

'There was an accident last night,' I said. 'He just wants to talk to anyone who was there earlier in the evening.'

'Accident? What sort of accident? I don't remember an accident,' Pam said.

'It was after you left.' I wondered why Mallory wanted to talk to them. Pam had left early but Eric had run Lance to the Hare and Hounds to meet her later. It did seem odd.

'But I don't understand.' Pam sounded nervous. 'Is it about what happened in the pub last night?'

'The pub?' I said.

Pam pulled me into the entrance to the fire exit. 'I didn't mean anything by it,' she said.

'Why don't you tell me what happened?'

'I was talking to the bloke who runs the community shop—'

'Simon?'

'That's right,' said Pam. 'We were just chatting at the bar and I mentioned I used to work for the Earl of Denby at Carew Court and that we got evicted.'

'Ah.' I nodded. 'Simon's not a fan of the ruling classes.'

'You're telling me!' Pam said. 'Anyway, Eric – the one with the bushy eyebrows – turns up with Lance, and Simon's still banging on about how the Honeychurch lot get away with murder—'

'Figuratively, not literally,' I said quickly.

'Whatever,' said Pam. 'But when Simon started in on the

dowager countess, Eric went berserk. The landlord threw them both out!'

Eric's loyalty to the family was legendary but I couldn't see the connection to Harriet's accident. 'I'm sure he's just being thorough.'

'What if Eric says something to Lady Lavinia?' Pam's anxiety was contagious. 'I don't want Lance fired because of what I said. He's a good boy. It was nothing to do with him.'

'Exactly,' I said. 'Try not to worry. I'm sure it'll be fine.'

Pam seemed to relax. 'Thank you. Oh, I saw that the Barbie doll is back.'

I smiled. 'She never really left.' I had a sudden thought. 'You start at eight here, don't you?'

'Yes, every morning.'

'So you must have the code to get in and disable the alarm?'

Pam nodded. 'That's right.'

'Was anyone else here that early? Like . . .' I hesitated '. . . Di, perhaps?'

'No. Why?' Pam regarded me with curiosity.

'I just wondered,' I said.

'I saw a white van – it had the UPS logo – parked outside the main entrance when I got here this morning,' said Pam. 'I can't sign for packages and I told him to come back at nine.'

'You spoke to the driver?' I said sharply. 'Do you remember what he looked like?'

Pam shrugged. 'He had a brown cap and shirt that said UPS. Little pencil moustache and a goatee.'

'And you're certain it was UPS?' The UPS vans I'd seen

around were never white, always brown with their trademark logo. But this was a white van. And a van that had arrived and left before Nigel had begun his day. It might be significant.

Telling Pam I'd see her later at the Hall, I had a quick word with Willow, who confirmed she'd witnessed the ugly fight between Eric and Simon in the bar.

'Gran says that Eric would do anything for that family,' Willow confided.

Even murder? It wouldn't have been the first time that Eric had protected the family from scandal. But, as far as I knew, he didn't follow social media so it was unlikely he would have seen Harriet's damning video.

I felt a wobbly coming on. I had tried to push Harriet Bone to the back of my mind and, for a moment, the return of Emerald Barbie had allowed me to do that. But now I had to face two different realities. Was Shawn right that Harriet had been murdered? And had Di really returned the doll?

As I headed to Sunny Hill Lodge I rehearsed what I planned to say to her.

Twenty minutes later I turned into the entrance. It was one of the most expensive residential nursing homes in the south-west. Reindeer, draped in fairy lights, were strategically scattered along the grand drive, which was flanked by deciduous shrubs covered with snow. The road had been gritted and I noted that, unlike other lanes in Devon where the snow plough had done its job, the mounds of snow had been taken away.

Sunny Hill Lodge was a gracious Georgian house with large bay windows, a portico, and exquisitely manicured grounds. A pergola, which would be blooming with wisteria in spring, stretched the length of one wing. Clipped boxwood topiaries decorated with more lights flanked the front entrance.

A line of luxury cars – a Tesla, a fleet of Range Rovers and BMWs – were parked on the far side of the gravel. I pulled up and cut the engine, taking in the staggeringly beautiful view of Dartmoor with its snow-capped tors on the horizon.

Sunny Hill Lodge cost just under fifteen hundred pounds a week. The *Western Times* had done a feature on it only last summer. I didn't know much about Di's family background – it was something we hadn't really discussed – but obviously they had money.

In which case, why would Di steal Emerald Barbie?

I headed for the front door, which was adorned with a beautiful wreath. More topiaries covered with lights flanked the entrance.

I stepped into the vestibule and headed to the glass door that showed the hall beyond. It was lavishly decorated with antique furniture, artwork and rugs.

The home was a secure building. A buzzer and a panel with buttons were discreetly located behind the gold-rimmed frame of a painting.

I hit the buzzer. After a few moments, a woman in a tailored suit emerged from a side door. It looked as if she was expecting me because she tapped the sequence on the panel and gestured for me to come inside.

'Hello. Di asked if you could just wait here.' Her nametag said Belle. 'And please sign the guestbook and who you will be visiting.'

'I'm not visiting,' I said. 'I've just come to pick up Di.'

Belle gave a polite smile. 'We like to keep track of our residents as well as our guests. Everyone is required to sign the guestbook.'

I followed her inside. Classical music played quietly in the background and there was a pleasant smell of festive botanicals. It felt more like a five-star luxury hotel and that was the intention. Any equipment that held a hint of disability was hidden from view.

Belle led me to a pretty mahogany side table against a wall. The leather guestbook lay open beside a quality pen – there were no cheap biros at Sunny Hill Lodge. I looked for Di's name to see when she had entered the premises. It didn't appear on the page I was signing so I flipped back and saw she'd checked in at seven twenty-five that morning. That would have given her time to go to the Emporium.

'Is Margery Rook still the manager here?' I asked Belle. Last summer, I had been the toastmaster at one of the black-tie charity balls.

'Yes. But she's not here today.'

'Please tell her that Kat Stanford sends her best wishes.'

'Oh, yes, of course that's who you are,' said Belle, smiling. 'Can I bring you some coffee or tea while you wait?'

I declined. Belle gestured to a wingback chair, but I declined that too. I was far too jittery to sit. Belle drifted away and disappeared through a side-door labelled 'Office'.

Above the guestbook was an oak-framed notice board. It had the usual announcements – a list of church services,

Speedy Cabs, a flyer for the Honeychurch Hall Gala – but then I did a double-take.

A Mark 1 1978 Ford Fiesta in peppermint green with a black-and-white houndstooth interior was for sale. It was the same car that Nigel had seen in the Emporium car park. I distinctly remembered the number plate. There was no price, just an email address. I snapped a quick photograph so I could share it with Mallory.

But now I was unsure what to do. I didn't believe in coincidences. If I had needed confirmation that Di had had an accomplice, this could be it.

'Kat!'

I gave a guilty start and spun around to greet her.

Di was already dressed for the outdoors and wore a messenger bag over her shoulder.

She looked terrible, dishevelled, with bloodshot, puffy eyes. I could see she had been crying.

Instinctively, I gave her a hug. She felt so thin and frail. 'It's going to be okay,' I said gently. 'We'll sort it all out, I promise. Do you have all you need? Let's go.'

'I have to sign out,' she said. 'You do too.'

It wasn't until I started the car engine that Di burst into tears.

I felt conflicted – sorry for her, but angry at the same time. All I said was, 'Why don't you start from the beginning?'

Chapter Thirteen

'I just don't think I can do that to her,' Di said, finishing her story.

I kept my eyes firmly on the road, not daring to look at her and trying my best to suppress a building fury.

Di's need to tell me everything had had nothing to do with the theft and return of Emerald Barbie. In fact, I hadn't even had a chance to bring up the topic of the doll.

Di had got herself into trouble. It turned out that her mother's modest detached bungalow had been sold to pay for the nursing home. Di said her mother made the social climber Hyacinth Bucket from the well-loved TV show *Keeping Up Appearances* pale into insignificance. After Di's father had died, Ruth had gone on a massive spending spree with the purchase of a Mercedes coupé, five-star holidays (only flying first class) and jewellery. She had even taken out a reverse mortgage, not once but twice.

Then came the shock that Ruth had huge credit-card debts that she had kept secret for years. Di had been footing the bill, selling off what she could, but now she had run out of money and turned to a loan shark.

'I thought every week was her last on this earth,' Di went on miserably. 'I love her to bits but the Mum I knew left a year ago when Alzheimer's really took hold. It's such a cruel disease.'

I reached across and gave her hand a sympathetic squeeze. The obvious solution would be to move Ruth to an NHS-run facility but that wasn't for me to say.

'I know what you're thinking,' Di said, as if reading my mind. 'But the answer is no. She always made me promise not to put her in a home that smelt of cabbage and wee.'

'But she wouldn't know that now,' I said gently.

'No, she wouldn't,' Di agreed. 'But I would.'

I stole a glance at my friend, who wiped away a tear.

'And who is this loan shark?'

'I can't tell you,' Di said. 'I feel such an idiot. I can't believe I thought I'd be able to get out of it.'

'But you said you paid most of it back,' I pointed out.

'I did!' she wailed. 'But now they're adding on thirty per cent interest. They keep calling. I must keep my phone on in case something happens to Mum. But they're so persistent. When I do turn it off, there are literally dozens of voicemails from Vlad the Impaler.'

'Vlad?'

'My nickname for him. His accent is Eastern European,' Di ran on. 'It's awful. I can't carry on like this. They know everything about me, and they just don't care! I can't believe I've started smoking again.'

'Was that why you ran out of the Emporium yesterday?'

'Yes.'

'And that's why you left my space when the carol singers came through?'

'Yes. They just won't leave me alone.'

'You should have told me how much trouble you were in.'

'I tried. Remember?' Di sniffed. 'But you always changed the subject. Fiona is on my back as well because I'm a little behind with my rent. Someone's been shoplifting and I know she thinks it's me.' She took a deep breath. 'Have you ever pinched anything?'

'No,' I said, but then I remembered. 'That's not true. I stole a plastic cat from the girl next door when I was about seven.'

'A *plastic* cat?' Di exclaimed.

'It was very small,' I said. 'Squashed under the end of a see-saw and she didn't seem to care.' I thought of how guilty I'd felt when I'd sneaked it home in my pocket and hidden it in a drawer. 'I can't even remember her name now, but I still have the cat.'

Di chuckled, but quickly grew serious. 'Well, I have. It was a schoolgirl dare and I was the only one who got caught.' She gave a bitter laugh. 'That's why I keep an eye on Willow's friends. They remind me of what I was like at that age.'

'Well, the good news is that the doll has been returned.'

Di gasped. 'That is good news! I'm so pleased! When?'

'Willow told me she was back in her display case when she arrived this morning.'

'I told you!' Di crowed. 'Those girls did it for a prank. Willow has the code to the building, doesn't she?'

'Willow had nothing to do with it,' I retorted.

The problem was that Di had had every motive to take that doll and pass it along to those sharks to pay off her debt. But why would she return it? And what was the connection with the peppermint-green Ford Fiesta?

So I asked her about the car.

'A Fiesta on the notice board?' Di said. 'I have no idea who put that up. I never look. Why?'

I stole another glance. 'What car did your mother drive?'

'I already told you! And her Mercedes was repossessed a month ago.'

'The Ford Fiesta was driven by the man who left through the fire exit,' I said.

'Maybe he wanted to avoid the carol singers.'

'But weren't you by the fire exit around the same time?' I said.

'I didn't see anyone. Why does all this matter now?' Di sounded exasperated. 'You've got her back. End of.'

We fell into an uncomfortable silence. Di fumbled in her handbag for a tissue and blew her nose. She was in a terrible situation, and I felt bad for her. 'I think you should go to the police.'

'Seriously?' she said, with scorn. 'I knew what I was getting into when I took Vlad's money. I've already given them my car. So that knocked off five thousand. I lied to you about that. I have a moped but it's rubbish in this weather. I've also got a second job.'

'Doing what?' I said. 'How can you fit in a second job?'

'It's at night,' said Di. 'I'm driving a taxi. And you know what? I'll be driving around all those fancy partygoers for the gala too. I'm Cinderella!'

'If you remember, Cinderella did go to the ball.' I thought for a moment. 'Don't you have any relatives who can help?'

'Two cousins,' said Di. 'My mum was the youngest of six and all her siblings have passed away. They gave me some cash, but it was a drop in the ocean. And, besides, they just tell me to move her elsewhere and I won't. Can we change the subject?'

'What do you want to talk about?'

'I saw that footage on social media about the dowager countess's driving,' she went on. 'I was waiting for the doctor and went on my phone. Who is that woman anyway? And what's this secret she's threatening to expose? She certainly has an axe to grind. Is she local?'

When I told Di that the woman with an axe to grind had died and that I had found her body – I didn't elaborate on the details – she was appalled.

'Oh, Kat, I'm so sorry,' she said. 'That's terrible, and here am I just banging on and on about my awful life. I'm such a selfish cow.'

'It's fine,' I said. 'Really.' But, of course, it wasn't.

We turned into the car park. Nigel waved me on through. I stopped outside the main entrance to drop Di off first.

She kissed my cheek. 'You're a very good friend. Thank you for being there for me.'

I'd only driven a few yards when Shawn rang. He got straight to the point.

'You need to get back here straight away,' he said.

My heart dropped. 'What do you mean? What's happened?'

'Now, Kat,' said Shawn, tightly. 'I'll wait for you at the gatehouse.'

I dashed into the Emporium to pick up Emerald Barbie for her photo shoot with Lance later in the day, gave Willow some instructions about the stock, and hurried back to my car.

With a racing heart, I headed for home.

Chapter Fourteen

Shawn was waiting in his car when I pulled up behind him. His greeting was short and there was no customary hug. Something was terribly wrong.

My hands shook as I unlocked the door to the showroom and hurried inside to turn off the alarm.

He didn't take off his coat, just stood in the sitting room looking solemn. I put down my tote bag with Emerald Barbie inside but kept my coat on too.

I went and sat down.

'In Harriet Bone's suitcase were five of your mother's books,' Shawn said coldly. 'I believe the titles were from the Star-Crossed Lovers series.'

My stomach gave that all-too-familiar sickening lurch. Mum had written gazillions of books, but the Star-Crossed Lovers was what she was best known for. She had set that series at Honeychurch Hall. I'd read them all and Mum had been very cavalier when I'd warned her to be careful, that the places she'd described were distinctive, but she had pooh-poohed my fears and said no one cared. Better yet, no one recognised themselves in a book.

'But we've already established that Harriet was a fan,' I said. 'My mother has a lot of fans.'

Shawn delved into his jacket pocket and withdrew a battered paperback of *Forbidden* in a Ziploc evidence bag that had not been sealed. It was the book I'd seen in the shepherd's hut.

He passed me a pair of disposable gloves. 'Take a look, please.'

I pulled them on and took the book out of the plastic bag. 'Does Mallory know you removed some evidence?'

'Open it,' he said quietly. 'And no. Not yet.'

Vast passages had been highlighted in yellow. They weren't dialogue but descriptions. Descriptions of the Great Hall, the walled garden, the grotto, the ha-ha, the chestnut walk and, most worrying, the stumpery.

I met Shawn's eyes with dismay. 'Are you saying that Harriet Bone found out where my mother's books were set?'

'It looks like it.'

I was puzzled. 'But how? No one has Mum's address. It's just a PO box. Any mail is sent from the publisher to a PO box in the village in my name. Harriet Bone isn't even a local. She lived in Basingstoke.'

'I know,' said Shawn. 'Her husband has been notified and a social worker should be with him right now. Perhaps he'll be able to shed some light on her decision to come to the area.'

'I can tell you why she came,' I said. 'Harriet told me she needed to get away for a bit. It sounded like she and her husband were having problems. He had just retired, and I got the impression that she didn't want to be married any more.'

Shawn began scribbling in his pad. 'What did your mother and Mrs Bone talk about? Books?'

'I told you,' I said. 'Mum barely spoke two words to her.'

I felt Shawn's eyes upon me. My mother had a lot to lose if Harriet had indeed found out not only where she lived but that Iris Stanford was Krystalle Storm.

'You're implying that my mother had something to do with Harriet's death because she was afraid Harriet had discovered her true identity.' I could feel my temper rising but it was from fear, not anger. 'You've never liked my mother.'

'And she's never liked me,' Shawn shot back. 'I stepped away from my own case to come here this afternoon because it will all come out that your mother is Krystalle Storm. The passages in this book are highly incriminating.'

'They're not!' I shouted, but I was frightened. 'They're just highlighted! Don't you ever write in the margins or highlight passages in books that mean something to you?' I gave him the book back.

'Kat, stop!' Shawn put down his notebook, stood up and came to sit beside me. He took my hand. 'We knew that your mother wouldn't be able to keep up this façade for ever. I came here to talk to you first. Mallory is a good policeman. He'll find out. It's over.'

I bit back bitter tears. He was right. My mother had had so many close calls with keeping her secret. She had also put Shawn in an impossible position, many times.

'Mum will go to prison, you know she will,' I whispered. 'Martha Stewart went to prison for not paying her taxes so Mum will, too.'

'Kat ...' Shawn began. He squeezed my hand. 'I don't know what to say other than I'm sorry.'

Why had my mother decided to write in secret for all those years? Her guise as a wealthy widow was only possible from her earnings, but since she had moved to a new area and made a fresh start, people only knew her for what she seemed to be now – a rich, merry widow and the self-appointed Honeychurch historian.

It was hard to escape the irony that Dad had been a tax inspector. In fact, my parents had met when he'd been investigating bogus ticket sales at Bushman's Travelling Fair and Boxing Emporium, which was where their love affair had begun and why my mother had wanted to come back to live in the grounds of Honeychurch Hall all these years later.

And it wasn't just Mum who would go down. It would be Alfred, whom she had sent across the English Channel to her bank in Jersey to bring cash – illegally – into the country.

The cover story given to everyone – including Shawn – was that Alfred had been training circus horses in Spain when in reality he'd been serving time in Wormwood Scrubs.

And then my mouth went dry. What if Alfred knew that Harriet had found out? What if my mother had asked Alfred to lure Harriet to the stumpery, to the lookout, and to give her a little push? I didn't think Alfred's scruples matched my mother's. Alfred had just as much to lose by my mother's exposure – maybe much more.

Shawn squeezed my hand again. 'You can't help your mother, Kat. This is her problem, and she must face the consequences.' He stood up. 'I've got to return this book before Mallory's meeting.'

'You'll be there?'

'The dowager countess has asked me to be present,' he said. 'Besides, my grandmother and I were both at the Hall last night. So, yes, we'll be there.' He paused. 'You need to warn your mother about the books in Harriet's suitcase.'

I nodded. But in the end I didn't have a chance. When I got to the Carriage House Mum's red Mini had vanished and when I called her mobile, she said she'd bagged me a seat in the drawing room and was looking forward to Mallory's performance.

With utter dread, I headed for the Hall.

Chapter Fifteen

When I arrived, Mum and Delia were already seated in the drawing room. They were chattering away, seemingly oblivious to what lay ahead. In vain I tried to attract Mum's attention to see if I could entice her away for a few minutes of privacy.

I took in the drawing room with its elaborate cornices and decorative strapwork. Red silk paper shared the walls with tapestry hangings. Damask curtains fell graciously from the four casement windows that overlooked the park.

The furniture reflected the Hall's various incarnations from seventeenth-century oak court cupboards to an ugly twentieth-century drinks cabinet. There was the usual collection of side tables, lamps and gilt-framed mirrors, as well as an overwhelming number of miniatures that took up almost the entire wall to the right of the fireplace.

On a chair were some placards, red ropes and stands. It looked like future plans to open the Hall to the public were already in motion.

It was an elegant room but, sadly, the scene of rather too many performances, as Mum liked to say, with a detective starring in a leading role.

Mallory was talking to Rupert in hushed tones by the fireplace. I wondered if every crime scene had the compulsory Poirot-library moment when each person became a suspect to be dramatically revealed by the detective.

Alfred and Eric stood by the window in their outdoor coats and socks. Before the Cartwrights arrived, no one had thought twice about tramping through the hall in muddy boots.

I took a wingback chair and tried to stop my hands shaking. I felt as if I was about to witness a train crash and there was nothing I could do to stop it.

Lavinia and Marion came in together. Lavinia – in jodhpurs and with her hair squashed under a slumber net – was her usual dishevelled mess and Marion the height of polished sophistication. Both took their seats on one of the two sofas.

'We're just waiting for your colleague, Inspector,' said Marion. 'And Lance Price.'

'And Lady Edith,' piped up my mother. 'Where is her ladyship this afternoon?'

I felt dreadful when I thought of Edith, who Mum adored. In fact, the dowager countess featured in *Gypsy Temptress* as a young woman who was involved in a tragic love affair that had actually happened. What would Edith make of having her secret out in the open?

'Delia,' said Marion. 'You may as well go and organise the tea.'

Delia was wearing the green scarf. She left the room just as Shawn entered with Peggy Cropper. He looked over and gave me a reassuring smile. I felt as if I had swallowed a brick. Shawn settled his grandmother into another chair, then sat at the back of the room.

I did a swift headcount. Mallory, my mother, Alfred, Ryan, Marion, Rupert, Lavinia, Shawn, Peggy, Lance – when he got here – and myself. There was no way Delia could organise the tea on her own. It might give me a chance to talk to Mum alone.

I stood up. 'I'm sure Delia needs some help in the kitchen, don't you think, Mum?'

'Go right ahead, dear.' Mum leaned back in her chair and closed her eyes. I panicked. Was she tired? Was it because she'd been up all night murdering Harriet Bone?

'Mum, really, I think she could,' I said, more forcefully. My mother didn't answer.

Unfortunately, that meant I was now committed to helping Delia in the kitchen.

Out in the hall I found Pam and Lance looking lost.

'They're in the drawing room,' I said.

'You don't have to come with me, Mum,' Lance said.

'I'm coming,' Pam insisted.

I left them bickering and headed for the kitchen where Delia was setting up a two-tier hostess trolley.

'Oh, good,' she said, as I walked in. 'I could do with a spare pair of hands. Come on, what's the gossip? You have the inside scoop. We all know Harriet's death wasn't an accident, don't we? Otherwise, why else would we be summoned here?'

'I don't know,' I lied. 'Are these plates all going onto the trolley?'

Delia nodded. 'You found Harriet's body. Weren't you suspicious?'

'And you were the last person who saw her alive,' I pointed out.

Delia's eyes widened. 'She was alive when I left her in the shepherd's hut, but she was in a bad mood – the drink, I think. And then there's all the hullabaloo about who pulled the grille off her rental car and towed it back to the Hall.' She lowered her voice although she didn't have to. 'I think it was Ryan. I mean, he's an American.'

I wasn't sure how being an American affected Ryan's ability to pull a car off a bank.

'I'd stay out of it if I were you,' I couldn't help adding. 'You could be the prime suspect.'

Delia squeaked and dropped a plate. 'Now look what you made me do!'

I should have felt guilty, but I didn't.

As I helped her pick up the pieces, I noticed her hands. They were red and covered with ugly welts. 'What happened to your hands?' I said. 'Did you burn yourself on the range?'

Delia held them up for me to inspect. 'I woke up like this,' she said miserably. 'Marion said it was my fault for not wearing rubber gloves in hot water – which I do, I'm not stupid. She's insisted I wear white cotton gloves to serve the tea.'

I had to admit I would want Delia to wear gloves too. Gesturing to the scarf, I said, 'That colour suits you. It looks nice.'

Delia touched it. 'I know! I told Marion I needed some festive cheer and she said, "All right."' She gave a mischievous grin. 'Speaking of festive cheer, Iris and I are going to watch *Gladiator* tonight to see if we can spot Ryan in his loincloth.' She gave a dirty laugh. 'Iris wants to take a look at his weapon.'

'Delia!' I chided. 'You're as bad as my mother.'

I heard someone clearing their throat and, to my embarrassment, Ryan walked in.

'You wanted to know about my weapon?' he said. 'I had two. A fascina, which is a three-pronged trident, and a weighted net called a retes. It's pronounced reetees.'

Delia caught my eye. 'Oh, I think Iris would love to be caught in your net. She has such a crush on you.'

Ryan paled.

'But don't worry! She knows you're never going to leave Marion.' Delia caught my eye again and winked. It was obvious that Mum had shared her love of teasing Ryan with Delia too.

'I came in to give you ladies a hand,' Ryan said, suddenly all business. Deftly, he took control of the trolley, rearranging the cups and saucers to make room for the cake plate with smooth professionalism. 'When Marion and I were in Bel-Air working for this celebrity family, there was a staff of ten.'

'Who?' Delia cried. 'Please tell. Was it the Kardashians?'

'I'm afraid I can't,' said Ryan. 'We signed an NDA.'

'A what?' said Delia.

'It's a non-disclosure agreement,' I said.

'Pity,' said Delia. 'You could have written your autobiography starting with your starring role in *Gladiator*.'

'And let's not forget my stint in *Waterworld*,' said Ryan.

Delia's eyes bugged out. 'With Kevin Costner?'

'No. *Waterworld* at Universal Studios. I was a stunt man,' said Ryan. 'I was set on fire four times a day and had to fall from a tower into the water.'

'No!' Delia's jaw dropped. 'Wasn't that a bit hot?'

'We all wore fire-retardant suits.' Ryan touched the sides of the teapot. 'And this isn't hot. The water needs to be boiling when it goes into the teapot, Delia. Go and make it again. Is anyone having coffee? Where's the French press?'

'No one drinks coffee in the afternoon in England and, besides, we call it a cafetière,' said Delia, clearly annoyed by Ryan's tone. 'And I do know how to make tea.'

'I enjoyed doing stunts but that was another life.' Ryan fell quiet, then added wistfully, 'Marion and I have certainly had some adventures.'

'But no children,' said Delia, with an exaggerated sigh. 'Well, Marion's too old to have any now, isn't she, and who wants to be changing nappies at your age?'

'Okay,' I said loudly. 'Let's get this show on the road.'

'Well,' said Ryan. 'Delia's right. I think the kids' ship has sailed for us. But I wouldn't want to be with anyone else. Honestly.'

Sometimes I wondered if he was just reassuring himself about his marriage.

Ryan suddenly noticed Delia's hands. 'Whoa! Whoa!' He took a step back. 'What's going on there?' He peered at them cautiously, as if inspecting a dead mouse. 'You need a doctor. That looks contagious.'

'Rubbish,' Delia said. 'You Americans are such hypochondriacs! I'll see how they are tomorrow.'

Ryan shook his head. 'You can't serve the tea like that.'

'Marion gave me some white gloves to wear,' Delia protested.

'I'll do it,' said Ryan. 'And take off that green scarf. Didn't Marion tell you that the only accessories permitted are pearl earrings?'

'Marion said I could wear it,' Delia cried.

'I don't care what Marion said. This is a professional establishment. Please remove it.'

Delia did as she was told.

I gasped at the unsightly rash around her neck and immediately thought of my mother. How odd. The scarf had irritated her skin, too. 'Good grief. That looks sore.'

Ryan sprang back again. 'Omigod! Are those hives? Are hives contagious?'

'It's only on my hands and neck,' Delia remonstrated. 'Why? Do you want to see if it's anywhere else on my body?' And, with a mutinous glare, she retied her scarf around her neck, donned the white gloves and flounced out of the kitchen.

Ryan turned to me. 'She really should see a doctor.'

Chapter Sixteen

Edith was sitting in another wingback chair dressed in her usual side-saddle habit and riding boots, which, to my amusement, had tramped a trail of wet mud across the carpet. She did not look happy. Lance and Pam had each taken an upright chair that flanked a mahogany sideboard. Having nowhere to put her fake-fur coat, Pam sat with it bundled on her lap. She wore a peculiar expression on her face and I noticed that her eyes flicked repeatedly from Marion to Ryan and back.

Ryan set the trolley by the window where Delia poured out the tea. He proceeded to distribute the cups and saucers with great finesse, keeping his left hand behind his back and giving a little butler bow with each delivery.

Marion followed him with sliced Tunis cake on small plates, which prompted a comment from my mother.

'This cake reminds me of when I was a girl,' Mum said. 'The ones they sell in the supermarket are rubbish. The chocolate is too thin and the marzipan fruits too small.'

'It's homemade,' said Marion. 'Mrs Cropper gave me the original recipe.'

'And it's frightfully yummy,' said Lavinia. 'Have two slices, Lance. You need fattening up.'

Neither Lance nor Pam needed encouragement: both took another slice each.

Mallory refused both tea and cake, and so did I. I was a bag of nerves.

Mallory waited until everyone had settled down and enjoyed a few mouthfuls before saying, 'I'll get straight to the point. I'm afraid Harriet Bone was murdered.'

If Mallory had been hoping for a universal cry of horror, he was disappointed.

'Tell us something we don't know,' said Mum.

'Who is Harriet Bone?' asked Pam.

'You said you wouldn't talk, Mum,' Lance hissed.

'Yes, but if there's a killer on the loose, I think I have a right to know,' said Pam.

Marion raised her hand. 'With all due respect, Officer, Mrs Price wasn't at the staff meeting. I don't think she needs to be here.'

'Mrs Price should stay,' Edith said firmly. 'We can't have her wandering around the Hall, can we? She might be tempted by the silver. Let's keep Mrs Price where we can see her.'

The implication was plain and highly embarrassing. Pam gave Edith a look of pure hatred.

Lavinia opened her mouth to say something but thought better of it.

I felt the twinge of suspicion about Di's involvement in Barbie's theft again. What if Di had been in cahoots with Pam all the time? Mallory had already searched Pam's locker and found nothing, but that didn't mean that Di hadn't hidden the doll among her own possessions.

'I'd rather stay,' Pam said. 'You never know, I might have noticed something important before I left for the pub. Don't they say that the devil is in the details?'

'Ah, indeed he is.' Mallory smiled. It was one of his favourite phrases.

'Yes.' Pam looked directly at Marion. 'I'm very observant. Very.'

Mallory flipped open his notebook. 'Let's recap,' he said. 'There was a staff meeting yesterday when each of you present was assigned a role for the upcoming gala.'

'That's correct, Officer,' said Marion. 'Apart from Mrs Price, of course. Although perhaps we could speak afterwards, Mrs Price. At the moment we don't have anyone taking care of the toilets and I think you would be a perfect fit for the position. After all, that is one of your skills.'

Far from being insulted. Pam smirked again. 'As you well know.'

Marion gave her flight-attendant smile. 'You'd be able to come to the gala and watch your very talented son in action.'

The exchange was weird. We had assembled to discuss Harriet Bone's murder and Marion and Pam were discussing cleaning toilets.

'You can sort that out later,' Mallory cut in firmly.

'I understand that Harriet Bone was at the staff party. Was she involved in the gala?'

Marion dragged her eyes away from Pam. 'Of course not,' she declared. 'It being Christmas, we invited her in for a drink. It was all very amicable.'

'Amicable' wasn't the word I would have chosen. And with Marion being so dialled into social media I found it hard to believe she hadn't seen Harriet's explosive footage.

'I believe there was an altercation between Harriet Bone and your ladyship.' Mallory gave a nod to the dowager countess.

I raised my hand. 'Harriet was upset about her car being damaged when it was towed off the bank at Bridge Cottage. The grille was pulled away—'

'Well, don't look at me,' said Eric. 'What kind of idiot attaches a rope to the grille?' He pointed a finger at Ryan. 'Why don't you just own up to it?'

Ryan turned red. I knew that Eric and Ryan didn't see eye to eye, especially given Ryan's lofty position as the estate manager.

The two men couldn't have been more different. Apart from Ryan's obvious physical attributes, Eric had been endowed with the most frightening eyebrows, which had earned him the nickname Beetlebrows, and was the cliché of a burly farmer in need of a good dentist and a bar of soap.

Ryan raised a hand. 'I'll own up to it,' he said, to everyone's surprise. 'And I'm sorry.' He looked sheepish and gave us his charming boyish smile. 'They don't make cars like they used to.'

'Ryan was always going to tell but he didn't get a chance.' Marion sprang to her husband's defence. 'It only happened last night, and Ryan was going to offer to pay for the damage. He even went to try to find Harriet this morning. Didn't you, darling?'

'You did what?' said Mallory, sharply. 'What time was this?'

'Around nine thirty,' said Ryan. 'Her car was where I left it. I went to the shepherd's hut, knocked but there was no reply. I thought she must be still sleeping.'

That explained the set of footprints I'd seen in the walled garden.

'Interesting.' Mallory made a note on his pad. He turned to Lavinia. 'What time did you go to bed?'

'Oh, that's *frightfully* easy,' she gushed. 'Midnight. With my husband.'

'And your lordship?' Mallory fixed his eyes on Rupert. 'Unfortunately, a husband and wife supplying each other with an alibi is not acceptable but—'

'I can confirm I spent the night with my wife.'

'That makes a change,' Mum said, under her breath.

'Alfred?' Mallory asked. 'I assume that only the horses will be able to give you an alibi.'

'Yes. And I saw Delia and that woman cut through the stableyard,' he said. 'They were making a right rumpus and I had to tell them to be quiet.'

'A rumpus?' Mallory asked.

'Throwing snowballs,' said Alfred.

'How extraordinary!' Mum burst out. 'How immature!'

'I jolly well hope not!' Edith exclaimed. 'The horses need absolute quiet when resting.'

'But that's not true!' Delia burst out. 'I didn't throw any snowballs! Harriet got some snow and just shoved it down the back of my coat!'

'And why do you think she did that?' Mallory asked Delia. 'Why did she push snow down your coat?'

'I have no idea,' Delia said. 'She thought it was funny. If you ask me, it was weird. Like we were all girls together. If you know what I mean.'

'But you went back to the shepherd's hut with her,' Mallory pointed out.

'I'd told her to,' Marion chipped in. 'I wanted to make sure we had a happy guest because of . . . because of the incident with her car and the dowager countess.'

Delia nodded. 'I had a nightcap and got out of there as fast as I could. I practically had to fight her off.'

Mum began to titter.

'Not like that, Iris,' Delia snapped. 'She thought we were best friends. It made me feel uncomfortable.'

'What did you talk about?' said Mallory.

'Marriage. Errant husbands. The stumpery,' said Delia.

My heart skipped a beat. This was it. Mallory was going to bring up Krystalle Storm. But he turned to me and said, 'We'll come back to the stumpery in a moment. Kat, talk me through this morning.'

'Harriet was supposed to come to the gatehouse for a valuation. She had a necklace that she said was very valuable.'

Mallory's eyes narrowed. 'Did you see it?'

'Briefly,' I said. 'It was a string of Majorica pearls. They're quite popular purchases on cruises. Harriet's had five diamonds but . . .'

'But what?' Mallory prompted.

'I had my doubts about the diamonds,' I said. 'And Harriet did too. She had told me her mother-in-law suggested they weren't authentic. The light wasn't very good but I was pretty sure they were zircons. That was why I asked her to come to the gatehouse this morning.'

'And who else knew about that piece of jewellery?'

'She was showing it to everyone,' Delia said.

'I didn't see it,' Mum said.

'Nor did I,' Marion chimed in.

Delia blinked. 'Yes, you did. You told her that you had one very similar. Remember?'

Marion frowned, then brightened. 'Oh, yes. I apologise. I have a lot of jewellery.'

'A similar necklace, you say?' Mallory turned his attention to Marion. 'Can we look at yours?'

Marion shrugged. 'Of course, Officer. It's at my cottage but I can bring it to you later today. Can I ask you why you need to see it?'

'Among Harriet's possessions was an empty Majorica jewellery case,' said Mallory. 'The deceased was not wearing her necklace and there was no sign of it in the shepherd's hut.'

Lavinia raised a hand. 'But . . . are you implying that one of us here would steal a pearl necklace that had been bought in a souvenir shop?'

'Not a souvenir shop,' I put in. 'Majorica pearls are reportedly the best man-made pearls in the world. They're manufactured in Mallorca. The exact process is a closely guarded secret. The company started in 1890 and . . . Never mind.'

'Kat knows these things,' Mum asserted proudly, but shot me a puzzled look. I blushed. What did it matter about the process? I was a nervous wreck and it showed.

Lavinia raised her hand again. 'I don't think any of us here are guilty of theft.' But she couldn't help glancing at Pam.

Pam gave a harsh laugh. 'Seriously? First, I never met the woman or knew she had a necklace. Second, I don't know where the shepherd's hut is or the . . . What did you call it? Stumpery! And third, I was in the pub. You can ask anyone in there.'

'We already have,' said Mallory, smoothly. 'Which is why I'm asking everyone now where they were between the hours of midnight and six this morning. It seems that none of you have firm alibis, so we turn to motives.' He looked keenly around the room. 'The pearl necklace is missing but Harriet's purse was untouched. Theft? Possibly, but, as Kat has just pointed out, would a Majorica pearl necklace be worth killing for and why not just take it in the shepherd's hut? Why lure the victim to the stumpery?'

The room fell silent. Every time Mallory mentioned the word 'stumpery' I felt nauseous, and, whenever he did, I glanced at my mother, who sat placidly in her chair as if she didn't have a care in the world.

Mallory spoke again. 'We found Harriet Bone's mobile in her handbag. She had posted a particularly unpleasant piece about . . .' he hesitated, as if trying to find the right words '. . . the dowager countess on social media.'

Everyone except Marion and Ryan looked puzzled.

Lavinia said, 'We don't do social media, Officer.'

'Where was it?' Delia said. 'I'm on Facebook.'

'Me too,' Mum said. 'But I didn't see anything either.'

'It was on Instagram,' I said.

'Yes. We saw it,' said Marion. 'But since she didn't mention the gala, we weren't concerned, were we, Ryan? But now . . .' She and Ryan turned to Edith. 'We may have to put out some fires.'

'The footage was posted at twelve-oh-seven,' said Mallory.

Delia raised her hand. 'That would have been after I left her and after she was shouting outside my window.'

'Shouting?' Mallory said. 'Shouting about what?'

Delia shrugged. 'She was shouting that she knew everything.'

'We didn't hear her,' Marion said. 'Did we, Ryan?'

Ryan shook his head.

'What about you, Eric?' Mallory asked.

'Yeah, I heard shouts but I ignored them.'

Mallory scanned the room again, looking at each of us in turn. It was unnerving. 'The footage on Harriet's phone hinted at a further revelation,' he said. 'I quote, an exposé.'

I heard a sharp intake of breath and realised it had come from me. I was glad that Shawn was seated at the rear but, even so, I could sense his eyes boring into the back of my skull.

'They say that people are killed for four reasons,' Mallory began, and started to tick off his fingers. 'One, they saw something; two, they know something; three, they have something; and four, they heard something.' He paused to allow us to take this in before adding, 'And that's why Harriet Bone was lured to the stumpery.'

'I have no idea what you're talking about.' Edith got to her feet. 'If you don't mind, Alfred and I have horses to feed, and this has nothing to do with me.'

'I have just one question, if you don't mind, your ladyship,' said Mallory, gently. 'I'm afraid I must ask. Where were you between the hours of twelve and six this morning?'

Edith's eyes were cold. 'I have no alibi. That woman was trouble. She was aggressive and antagonistic. I won't pretend that I'm sorry she's dead, but I can assure you that, at my age, the last thing I would do is venture out in below freezing conditions to push her off a ledge in the stumpery.'

Shawn jumped up and hurried over to Mallory, drawing him aside and whispering in his ear. I saw Mallory's eyebrows rise and a flicker of annoyance cross his features, but he gave a curt nod and muttered, 'All right.'

'Your ladyship,' he said. 'We will be discussing the topic of your expired driving licence, but since it is Christmas, I intend to do that in the New Year.'

'You are free to go, milady,' said Shawn.

Edith sprang up with surprising agility, gesturing for Alfred to follow her. Their exit seemed to break up the party.

Marion stood up. 'Are we free to go now?'

'Not quite yet,' said Mallory. 'Are you familiar with the international romance writer, Krystalle Storm?'

Chapter Seventeen

'Oh, yes,' Lavinia trilled. 'I love her books. Love them! Love them!'

I looked steadily at my hands.

'It would appear that Harriet Bone was a great fan,' said Mallory. 'We found in her possession, a number of titles—'

'Which ones?' Lavinia said. '*Gypsy Temptress*, *Forbidden*, *Ravished*, *Betrayed*, *Addicted*, *Exposed*? I've read them all.'

Mallory gave Lavinia a nod of acknowledgement, clearly having done his homework.

'A number of passages had been highlighted,' he went on. 'In fact, the deceased had been very prolific with her yellow highlighter. All the books written by Krystalle Storm in her possession had passages highlighted – a grotto, a sunken garden, a chestnut walk, an ornamental lake with a summer-house, to mention just a few landmarks.'

'But stumperies are two a penny,' I heard myself say. 'You just need to look at any National Trust or English Heritage or Historic House. It was part of the way things were in the Golden Age of the country house.'

'Kat's right,' Mum agreed. 'And grottos and sunken gardens. Really. They were two-a-penny.'

'That's as may be,' said Mallory. 'But the stumpery scene in *Forbidden* has specific details, such as the treads in the bank that lead up to the lookout and a pair of initials carved on the trunk of an oak tree.'

My mother had turned ashen. She stared straight ahead at nothing in particular.

'I quote,' Mallory went on. '"At the bottom of the tree was a fairy ring . . ."'

'". . . where Viola had shared sweet kisses with her Reginald,"' whispered Lavinia, in a breathless voice. '"How her body yearned for the forbidden touch of his fingers—"'

'Lav!' Rupert exclaimed, mortified. 'Stop, please.'

I felt sick. Shawn was right. This was it.

Mallory regarded Lavinia with curiosity. 'You are a fan indeed, milady.'

'Viola Honeychurch and Reginald Carew,' said Lavinia. 'That's what VH and RC stand for. Our two families have been having a bit of rumpy-pumpy for centuries.'

'Lav! For Heaven's sake!' Rupert's face was scarlet with embarrassment.

'Ah,' said Mallory. 'I wasn't sure what the initials stood for.'

'Well, they don't say Honeychurch or Carew in the book,' Lavinia blundered on. 'But I did have a great-great-great-uncle Reggie. You should ask Iris if there's a Viola on the

Honeychurch side. She knows everything about the family tree.'

'No, there isn't,' Mum said quickly, and gave a sickly smile.

'Interesting,' said Mallory again. 'Lady Lavinia, may I ask, are you, perhaps, a writer?'

'You mean? Am I Krystalle Storm?' Lavinia gave an unattractive snort. 'Golly, I wish.'

'Apparently Krystalle Storm lives in the South Hams,' Mum said suddenly. 'Perhaps she visited the Hall at some point.'

I let out a cry of shock that I quickly turned into a cough.

'Are you all right, Katherine?' Mum said innocently. 'I hope you haven't got a cold coming on.'

'Krystalle Storm was here!' Delia exclaimed. 'But when?'

'The Hall has been open a few times to the public,' Mum said. 'And we had the opera here last summer. Remember? The place was crawling with singers and a fleet of technicians and whatnot as well as all the people who attended the performances. Then there was the Civil War re-enactment. The place was teeming with soldiers roaming the grounds. Perhaps Krystalle Storm was here then. It would have been easy for her to sneak away to get inspiration for her next blockbuster.'

Lavinia's eyes were out on stalks. 'Golly. She was here and no one knew!'

'I did some research about this reclusive author,' said Mallory. 'She never gives any interviews or appearances, and it seems that no one knows her real name.' Mallory scanned the drawing room. 'There would be a lot of media interest if the real Krystalle Storm was unveiled, don't you think?'

'But she also has a house in Italy,' Mum put in. 'And, besides, doesn't she have a dog? I've not seen any Pekinese dog called Truly Scrumptious strolling around Little Dipperton.'

'Neither have I,' said Lavinia.

'What if Harriet Bone discovered her real identity?' said Mallory, quietly.

Mum started to laugh and kept on laughing. It smacked of vaudeville and it wasn't just me who looked at my mother as if she had gone mad.

'I'm sorry. That's just so funny,' she gasped. 'Are you saying that Harriet Bone discovered the true identity of this Krystalle Storm person who – and this is hard to believe – is living among us on the Honeychurch Hall estate? Somehow this Krystalle Storm lured Harriet to the stumpery – why there? If she wanted to kill Harriet, why not just poison her in the shepherd's hut? Lace her drink with arsenic, perhaps.'

'It's obvious,' Lavinia said suddenly.

We all swivelled to look at her.

'She wanted to prove her point,' Lavinia said. 'Krystalle naturally would have denied it, but Harriet would have said, "Come with me and I'll show you exactly where Reginald made passionate love to his Viola next to the fairy ring."' She gave a wistful sigh. 'Yes. I think that's what happened.'

Mum started to laugh again. 'I'm sorry, Officer, so who in this room is Krystalle Storm?' She sniggered. 'I know it can't be Delia and it's certainly not me, Alfred, Kat or Peggy

Cropper. I doubt it's Pam or Lance since they don't live here, which leaves Eric, Lady Lavinia and Marion.'

'Me?' Marion gasped. 'I don't read that kind of book.'

'But you would say that, wouldn't you?' Mum said sweetly. 'Writers can write anywhere. Don't you have a villa somewhere in Europe? And what if you made up all that stuff about living in Italy and having a Pekinese? Posing as a domestic couple with your handsome husband would be the perfect cover for your true identity.'

Marion had gone deathly pale.

'You're crazy,' Ryan exclaimed.

'We all heard Harriet say you looked familiar,' Mum went on. 'Come to think of it, you do look a little like Krystalle Storm. I checked her website. You've got her blonde hair. She might be a little bit older than you, but we all know what Photoshopping can do – and, besides, wouldn't that be part of the ruse?'

'Oh, yes,' Delia agreed. 'Marion's got her wide mouth.'

At that comment it was all I could do not to laugh.

Mum looked daggers at Delia. 'Krystalle Storm does not have a mouth like a letterbox.'

'Iris! Seriously?' Marion exploded. 'This is utterly ridiculous, Officer. Surely you can see that. I've never heard such rubbish!'

'Yeah. Totally,' Ryan chipped in.

'You'd be surprised at what I hear on a daily basis,' said Mallory, drily. 'At this point in the investigation I'm not dismissing anything, but I would like to show you something.'

He withdrew a Ziploc bag. I could make out a piece of

folded paper. 'This is a map that was found among Harriet Bone's possessions.'

'I think you'll find that it's the estate map showing various footpaths, carriage drives and landmarks,' said Marion.

'Marion designed it,' Ryan said proudly. 'She's an awesome artist.'

'Not this map she didn't,' said Mallory. 'This map was most likely drawn by the deceased. We'll obviously check her handwriting but I'd like you to take a look to see if it makes sense.' Mallory kept the map in the Ziploc bag and stepped forward to hand it to Lavinia. 'Pass it along, please.'

Lavinia did as she was told and, eventually, the map made its way to me.

'Harriet Bone was completely sure of those landmarks,' Mallory went on. 'She has put asterisks and marked the distances in terms of minutes from one to the next. For example, according to this, it takes ten minutes to get from the chestnut walk to the stumpery. Why would she have done that? What had she been looking for?'

'Buried treasure,' Mum said suddenly. 'That's what she must have been looking for. This has nothing to do with Krystalle Storm! It's about buried treasure! Don't you agree, milord?'

There were rumbles of excitement.

'As you know, I'm the Honeychurch family historian, Officer,' Mum began. 'During the Civil War, this house was a Royalist stronghold. The ladies of Honeychurch Hall held out for a year while their men went off to fight Cromwell. They used a secret tunnel to bring in supplies.'

'A secret tunnel?' Ryan's eyes shone with boyish excitement. 'Cool. That's rad!'

'Everyone knows some of the family silver and coins were buried in the grounds so the Roundheads wouldn't get their hands on them.' Mum was warming to her theme. 'Don't you agree, milord?'

Rupert nodded slowly. 'There are rumours, it's true.'

'And Eric is always digging up the odd skeleton or two. Roundheads, usually,' Mum continued. 'I think Harriet must have heard about the buried treasure – people are always talking about it in the village – and voilà!'

'But what about Krystalle Storm?' Lavinia sounded disappointed.

Mum ignored her. 'As I mentioned earlier, we had the Civil War re-enactment last summer . . . or was it the summer before? I think she must have been part of that. It certainly would go a long way to explaining her knowledge of the grounds.'

She sat back and folded her arms with a satisfied grunt.

'Well,' Mallory said slowly. 'It's not something I'd considered but . . .'

'You're not local, you see,' Mum said, with a sigh.

'All right. There's no harm in looking into it,' Mallory said. 'Hopefully Harriet's husband will be able to help us. He'll be arriving tomorrow.'

Mum suddenly clicked her fingers. 'Perhaps that's why Marion and Ryan decided to come to Honeychurch Hall.' She laughed. 'They're hunting for buried treasure! I can't think why else you two would want to hide away in rural Devon.'

'We came here because my mother is very poorly, Iris,' Marion said coldly. 'As well you know.'

'And to put on the gala,' Ryan said, as if we'd all forgotten.

'I think I have enough to go on for the time being,' said Mallory. 'Anything more to add, Shawn?'

We all turned to stare at Shawn. His expression was grave but all he said was, 'Nothing to add.'

And with that, we were dismissed. I had never seen my mother move so quickly as she darted out of the room. I resolved to have words with her later.

Shawn pulled me aside in the reception hall. 'Clearly, you didn't have a word with your mother about this.' His voice was tight and I knew he was annoyed.

'I didn't have a chance,' I protested. 'But I'm going to talk to her right now.'

'Please do,' said Shawn. 'I mean it, Kat. If you don't there will be serious consequences and not just for Iris.'

'What's that supposed to mean?' I demanded.

'For us,' he said curtly and, without so much as a peck on my cheek, he mumbled, 'I'll see you around seven this evening.' And he left.

'Everything all right?' Mallory said, as he joined my side.

I forced a smile. 'Yes, fine.'

'You left a message about the doll being returned,' he said. 'What happened?'

'I'm not quite sure yet,' I said. 'Willow told me that when she got to my space this morning Emerald Barbie was back in her display case.'

'I see.' Mallory frowned. 'You think Di returned it? Have you spoken to her yet?'

'She denied it,' I said. 'She thinks Willow and her friends are involved. I think I want to drop it now. The doll is back. No harm done.'

Mallory regarded me with concern. 'Are you sure?'

'Yes.' I smiled. 'It is Christmas after all.'

Lance appeared at my side with Pam in tow. 'Shall we take the photos now?'

I looked at my watch. 'Let's go.'

Chapter Eighteen

'Well, this is posh,' said Pam, as I let them into the gate-house. While Lance went back and forth to the silver Polo to bring in his lighting equipment, Pam made herself at home. She took off her coat and sank onto the sofa. 'Is there really buried treasure here? You hear about that kind of thing all the time. I could do with finding some silver coins. Get my Lance off to film school.'

'Mum,' Lance said, exasperated. 'How many times do I have to tell you I don't want to go to film school?'

Pam rolled her eyes. 'All right. But Kat here is going to see if she can get you a job in TV.'

Lance muttered something derogatory under his breath and turned his attention to setting up the lighting.

'I know what's good for my son,' Pam went on. 'He'll rot if he stays here. Make him see sense, won't you, Kat?'

I changed the subject. 'Do you want another cup of tea?'

'No, thanks,' said Pam. 'I'd like a look at that doll, though.'

I collected Barbie from the safe and returned to the

showroom. Pam's eyes widened and she seemed genuinely enthralled. 'My word. So that's what a real emerald looks like.'

If I had had my suspicions about Pam's involvement in the theft, they vanished. Her reaction and childlike enthusiasm couldn't have been faked.

'I had a Tressy doll when I was a kid,' she said. 'You could make her hair grow. I remember pulling it out to see how long it would be and then I couldn't get the hair back in again.' She laughed. 'I got a clip around the ear from my mum.'

As Lance took photographs of Barbie, I saw a different side of Pam, the one before she had been beaten down by life's troubles. If what Di had said was true, she had loved her cottage and her life on the Carew estate. She'd had a husband who had clearly enjoyed his job and then, suddenly, everything had changed. Pam had lost him in the cruellest way and been left alone to support herself and her son. I understood that Lance didn't want to live out his mother's dream, but I could see why she wanted a bigger life for him.

Half an hour later, Lance had finished.

'Some questions now about the stone,' said Lance, once he'd packed away his equipment and loaded up the car. '*Dolls Galore* magazine need some content. Is it okay if we record our conversation?'

'I'll do it.' Pam brought out her mobile and perched on the edge of the sofa. 'I can't believe she's worth thousands and thousands of pounds,' she said. 'How do you know if the emerald is the real thing?'

'Out of all the precious gemstones,' I said, 'emeralds are probably the easiest to tell if—'

'It's a fake or a treasure?' Lance grinned.

I smiled back. 'Exactly.'

'Take a look at the stone.' I handed him my jeweller's loupe.

'Where do emeralds come from?' Pam asked.

'They're mined in Zambia, Colombia and Brazil,' said Lance. 'That's right, isn't it?'

'The authentic stones, yes,' I said. 'To manufacture a fake there are two very different types of process. The flux-melt method and the hydrothermal technique. It's a bit complicated.'

'I'm sure we can keep up,' Pam remarked. 'Lance is very bright.'

'I know he is.' I said. 'In 1888, two scientists called Hautefeuille and Perrey used lithium molybdate—'

'On second thoughts,' Pam cut in. 'Just tell us the basics.'

'A genuine emerald is flawed,' I said. 'Almost all emeralds have eye-visible inclusions. Eye-clean emeralds are so rare, I've never seen one.'

'Can I go over to the light?' Lance didn't wait for an answer. He got up with Emerald Barbie, settled into my chair at my desk and switched on the angled desk lamp. Wedging the loupe into his eye socket once more, he said, 'What sort of eye-visible inclusions?'

'Crystals, fractures, needles, fingerprints, growth tubes or liquid inclusions,' I said. 'If you have an emerald with few or no flaws, you can absolutely assume it's a fake.'

Lance quietly continued to scrutinise the stone for what seemed a very long time until he put the doll down and said, 'So, this emerald is a fake.'

I laughed. 'Of course it isn't.'

Pam gasped. 'The emerald is a *fake*?'

'You just told me that an emerald would have eye-visible inclusions,' said Lance. 'Unless I'm going blind, this stone is flawless.'

Pam leaped up with lightning speed. 'Let's have a look. Give it to me.'

'Go ahead, Pam,' I said calmly. 'But I can assure you that the stone is absolutely not a fake.'

Lance rose from my chair and Pam took his place, hunched over the doll and adjusting the loupe several times until she began nodding vehemently.

'Well I never! It *is* a fake.' She sat back and laughed.

I held out my hand for the return of the loupe and the doll. 'I'll explain what I see.'

Pam rose from my chair and gestured that we switch places.

I leaned over the desk to peer at the stone and my heart all but stopped. I can't remember the last time my entire body went cold.

They were right. The stone was synthetic.

The room began to spin. I tried to clear my head. How could this be possible? I had studied the stone so many times and I knew that the emerald had been real.

And then it hit me. The stone had been switched overnight. It was just as I had always believed. The theft had been the work of a professional.

'Judging from your reaction, I think you weren't expecting that,' said Pam, very slowly.

And from Pam's reaction, she hadn't been expecting it either.

Lance seemed as lost for words as I was.

I struggled to compose myself, unsure of what to do next. I had an idea.

'My mistake,' I said smoothly. 'I have two dolls—'

'Oh, *please*!' Pam rolled her eyes in mock despair. 'Seriously? You think we believe that this is one you made earlier?'

I barely knew her but, from what I'd seen so far, Pam was tricky. I decided to be honest and told her the truth.

'This happened on Sunday, didn't it?' Pam exclaimed. 'I *knew* someone had moved my trolley. They'd upset my cleaning chemicals!'

'If you do remember anything strange or unusual – and I can tell you're very observant – it would be really helpful.'

'What's it worth?' Pam said slyly, and glanced pointedly at her mobile phone. Of course she'd recorded the discovery. I was stunned. Surely she wasn't trying to blackmail me.

'I'll do whatever I can for Lance,' I said, shooting a look at him in the hope that for once he wouldn't protest. He didn't.

'Sounds fair.' She smirked.

'Do you remember seeing a tall man, wavy grey hair, heavy-rimmed glasses and a moustache that morning hanging around the Gents? He drives a peppermint-green Ford Fiesta.'

'You mean Oliver?' Pam said.

'Oliver?' I gasped. 'You know him?'

'I don't know his surname or what he drives but I've seen him a few times at the Emporium,' Pam went on. 'You should ask the girls in the café. I think he's a widower and looking for a bit of company.'

My heart sank as quickly as my hopes were raised. Oliver would hardly be a suspect if he was such a regular. The thing is, I'd never noticed him but, then, I wasn't at the Emporium all the time.

'What about Annie, the homeless woman?'

Pam shrugged. 'What about her? There but for the grace of God go I, is what I say. Why?'

'She got caught up in the carol singing on Sunday and fainted,' I said.

Pam shook her head. 'I heard about that but didn't see anything. I was doing my job.'

I thought for a moment. 'Has Annie ever come into the Emporium before? Maybe to use the facilities?'

'No,' said Pam. 'Fiona Reynolds gave me strict instructions that she wasn't allowed to do that.'

And, knowing how formidable Fiona could be, I was pretty sure that Annie wasn't about to start now. It made her appearance on Sunday all the more suspicious.

I must have looked disappointed because, in a rare show of warmth, Pam reached out and gave a sympathetic smile. 'I wouldn't want to be you for all the tea in China.'

I took a deep breath. I had to ask her. 'Was Di anywhere near the toilets on Sunday?'

Pam just blinked. 'No.'

I thought back to the Ford Fiesta on the notice board at Sunny Hill Lodge where Pam still had her cleaning job – and Di's mother lived. I didn't believe in coincidences. Pam was lying and there was nothing I could do about it.

'Well, if I remember anything else,' said Pam, as she gathered up her things, 'I'll be sure to let you know. Lance, are you ready? Let's go.'

Pam pulled on her coat and all but skipped out of the gatehouse.

Lance hung back. 'I'm sorry. I didn't know the stone was a fake. I shouldn't have said anything. What are we going to do about *Dolls Galore*? Shall I still email the photos?'

Ugh. I hadn't thought about that. 'Let me talk to Marion about it first – and, Lance, please persuade your mother not to share the recording.'

'I'll try,' he said, but he didn't seem too sure about it.

Moments later Pam's car started and, with three cheerful toots on the horn, they sped away.

I went straight back to the emerald and this time I noticed that the setting had been altered to accommodate the synthetic stone. Why hadn't I thought to give Barbie a thorough once-over when she'd reappeared?

I felt depressed. I had to go back to Mallory and Shawn and tell them I'd made a mistake. The Cartwrights would have to be told the truth too. I couldn't avoid it any longer.

But, first, I had another pressing problem.

Krystalle Storm.

Chapter Nineteen

'I'm not stupid, Katherine,' Mum said crossly. 'It's obvious that Harriet Bone tracked Krystalle down to Honeychurch Hall.'

'Tracked you down, you mean,' I shot back. 'And why draw attention to yourself with your theories?'

Mum shrugged. 'I thought the buried treasure idea was genius. Did you see Marion's face? She was furious!'

It had taken exactly five minutes for Mum and me to get into a full-scale argument. I was already a mess, wondering what to do about Pam and the wretched fake stone. But in the great scheme of things, my mother, who would be looking at a lengthy prison sentence when – not if – it all came out, trumped a cancelled gala and all the headache and financial implications that went along with it.

'I don't know why you're creating such a fuss,' Mum went on. 'No one suspects it's me. I fooled everyone in the drawing room—'

'Apart from Shawn,' I reminded her.

Mum gave a dismissive wave. 'He doesn't count. You're overreacting.'

'Somehow I doubt it,' I said. 'Mallory is very smart. But that's not the point. Who wanted Harriet dead? And if it wasn't you—?'

'Excuse me? *If* it wasn't me? Of course, it wasn't me. I don't know her from Adam.' My mother frowned. 'My money's on the dowager countess – or, rather, Eric. He'd do anything to protect the family and we know he's done it before.'

'He may have taken the fall but not murder,' I said.

'As far as we know,' Mum said darkly. 'Maybe Harriet's husband had something to do with it. Why didn't he come down immediately to see the body?'

I admitted that the thought had crossed my mind, too.

'Perhaps he took out a hefty life-insurance policy on her,' Mum suggested.

'But that doesn't explain what made Harriet go to the stumpery in the middle of the night.'

'Unless she was killed in the shepherd's hut and Eric carried her body to the stumpery in the hope that some wild animals might finish her off.'

I rolled my eyes. 'I can see why you're a writer. Your imagination has no connection with reality whatsoever.'

'And how was Harriet killed anyway?' Mum mused. 'Mallory didn't elaborate. We want details! Was it by candlestick, the lead piping, a rope, or a dagger?'

'This is not a game of Cluedo,' I said. 'It's not funny, Mum. The passages describing the stumpery were highlighted in your book. She went there for a reason.'

'Well, I don't know what you want me to say,' Mum grumbled.

'Let's not argue,' I said.

'Who's arguing?' Mum gave a heavy sigh. 'Can we change the subject? Let's have a gin and tonic.'

'Good idea,' I said.

We fixed our drinks and returned to the kitchen table with a packet of cheese straws.

'Did you get hold of the publisher today?' I asked.

Mum looked blank.

'The publisher, Mum,' I reminded her. 'You were going to ask if that new intern had given out your PO box address, remember?'

'Oh, that,' Mum said. 'In all the excitement I completely forgot. Speaking of which, didn't you say there was another package for me? I'm missing a hat.'

'I'll get it.' So I did. The package had rolled under the front seat.

'Aha. Same brown paper. Same Christmas stickers.' Mum tore it open. Inside a small gift was wrapped in Christmas paper.

'And, just like the gloves and scarf, it was sent directly to your PO box,' I said. 'Not via Goldfinch Press.'

'It's the hat,' Mum said, as she pulled out a cashmere beret in the same shade of green as the scarf and gloves.

'Is there a note?' I asked. Mum pawed through the paper and handed a card to me. I read: 'A hat-trick for my favourite author from your biggest fan.'

Mum put on the beret, adjusting it to a jaunty angle.

'What do you think? Where's the mirror?' She stood up, pulled out a drawer from the oak dresser and took out a small hand mirror.

'It's cute,' I said. 'Very French.'

'Oh, yes, I do like it,' Mum agreed. She sniffed it. 'And you're right. It's very French. I'll keep this one, although I can guarantee that Delia will beg me to give it to her so she can have the matching set.' She looked at the clock. 'Delia will be here in a few moments. We're going to watch *Gladiator* tonight and see if we can spot Ryan.'

'You should be able to,' I said. 'He told Delia and me that he's the one with a trident and a net.'

'I should hope he *is* wearing his netting under a loincloth.' Mum grinned.

I groaned. 'Not that kind of netting. You're incorrigible.'

'Stay and watch it with us. Do.'

There was a knock at the door. 'It's open!' said Mum. 'That must be Delia now.'

But it wasn't Delia. It was Marion. Her face was flushed. She seemed upset.

'Merry Christmas,' said Mum. 'Would you like a gin and tonic?'

'No, thank you.' Marion regarded my mother with open hostility. 'I need to talk to you.'

'Fire away,' said Mum.

'Why did you say I was Krystalle Storm?'

'Maybe you are!' Mum laughed. 'I also said it could be Lavinia. Or Eric, even.' She shrugged. 'I suppose it was just something to say.'

'Well, don't,' Marion snapped. 'That's the kind of talk that causes trouble and starts rumours and I don't like it.'

Mum was taken aback.

Marion pointed a finger and went on, 'And it's none of your business why my husband and I decided to come to Little Dipperton.' She gave a bitter laugh. 'Small-town malicious gossip.'

'Malicious?' Mum seemed bewildered.

'Why do you think I couldn't wait to move away from Devon?'

Mum's eyes widened. 'We're all under a lot of pressure at the moment. It was a stupid thing to say and I'm truly sorry.' And I believed my mother meant it.

Marion's beautiful face crumpled. 'No, I'm sorry. It's been such a horrible day.' She stood there, mouth quivering. I thought she was going to cry.

'It was Kat who found the body,' Mum pointed out. 'So I suspect, in degrees of horrible, Kat could be winning.'

And since I was about to deliver the news about the fake Emerald Barbie, I was certain I'd be the winner.

Marion took a deep breath. 'I wish we could cancel the gala.'

My spirits lifted. 'That's a great idea!'

'But we can't!' Marion wailed. 'Our mystery guest turned down several lucrative movies as a favour to Ryan.'

Mum was excited. 'It's Maximus from *Gladiator*, isn't it? It's Russell Crowe!'

'Who? Of course not,' Marion responded. 'I think I will have that gin and tonic, after all.' She pulled out a chair and sat down in her coat. 'But I can't stay long. Ryan's in one of his fitness fads and won't eat after six thirty. Kale and boiled chicken. That's it. Every day.'

'And that's why he's so buff,' Mum put in. 'You're lucky to have a handsome husband who doesn't run to fat.'

'Yes, I know,' said Marion. 'But I shouldn't have said that. It's very disloyal. He's very stressed about the gala. Eating kale and boiled chicken is his way of feeling in control of *something*.'

I took a deep breath. 'I really think it *is* best we cancel the gala and I'll tell you why.'

'Because of that poor woman in the stumpery?' Marion said. 'I told Ryan so but he wouldn't have it.'

'And, yes, that too.' I nodded. 'But also because the emerald on the Barbie doll is a fake.'

Mum spat out her gin and had a coughing fit.

'*What?*' Marion turned white. 'Oh, my God. But . . . what do you mean? Why the hell didn't you know that from the beginning?' She put her head into her hands. 'Ryan is going to be so angry. Oh, no. This is a disaster!'

'It wasn't a fake. The doll was stolen on Sunday in broad daylight,' I said quickly. 'And she was put back before the Emporium opened this morning. The stone had been switched.'

'Another drink all round, I think,' muttered Mum.

Marion was stunned. 'But wait.' She held up her hand. 'Let me think.' She paused and attempted to frown. Mum had been right. Her forehead didn't move. 'But will anyone know that? Does it matter?'

'But I know it.' I was appalled. 'And it's my reputation at stake here.'

'But surely your reputation is already in the toilet since you only realised just now that it was a fake!'

'That's not true,' I shot back. 'The stone was switched. I told you.'

'But you would say that, wouldn't you?' Marion sneered.

'Excuse me?' I said.

'You made a mistake about the doll and now you're making up some bizarre story that someone came into the Emporium, took the doll from under your nose, switched the stone and put her back again?'

'That's exactly what happened,' I replied.

'How embarrassing for you.'

'It's not embarrassing for me,' I said. 'I'm not auctioning off a fake. I just won't do it.'

'And I agree,' Mum chipped in. 'That's unethical.'

'If I was to believe you, which I don't,' said Marion, 'what about the CCTV cameras? I've only been to the Emporium once, but everywhere has them now.'

'The police already have the CCTV footage—'

Marion gasped. 'Mallory knows the doll was *stolen*?'

'Yes, but he doesn't know about the stone switch yet because I've only just found out!' I was struggling to keep calm. 'It was a professional job, I know it.'

'Why do you say that?' Marion demanded.

'On Sunday I got a message from Shawn's office to meet him in the car park. It was a trick to get me out of the building,' I said. 'When I was away, the carol singers came through and a homeless woman called Annie fainted. It created enough of a diversion for the thief to make their move.'

'You mean, no one was watching the doll at the time?' Marion seemed incredulous.

I gave a heavy sigh. 'It's a long story. All I know is that a man called Oliver slipped out of the fire exit and drove off in a peppermint-green Ford Fiesta. Nigel got his number plate.'

'Well?' Marion snapped. 'Haven't you tracked him down?'

'I only discovered the man's name this afternoon,' I said. 'I was talking to Pam and she recognised him.'

'Pam Price?' Marion sounded surprised. 'Lance's mother?'

'I thought you knew Pam worked at the Emporium,' I said. 'Isn't that why you suggested she man the loos for the gala?'

'Oh, yes, yes, of course.' Marion seemed flustered now. 'And you say the doll was returned early this morning? Surely that would require assistance from someone on the inside. Someone who knows the alarm code.'

'Yes, I think so too,' I said. 'Pam also mentioned a UPS delivery van that arrived early but she told him to come back at nine.'

'Pam needs to share this information with Mallory,' Marion said. 'Although, if you say you think it was a professional job, I suspect the emerald is gone in the wind by now.' She stared miserably into her glass. 'I just don't know what to do about *Dolls Galore*.' She thought for a moment. 'No. I know what we'll do. We'll go ahead as normal. No one other than you knows about the fake stone, right?'

I bit my lip. 'Pam and Lance know.'

'What?' Marion shrieked. 'How?'

Marion's panic was contagious. By now Mum had started tittering. I knew she did that when she was nervous.

'It's not funny, Iris!' Marion shouted. 'We need to do damage control. Just shut up and let me think.'

'They were with me when I found out – actually, it was Lance who noticed it.' I didn't mention that Pam had recorded the whole thing in case Marion's head exploded.

She clapped a hand over her forehead. 'Ryan is going to freak out.' She thought for a moment. 'We'll pay them off. Tell them to keep quiet. At least until after the gala.'

'I'm not auctioning a fake,' I said firmly. 'You can have another doll from my own stock or find someone else to act as your MC. That's my decision, and I'm sorry if you don't like it. I still have to break the news to Cathy White that her emerald has been stolen. To be honest, the gala is the least of my problems.' I turned to Mum and gave her a pointed look. She rolled her eyes.

Marion slumped in the chair. 'Yes. You're right. We'll have to cancel. I'll talk to Ryan. But . . . it's the money! Refunding the tickets. Returning all the prizes and auction items – there are dozens and dozens. Then there's the sponsors.' Marion made a peculiar gulping sound and whispered something else about Ryan's temper.

'I think that is the best decision,' said Mum, gently.

'You don't know my husband,' Marion whispered.

'Well, hopefully I'm going to know him a lot better this evening,' Mum declared. 'Delia and I are going to watch *Gladiator*.'

Marion cracked the smallest of smiles. 'He's in the first combat scene with Russell Crowe. Ryan trained hard for that role.' Her smile faded. 'We had so much fun in those days. A lot of big dreams.'

Mum scratched her head and swept off her beret. A faint red mark was forming on her forehead.

'I love your beret,' Marion said suddenly. 'It's such a pretty shade of green. There's a special name for it.' She paused. 'Scheele's Green. The Victorians used arsenic in their dye to get that colour.' And then she seemed to pull herself together and stood up. 'Wish me luck.'

We heard the door slam.

'So, Ryan's the ogre,' Mum said. 'Behind the charming smile . . .'

But I wasn't listening to Ryan's attributes, physical or otherwise. I was thinking of Marion's comment about Scheele's Green. For a moment, I pushed away the emerald and all its implications and thought of the hat-trick – the beret, scarf and gloves – all the same green from the same fan. There was something sinister about the gifts that made the hairs on my neck stand up.

'Give me that beret,' I said suddenly. 'I want to check something.'

There was a shout of greeting from the inner hall and Delia strolled in. She removed her coat, green scarf and green gloves. I noticed that the red welt on her neck and the blisters on her hands had got a lot worse.

Delia took out a pair of cotton gloves from her handbag and pulled them on. 'I'm going to make an appointment with the doctor tomorrow. I can't get through Christmas with hands like this. It's so depressing.'

I had a suspicion of what could be causing it, but before I said something, I had to be sure.

I grabbed the brown wrapping paper from the dresser, snatched up the beret and, bidding them goodbye, left Mum and Delia to their gin and their gladiators.

Chapter Twenty

'Are you positive?' Shawn studied Mum's beret closely on my dining-room table. He'd arrived early and I was glad – and, to be honest, surprised. I'd half expected him to cancel.

'As positive as I can be without going to a lab,' I said. 'Yes. The scarf, gloves and this beret have all been laced with poison.'

I showed him my iPad where I had bookmarked a disturbing article on the arsenic-infused dye that was prevalent in Victorian times. There were photographs showing a range of blisters that bore a striking similarity to those on Delia's poor hands.

I told Shawn that in 1778 Carl Scheele announced the discovery of a new copper arsenate dye. It was used in artificial flowers, carpets, furs, dress fabrics, black stockings and wallpaper. Studies showed that even bedbugs could die in rooms that carried the new wallpaper. Another sign was a distinct garlic-like odour. Factory girls suffered the most because they were exposed to the toxins all day long. The images on my iPad were gruesome to say the least.

Unfortunately I knew that what I was about to tell Shawn would make things even worse for my mother.

I left him for a moment to scroll through the photographs while I fetched the brown-paper wrapping from the kitchen. Even though I suspected that Harriet had been the sender, I couldn't prove it.

'Mum received three items wrapped separately in brown paper that was covered with these festive stickers.' I set the paper on the coffee-table. 'They were sent directly to my PO box and not via the publisher.'

'PO box?' Shawn seemed confused.

'My mother's fan mail is always forwarded from the publisher to my PO box in the village,' I explained. 'The publisher keeps the parcels in their original wrapping and either puts them into a larger envelope or wraps them in brown paper. The beret, gloves and scarf did not go via the publisher. They were posted directly to my PO box.'

Shawn fastidiously donned his disposable latex gloves, which again seemed pointless since we had all been handling the brown paper, and began to study the wrapping.

After a few moments, he ripped off his gloves. A tic started to quiver in his forehead. I knew that sign well. He was furious.

'Let me get this straight,' he said. 'A fan sent the gifts directly to your PO box that was specifically set up for your mother. Ergo, this fan, assuming it was Harriet Bone, knows exactly where your mother lives.'

'Well, she didn't have the exact address,' I said.

'Don't split hairs,' said Shawn.

'It could still be a leak from the publisher. Mum is calling them in the morning to find out.'

Shawn sat back. 'And why do you think Harriet Bone sent these items of clothing?'

'Harriet was with me when I went to pick up Mum's post,' I said. 'As you can see, the wrapping is very distinctive with the festive stickers. She must have recognised them.'

'But why send three different parcels?'

I shrugged. 'I have no idea.'

'And you believe the items were deliberately soaked in this poisonous dye out of spite?' Shawn sounded incredulous.

I shrugged again. 'Harriet told me she had been a chemist. Mum gave the gloves and scarf to Delia.' I pointed to the iPad. 'Delia came out in welts and blisters very much like those illustrated here.'

'Was that why Delia was wearing white cotton gloves this afternoon?'

I nodded. 'And, what's more, Mum wore the green beret for all of twenty minutes. When she took it off, she had a rash.'

'After so short a time?' He shook his head as if not believing any of it. 'And what made you connect this with so-called Scheele's Green?'

'I didn't,' I said. 'It was Marion who mentioned it. I did some research and, well, you can see for yourself.'

Shawn seemed puzzled. 'Go on.'

'Harriet came to the Hall on Sunday evening after the

staff meeting in the ballroom,' I said. 'She came because she was upset about the damage to the grille on her hire car.'

'Go on,' said Shawn again.

'Harriet saw Delia wearing the gloves and scarf.'

'And this beret?'

'No,' I said. 'That was still in my car.'

'And why was Delia wearing the gloves and scarf that were sent to your mother?'

'Mum gave them to her,' I said. 'So Harriet assumed that Delia had to be Krystalle Storm.'

'Oh,' said Shawn.

'My mother was telling the truth when she said she'd hardly spoken to Harriet,' I said. 'I think it was a case of mistaken identity, at least as far as Krystalle Storm is concerned.'

Shawn folded his arms. 'Harriet was obviously a fan of Krystalle Storm judging by the books in her possession.'

'Exactly.'

'And a fan who, for some strange reason, was so upset that her adoration turned to malice. A fan who went to a lot of trouble to make poisonous clothing and send it as gifts to her former idol. And a fan who managed to track your mother down to Honeychurch Hall.'

'Yes.'

'Which suggests to me that Harriet Bone would have had no qualms whatsoever about revealing your mother's true identity to the world,' Shawn went on. 'And your mother knew it.'

'Mum did not!' I said hotly. 'I know she didn't!'

'It's obvious that Iris was going to be exposed, Kat,'

Shawn said. 'And if it wasn't your mother who killed Harriet Bone, who did? And why?'

'I don't know,' I wailed. 'And I also don't know how she ended up in the stumpery. Why do you say she was murdered?'

'I'm afraid at this point in the investigation I'm not at liberty to say.'

I stifled a wave of frustration. 'Do you know how infuriating you are when you say that? Why can't you tell me?'

'Because it's not my case,' he said simply. 'Have you told Mallory about your mother yet?'

'No,' I said. 'Because I think that should come from her.'

'You know my feelings on this. You're putting me in a very difficult position. I'm sorry, Kat—'

'And I'm sorry, too,' I said.

'If you won't tell him, I will.' Shawn reached for his mobile.

'Shawn! Please don't,' I cried. 'I'm begging you to wait.'

But, to my dismay, he made the call all the same and left a message asking Mallory to come to Jane's Cottage as soon as possible.

I stood up, mumbling about having to check on dinner. I was gutted and felt incredibly betrayed.

Shawn was right behind me. 'When are you going to accept that your mother is not the angel she portrays herself to be?' he said angrily. 'And what do you expect me to do with this information? I have a duty to report it!'

I spun around. 'You don't have a duty to report it,' I shouted. 'As you keep telling me, it's not your investigation. I'm sharing this with you because you're my boyfriend!'

There was a knock on the front door.

We stopped in our tracks.

The knock grew louder.

'Good grief. It must be Mallory,' said Shawn. 'That was fast.'

'Please, Shawn, please don't tell him. Not yet,' I begged again. 'Don't.'

But Shawn had already left the kitchen. I heard the door open and the men exchange greetings. There was a loud crack and a curse word. Mallory must have had hit his head again on the door frame.

I pinched my cheeks, checked my reflection in the kettle and put on my game face.

When I walked into the living area, I felt a glimmer of hope. The beret had been scooped up in the brown wrapping paper and deposited in the corner on the floor by my reading chair.

Shawn wouldn't look at me.

Mallory was rubbing his forehead. 'When will I learn?' His smile faltered. 'Have I come at a bad time?' The atmosphere must have been thick enough to cut with the proverbial knife.

'Not at all,' I said, with forced cheerfulness. 'A glass of wine? A beer?'

'I'm driving but I could have a small cider if you have some.' Mallory took off his coat and outdoor boots. I noticed thick grey sensible socks.

'And you should stay for dinner,' said Shawn. 'Kat is an excellent cook. She has some news to share.'

I blinked and nodded. 'I'll get your cider.'

The two men made small-talk. It was obvious that Shawn was not going to tell Mallory about my mother. He was leaving that up to me.

'I got Shawn's message, but I was on my way here anyway.' Mallory flashed a smile. 'I want Kat to take a look at Marion's pearl necklace, which she very kindly gave to me after our meeting.'

I had set out a wine glass for Shawn but instead he asked for Perrier. I knew that meant he had changed his mind and was not going to stay over. Resentment, mixed with despair, hit me afresh.

This was my mother's fault. The rift between Shawn and me was forcing me to choose between my boyfriend and the loyalty I felt to her. It just wasn't fair.

Mallory brought out a velvet drawstring pouch. He tipped out a pearl necklace but instead of five interspersing diamonds, this had three. It was very pretty.

'With the theft of the necklace,' said Mallory, 'I wanted to get an idea of value.'

'Harriet's was very similar to this but hers had five stones.' I retrieved my ever-ready jeweller's loupe from my tote bag. I didn't need to study the gems for very long. I already knew the diamonds were real.

'Well?' said Mallory.

I hesitated. 'In terms of value, this could be around fifteen hundred to two thousand pounds because these are real diamonds.'

'Yet the two necklaces were bought at the same place,' Mallory mused.

'Not necessarily,' I said. 'It just so happened that Harriet had bought hers on an island where they were manufactured when she was on a cruise in the Mediterranean.' I thought for a moment. 'Marion said she bought hers in Madrid.'

'Timothy Bone, Harriet's husband, is coming tomorrow,' said Mallory. 'Perhaps he can shed more light on this mystery.'

We fell quiet. Shawn cleared his throat. 'Speaking of mysteries, Kat has something to tell you.'

'Yes,' I said quickly. 'Let's eat.'

I knew what Shawn meant but I pretended I didn't. At last, the three of us were seated at my small dining-room table.

Shawn reached over and squeezed my hand. He gave me a nod of encouragement. 'Go on. Tell Mallory what you told me.'

Chapter Twenty-one

'First, I have a question,' I said. 'Harriet had broken her neck from a fall. That doesn't sound like murder to me.'

Shawn abruptly dropped my hand and picked up his cutlery with a lot of noise.

'Shawn won't tell me,' I said.

Shawn's jaw hardened. 'Because it's not my case.'

If he said that one more time I just might scream.

'We know it was murder,' said Mallory, 'because of a puncture wound behind the victim's ear.'

'What?' I was shocked. 'You mean like a poison-tipped umbrella?'

Mallory smiled and even Shawn grunted amusement.

'Nothing as sophisticated as that,' said Mallory. 'Our victim was not a Russian dissident.'

I smiled too. 'It's just a weird thing to do.'

'My theory is that it took the victim by surprise and prompted her fall.'

I thought the idea too far-fetched and said so. 'What do you think, Shawn?'

Shawn ignored me.

'We'll know more in the next few days, but for now,' said Mallory, 'I'd like to keep those details quiet.' He took a sip of cider. 'I believe that the victim was persuaded to go up to the lookout. The killer jabbed her with a sharp object, which prompted her fall. As I said, it's just a theory.'

'We have a few partial footprints on the treads—' Shawn began.

'Some might be mine,' I pointed out.

'—and on the slab,' Shawn continued. 'But, yes, they are probably Kat's. You weren't to know you were tramping all over a crime scene.'

'I wasn't expecting to find a body,' I protested.

'There's no need to get defensive,' said Shawn.

'I wasn't getting defensive,' I retorted.

'I told Mallory your shoe size so at least we could eliminate *you* from our enquiries,' Shawn said, with a tinge of sarcasm. I knew exactly what he was implying. He could eliminate me, but my mother was still a suspect.

Mallory looked to Shawn and back to me again. He'd have to have been blind not to realise we were in the middle of a hideous row. 'We won't know more until after Christmas,' he said. 'Unfortunately, unlike television, results take weeks to come back, not hours.'

Shawn gave a tight smile.

We continued to eat in silence. For a few moments, all

that could be heard was the clank of cutlery on the plates. I just picked at my food. I wasn't hungry.

'Well,' Mallory said finally, 'I got your message about the return of Emerald Barbie. That's very good news.'

'I did too,' Shawn added. 'Yes. Good news.'

'Not good news any more,' I said ruefully. 'I'm afraid the emerald was switched during the theft. It's a fake.'

Swiftly I explained the embarrassing conversation I had had with Lance and his mother Pam at the gatehouse and that it had all been recorded.

Shawn shook his head. 'You've put yourself in a vulnerable position, Kat. You've opened yourself to blackmail.'

'I realise that, but it was hardly deliberate!' I exclaimed. 'I do think there's something Pam isn't telling me, though. It's as if she has a secret but she doesn't want to share it.'

'She must have been involved in the theft,' Shawn opined.

'I just don't know,' I said. 'Her reaction to the discovery that the stone was a fake seemed genuine but she cleans at Sunny Hill Lodge, which is where the Fiesta is for sale on the notice board . . .'

'. . . and Di Wilkins' mother lives there,' Shawn finished.

'Yes, but this isn't anything to do with Di,' I protested. 'She wasn't at the Emporium this morning and whoever returned the doll did it before anyone was there. It's a coincidence.'

'A coincidence?' Shawn gave a snort of disdain. 'Your loyalty is commendable.'

I knew what he was insinuating but I ignored it. 'Di wouldn't know the first thing about switching an emerald for a fake. This was a carefully thought-out plan. You can't just pick up a synthetic stone that fits the setting by chance.'

'But she could have been an accomplice. Di sells vintage jewellery,' Shawn pointed out. 'She's hardly a stranger to that world. Don't rule her out.'

'Yes, I know that, Shawn.' I was getting annoyed.

'I'm afraid Shawn has a point.' Mallory relayed his conversation with Fiona Reynolds about Di's financial woes. 'And there have been several cases of shoplifting over the past few weeks as well.'

I thought of Willow's friends and Di's accusation and suddenly felt incredibly tired. I was weary of fighting everyone else's battles. I needed to focus on my own problems, namely the recovery of the real emerald. And then there was my mother.

'And for the record,' I said, 'Di told me about her shoplifting past, and it wasn't proper shoplifting. It was for a dare.'

Shawn shrugged. 'Maybe Kat should call her old boyfriend. He's a world-famous art investigator.'

'David, you mean,' I said, ignoring the dig. Shawn had never liked David even though he had no reason to be jealous. 'And, yes, I was planning on doing that, but I wanted to discuss it with you first.'

'Me?' Shawn said, clearly sulking. 'It's Mallory's case. But it sounds like you're looking for a needle in a haystack. You may as well accept defeat.'

'Ah, as the saying goes, not so fast, my friend.' Mallory took another sip of cider. 'I traced the owner of that car and the name.'

'Yes, it's Oliver—'

'Oliver?' Mallory looked surprised. 'No. The car is registered to an Arthur Matthews of nine Bradninch Rise, North Brent.'

'Are you sure?' I said.

'Perhaps he changed his name,' Shawn said, looking at me. 'Lots of people do. Usually to hide something illegal.'

'I'll be heading there first thing tomorrow morning,' Mallory said, looking at Shawn and me again with curiosity. 'It could be a wild-goose chase but we have to rule him out. We'll also take another look at the CCTV cameras since you mention the doll was returned before the Emporium opened.'

'Pam told me that a delivery driver attempted to drop off a package,' I said, 'but she sent him away.'

'I'll have another word with her.' Mallory sat back in his chair. 'That was delicious. Thank you for inviting me. You're an excellent cook.'

'I try,' I said, with a smile, and downed the rest of my wine.

Shawn made an exaggerated motion to check his watch. 'I've got to go,' he said. 'My mother-in-law wants to leave by ten. I'll call you tomorrow, Kat.'

It was a slap in the face. Mother-in-law. A reminder that Shawn had been married – happily married – before. He hadn't referred to Lizzie as his mother-in-law for a long time.

I was glad he was leaving but incredibly upset. I was stuck in the middle on all sides, but all I said was, 'I made a blackberry and apple crumble.'

'Another time.' Shawn stood up.

'I'd love some,' Mallory said.

'I'll see you out.' I followed Shawn to the front door, and whispered, 'Please stay.'

He gestured for me to step outside. It was bitterly cold, but I followed him in my slippers.

Shawn pulled the door closed behind him, not quite on the latch. I started to shiver.

He took my hands and pulled me towards him, gently brushing my hair from my face. 'I'm sorry, Kat,' he said quietly. 'I can't sit there with a colleague I respect and keep this secret of your mother's.'

'But—'

'Ssh!' He put his finger on my lips. 'This isn't the first time that Iris has been in this situation. You've chosen your side and I understand. Until you come clean with Mallory, I can't see you. It's just too difficult for me.'

My jaw dropped. I couldn't believe it. 'You're breaking up with me?'

'Of course not.' He kissed my forehead. 'I love you. But you need to make some hard decisions. Let's just take a few days apart.'

'But what about the gala?' I said.

'You know I hate that kind of thing,' said Shawn. 'I already told you I wasn't sure I could make it. Babysitters and—'

'You've known about the gala for months.' I was desperately disappointed. 'You just don't want to go.'

He didn't answer.

'You never want to go to anything with me.' I knew I sounded like a needy girlfriend, but it was yet another bone of contention. We rarely went anywhere together. Most of our couple time was spent in my house or his watching TV.

Shawn looked deep into my eyes. 'It's no reflection on not wanting to spend time with you,' he said. 'I'm just not a social kind of person.'

'Can we at least speak on the phone?' I asked.

'Let me know when you've told Mallory and then we'll see,' said Shawn. 'I'm sorry, Kat. Truly I am.'

I watched his car pull away and the lights disappear down the service drive. When I stepped back inside, I was fighting tears.

Mallory wasn't in the living room. I could hear running water and the clunk of crockery. I noticed that he had cleared the dining table.

I found him at the kitchen sink with a tea towel draped over his shoulder, rinsing the plates, and stacking them on the overhead wooden rack. The blackberry and apple crumble sat on a trivet covered with aluminium foil. He clearly knew his way around the kitchen.

'You didn't need to wash up,' I said.

'You look cold.'

I promptly burst into tears.

Mallory set down the plates and hurried to my side. He pulled me into his arms and didn't say a word. I felt oddly safe. Neither of us spoke until I pulled away.

'You've had a horrible day,' he said, with a gentle smile.

'That's an understatement,' I muttered, thinking that finding Harriet's body had been the tip of the iceberg.

Mallory tore off a piece of kitchen roll and handed it to

me. I dabbed my eyes and nose, remembering that Mum always said I sounded like an elephant whenever I blew it.

'And I still want some crumble,' he said. 'I assume you don't. How about a brandy?'

I nodded.

'Go and sit down,' he said. 'I'll find it. I'm a detective!'

I went back to the dining table and pulled out a chair. Mallory brought in a balloon of brandy for me and the crumble for him with lashings of clotted cream.

'I would have made custard,' I said, 'but I got sidetracked.'

My heart began to pound again. This was the time I had to tell him about Mum. *Do it, Kat. Say it!*

I took a deep breath. 'I have to tell—'

'Tell the Cartwrights about the emerald,' Mallory said. 'Absolutely.'

'Oh – yes. No, I mean. I already told Marion this afternoon,' I rushed on. 'She knows it's a fake and wants to go ahead regardless.'

'Go ahead with the auction?' Mallory's eyes widened. 'And how do you feel?'

'I can't do that! I can't auction something I know to be fake!' I took a long sip of brandy and felt comforted by the warmth as it flooded through my body.

'Have you told the donor yet?'

I shook my head. 'No. Cathy's away until Thursday. I don't want to ruin her holiday.'

'Did you find an alternative?'

'I have something in mind,' I said.

Mallory stood up and took his bowl to the kitchen.

'I must go. This new development has got me thinking. It's critical you continue as if the emerald has not been switched. Keep the Barbie doll at the Emporium. How many people know it's a fake?'

'The Cartwrights, Lance and Pam, my mother, you and Shawn,' I said.

Mallory frowned. 'We need to tell them to keep this quiet, at least until I've tracked down Arthur Matthews, a.k.a. Oliver, in North Brent. I will also talk to Di—'

'I don't think—'

'I know!' Mallory cut in gently. 'But perhaps there were details she missed the first time around. The same goes for Willow.'

'Okay.'

'Timothy Bone is coming here tomorrow,' Mallory went on. 'Are you certain that the diamonds in Harriet's necklace were zircons?'

'Ninety-nine per cent,' I said. 'When I saw Marion's, it was obvious those were real. Why is he coming here? Isn't Harriet's body in the morgue?'

'Mr Bone is adamant that he sees the exact location where his wife was found,' said Mallory. 'It's clear that the stumpery is significant, and I need to find out why.'

'I . . . yes. It must be important. Um. Yes.' *Tell him, Kat!* But my courage failed me again.

Mallory's eyes were full of concern. 'Are you okay?'

'Yes. Fine,' I whispered. 'Just a bit tired.'

I felt wretched as I waved goodbye to Mallory. He had been so kind.

There was no exchange of goodnight texts with Shawn.
He was right. I had a big decision to make.

Chapter Twenty-two

After a hot bath and a cup of lavender and camomile tea, I slept like a log and rose early. I felt despondent over Shawn and our future but I couldn't afford to feel sorry for myself. One of my pet peeves was that awful phrase 'It is what it is.' But it summed up everything right now. I gave myself a pep talk. I could only deal with what was in front of me and push everything else to one side.

I had a busy day ahead. I had to call the insurance company, David, Margery Rook about the Ford Fiesta, and I had a valuation scheduled for eleven. I also had to drop Barbie off at the Emporium.

I went to David first.

My decade with him had only been hampered by the shadow of his estranged wife. We'd enjoyed the same things, had a wide circle of friends, travelled together and he made me laugh. With Shawn, our relationship was hampered by the shadow of his dead wife. The two men did the same thing, investigated crime, but couldn't have been more different in their approach. With David, it had always been an adventure. With Shawn, everything was so serious – apart from his peculiar hobby of trainspotting. I did love Shawn. I was sure I did.

After the initial few months of hurt feelings and upset, David and I were able to maintain a professional relationship, even a friendship of sorts. His divorce had finally gone through and the last I knew was that he was dating.

I called him.

Knowing me well, David picked up on my mood and even asked me if everything was okay. He didn't make the usual barb about my mother. Sometimes I wondered if I'd spent all those years training him for another woman to reap the benefits. I even felt a pang of nostalgia and thought back fondly to our hectic and very exciting social life in London. How had I ended up in rural Devon holding my mother's hand and dating a stuffy, pompous policeman?

After exchanging small-talk, I told David about the emerald. His voice became animated. 'I've heard of such a set-up.' He went on to tell me of numerous thefts in Amsterdam, London and Rome where sleight of hand and a jewel switch had only been captured on CCTV cameras long after the theft had been discovered.

'We're talking months,' David went on. 'The MO was usually a customer asking to see raw stones. The moment the sales assistant's back was turned, the stones would be switched.'

I could hardly believe it. 'In the showroom?'

'Oh, yes,' said David. 'It's not usually a one-man show. It's often a gang who can move the stones along on the black market, but I'll be honest, I don't hold out much hope for the return of your emerald, and certainly not in time for your gala. Send over some photographs and I'll put out the word.'

'I have plenty of those,' I said. 'I took them for insurance purposes.'

'I knew you would,' said David. 'If and when the stone resurfaces, it will be easy to identify. That's the beauty of emeralds. Each one is distinctive because of its flaws. Rather like you.'

'Very funny,' I said, and laughed.

'Take care, Kat,' said David, warmly. 'I'll let you know the moment I have news. And good luck on Friday. Whatever happens, you'll find a solution and save the day. You always do.'

I felt marginally better after hanging up. David was the best out there in international art fraud and theft. If anyone could find it, it would be him.

But not before Friday.

As Mum liked to say, there's no point in crying over spilled milk. It looked like the gala was still going ahead. I'd have to find a replacement, and fast. I might not have Emerald Barbie, but I had enough unique antique dolls to choose from. I took poor Emerald Barbie and headed to the Emporium, planning on being back in the showroom for my valuation by eleven.

The next hour was busy with shoppers. Telling Willow I would return after lunch I made a quick stop at the toilets before heading to my car.

The toilets were in a state of disarray. No loo paper and piles of discarded paper towels on the floor. There was no sign of Pam.

I returned to my car and was just leaving the car park when Lance appeared on his moped. He flagged me down.

I pulled over and opened my window.

Lance removed his helmet. 'Have you seen my mother today?'

I thought back to the state of the toilets and didn't think Pam had been in. 'Why? Is everything all right?'

'I'm not sure,' he said. 'I heard her go out late last night, and when I woke up this morning, her car wasn't outside. She's not answering her phone either. She always starts work at eight but her car isn't here.'

'Have you asked the police if there have been any accidents? Even though the snow is melting, there was a lot of black ice last night.'

'Yes, and I've driven our usual route as well.' He looked worried.

'I'm driving back to Little Dipperton,' I said. 'I'll keep an eye open. Will you let me know when you find her?'

Lance nodded. 'By the way, Marion asked me for the *Dolls Galore* photos this morning. I had to give them to her. I'm sorry.'

My heart sank. I had decided to tell Marion we needed to pull the article. 'Oh, Lance, I wish you'd checked with me first.'

'She insisted,' said Lance. 'Marion had already paid me up front, so it was hers to do what she liked with.'

I could have kicked myself. With everything going on I

had completely forgotten about the wretched magazine. 'Don't worry, Lance. I'll contact her and sort it out.'

'But then she'll ask for her money back.' Lance thrust out his jaw. 'That's not fair. It's not my fault the stone is fake. I did a job, and I should be paid for it.'

I saw Lance's point, and I also saw a side to him I hadn't noticed before. It looked like he could stand up for himself after all. 'I'll ask Marion if I can see the copy. Perhaps we can take out the incriminating stuff. Okay?'

My answer seemed to satisfy him. He put his helmet back on and we parted ways.

In the car, I called Marion. As usual she was driving and put me on speaker phone.

'Too late,' she said. 'It's been accepted. Sorry – going into a bad area.' And we were disconnected.

Stifling my annoyance, I got back to my showroom in good time for my appointment at eleven and was just about to make a coffee when there was a knock at the door. 'It's open,' I called.

A man in his mid-sixties, dressed in a camel car coat and winter boots, stepped inside. 'Am I in the right place?'

'Yes,' I said, and offered my hand in greeting. He took it and held it for just a second too long. 'Can I take your coat? Would you like a cup of coffee?'

The man seemed surprised. 'Well, that's service for you. I don't mind if I do.'

He took in my showroom with teddy bears and dolls ranged on shelves. I'd added a festive touch with a Christmas tree but I hadn't gone overboard.

'Kat's Collectibles, eh?' he mused. 'And you're Kat Stanford.'

'Do you need help bringing them in from the car?' I asked.

The man seemed puzzled. 'Bringing in what?'

'The military memorabilia?' I said. 'The medals?'

'I haven't come to see you, love,' he said. 'I'm Timothy Bone.'

'Oh.' I felt my face redden. How horribly awkward. 'I'm sorry for your loss.'

'You heard what happened?' he asked.

I nodded. I could hardly say that I had been the person to find Harriet's body. Mallory had specifically told me to say nothing. 'The Hall is about a mile up the drive.'

'I was told to come to the gatehouse by a Detective Inspector Mallory. He said he'd meet me at the entrance.'

'Ah, right.' This was news to me. 'I'll just let him know you're here.'

Mallory picked up on the first ring. 'He's early and I didn't expect you to be there,' he said. 'I was going to meet him at the bottom of the drive. Sorry, Kat. I'll be there in twenty minutes. Obviously, I don't want you answering any of his questions. All he knows is that his wife had a fall. You know that the spouse is always a suspect so the least said the better.'

There was a beep in my ear signifying a call waiting. Unfortunately, I couldn't switch over in time and I dropped both. Luckily, the second caller left a voicemail. It was my client cancelling his valuation appointment because of the bad weather.

I was stuck with Timothy Bone.

Twenty minutes sounded like an excruciatingly long time. I didn't relish the thought of making small-talk with a man whose wife had just been murdered.

'Have you come far this morning, Mr Bone?' I asked.

'Basingstoke,' he said. 'Three hours and twenty-seven minutes, excluding a stop for petrol. The roads were clear, except for the A303 by Sparkford. They're building a new dual carriageway, which should shave off another nine minutes. Maybe ten.'

'Oh. Good.'

'I'll have that coffee now,' he said. 'Instant. Not that ground muck that people serve up, these days. Nescafé would do nicely. A level teaspoon, mind, and one sugar. White. Splash of milk, not that semi-skimmed muck, but proper milk.'

I had none of those things. 'I can offer you tea. PG Tips.'

'I suppose that will have to do.'

I stifled a smile. Harriet had mentioned her husband used the word 'muck' a lot. She was right. No wonder she'd wanted to get away for a few days. I would too.

I returned with a mug for me and a cup and saucer for him. Somehow I could tell he wouldn't approve of a mug. He had removed his coat, fastidiously folded it with the lining exposed and laid it on the arm of the sofa. He jerked up his neatly pressed trousers and sat down.

'Harriet mentioned you'd retired,' I said, as I perched on the desk, sending pencils tumbling to the floor. I bent to pick them up. He made no move to help me. 'What did you used to do?'

Timothy's eyes narrowed. 'Why are you asking?'

'I just wondered.' But then I remembered. 'She mentioned you worked for the post office.'

Timothy stirred his tea and didn't comment.

I struggled for something safe to say. 'My father was a tax inspector.'

'Poor sod,' said Timothy.

'Actually, he enjoyed his job,' I said.

'Bet he didn't have many friends.'

Silence stretched between us. Timothy continued to stir his tea. The ting-ting-ting of the teaspoon began to grate on my nerves, just as Harriet had said.

'I suppose being retired frees up some time to take more cruises,' I said, then regretted saying it. How could I have been so thoughtless? He'd hardly take a cruise on his own now.

'Expensive things, cruises,' said Timothy. 'Harriet always wanted to take the offshore tours. They weren't included in the price, you know. Total rip-off. And then she always wanted the jewellery and clothes and souvenirs. All marked up.'

'Ah. Yes.' I thought of Harriet's pearl necklace. 'Harriet showed me a beautiful pearl and diamond necklace that you bought for your thirtieth wedding anniversary.'

'That set me back a couple of thousand pounds,' said Timothy. 'I suppose she asked you to value it. My mother insisted that the diamonds were zircons but Harriet wouldn't have it.'

'Unfortunately, I never got the chance to see it.' It was a lie of sorts, but with the necklace still missing, it could get awkward.

'Bought it in the Majorica factory shop when we stopped in Mallorca,' he said. 'That cruise was a disaster, and you don't get a refund, you know.'

'Oh? What happened?' I said.

'There was an incident. Someone fell off the balcony. Harriet heard the splash. She was the one who raised the alarm. We all had to get off and go home. All the other passengers got a refund, but because Harriet had won it in a contest, we didn't! Had to fly back to Heathrow on our own dime.'

'Oh dear,' I said.

We fell into another uncomfortable silence, except for the sound of Timothy Bone's spoon clinking in the teacup. It was all I could do not to grab it out of his hands and hurl it against the wall.

Where was Mallory? But then I had a thought. Mallory's delay could work to my advantage. True, I'd promised not to answer any of Timothy Bone's questions, but I could certainly ask them.

'I understand your wife was a great reader,' I said. 'She told me she was a big fan of Krystalle Storm.'

'Fan?' Timothy said, with a sneer. 'She idolised her. She wanted to *be* Krystalle Storm. That was all she talked about. But then last year she wanted to be Salome Steel until she found out who she really was.' He laughed. '*Paparazzi Razzle* had a field day with that one.'

I distinctly remembered Harriet mentioning *Paparazzi Razzle*. I felt faint at the thought of how close my mother's identity had come to being exposed.

'Harriet mentioned she had contacts with that, er, sort of publication,' I said.

'She got a taste for fame, and it never left her. She changed.' A flicker of sadness crossed Timothy's features but was swiftly gone.

And then I was struck by a bizarre thought. Had Harriet sent arsenic-laced clothing to other authors she'd been infatuated with?

'Harriet mentioned she used to be a chemist?' I ventured.

'Is that what she told you?'

'Wasn't she?'

Timothy put the spoon back onto the saucer and regarded me with suspicion. 'You had a long chat with her, then?'

'Not really. More . . .' I was about to say 'muck' '. . . tea?'

I heard a car pull up outside. 'That must be Detective Inspector Mallory.' I hurried to the window, but it wasn't Mallory at all.

It was my mother.

Chapter Twenty-three

'Oh, sorry, darling,' said Mum, cheerfully, as she strolled in. 'I forgot you had a valuation this morning.'

Timothy's face lit up. He set down his cup and saucer and got to his feet, gesturing for my mother to sit down. 'Allow me. Can I take your coat?'

His entire demeanour had changed. I thought of Delia's comment about her former cheating husband and how the two women seemed to have bonded over infidelity.

I made the introductions. 'This is Timothy Bone, Harriet's husband,' I said, giving Mum a meaningful look. 'And this is my mother, Iris Stanford.'

'Oh, I'm so sorry for your loss,' Mum said, as she handed him her coat. 'Awful business. And, of course, who would want to do such a vile thing so close to Christmas?'

Timothy's eyes narrowed. 'Do what?'

'No one knows the details about Harriet's *accident* yet, Mum,' I said quickly. 'We're just waiting for Detective Inspector Mallory now.'

Mum turned pink. Fortunately, she'd got the message. 'I hear your wife was a great reader of Krystalle Storm,' she said.

I regarded my mother with astonishment.

'I happen to love her books,' Mum enthused. 'Don't I, Kat?'

'Harriet was a writer too,' Timothy Bone added. 'Or liked to think she was.'

'A writer?' Mum echoed. 'Fancy that, Kat. Harriet was a writer. How wonderful.'

'No, it wasn't wonderful,' Timothy Bone said. 'She sent off her manuscripts to Krystalle Storm's publisher but never got a reply. I told her she was wasting her time.'

'It's hard to get published,' Mum said. 'Very difficult.'

'No, not published,' Timothy said. 'Harriet wrote . . . What's it called? Fanfiction. You know, she made up her own version of Krystalle Storm's stories.'

Mum's jaw dropped. 'Goodness. Is there such a thing?' She turned to me. 'Is that legal?'

'In some forms, yes,' I said.

'And you say that your wife sent her stories to Goldfinch Press?' Mum said faintly.

Timothy frowned. 'You've heard of Goldfinch Press? How?'

'It's on the spine of all Krystalle Storm's books,' I said quickly. 'She's very popular around here. Our former village postmistress was a huge fan.'

'I know,' said Timothy. 'Why else do you think my Harriet came to Little Dipperton?'

My mind was spinning. Harriet had written fanfiction. It explained why the passages were highlighted and possibly why Harriet had felt compelled to visit the stumpery, a place of many torrid encounters in the series so aptly recounted by Lavinia.

Mum had gone very quiet.

'But wouldn't it cause a problem for Krystalle Storm if she had read Harriet's stories?' I demanded. 'What if there was a similar idea, for example, and when it came out in print your wife felt she'd been plagiarised and decided to sue?'

Timothy seemed taken aback.

I pressed my advantage. 'I think that the publisher wouldn't have shown those stories to Krystalle Storm for that very reason. What do you think, Mum?'

Mum didn't answer.

'But they definitely reached the publisher,' Timothy insisted. 'Because they were signed for by a Monica Farley.'

'That doesn't mean Monica Farley is anyone important,' I pointed out. 'She could just be—'

'An intern,' Mum nodded, then gave an exaggerated sigh. 'I suppose we'll never know now, will we?'

Then we heard a car pulling up outside. A sharp rap on the door and Mallory entered, full of apologies. I had never been so happy to see him.

'I'm so sorry for keeping you waiting, Mr Bone.'

'These two ladies have kept me company,' said Timothy. 'Kat has very kindly offered to value Harriet's pearl and diamond necklace.'

I caught Mallory's eye.

'I'm afraid that won't be possible at the moment,' said Mallory, smoothly. 'Nor will the return of the hire car. At least for the time being.'

'What?' Timothy exploded. 'And why, pray, sir, is this?'

'Let's go somewhere private, Mr Bone,' Mallory said. 'And I'll explain everything. We'll take my car. I'm sure Kat won't mind you leaving yours outside.'

Timothy put on his coat and, with a nod of thanks, the pair left the gatehouse.

The moment I heard Mallory's car start, I breathed a sigh of relief.

'Harriet Bone wrote fanfiction,' I said. 'What do you think about that?'

My mother wore a peculiar expression that I could only describe as a mixture of guilt and panic. 'Do you really want to know what I think?'

'I'm not sure I do,' I said slowly.

'Now, promise you won't be cross,' she said. 'I think I have some of Harriet's fanfiction stories in my writing house.'

'You have *what*?' I exclaimed. 'Are you sure?'

'Not a hundred per cent, but on a scale of one to ten,' she said, 'I'm a nine. There were some envelopes forwarded to the PO box a few months ago.'

I clapped my hand over my forehead in despair. 'Jeez, Mum. Did you open anything?'

'I opened one, maybe two,' Mum admitted. 'I had no idea what they were. I just read the first few pages and thought it a load of rubbish.'

'But who on earth sent them to you?' I was incredulous.

'Not your publisher, surely.' My mind was reeling at this latest development. 'Did you keep any?'

'I put them in a drawer. I didn't want anyone going through my recycling bag,' Mum said. 'I called Goldfinch Press and complained, and they were angry. There was a new intern who had just started, Monica something . . .'

'Monica Farley, Mum,' I said wearily. 'Remember? She's the one Timothy Bone said signed for the manuscripts.'

'She should never have forwarded them to me,' Mum said. 'I think she got into a lot of trouble. And rightly so!'

I snapped my fingers. 'Then perhaps Monica was annoyed and gave out your PO box address to Harriet Bone.'

'Out of spite, you mean?' Mum's face fell. 'But why would Harriet send me such lovely gifts?'

'Ah, the gifts,' I said. 'There's something you need to know.'

When I finished telling Mum of my suspicions, she was so shocked she couldn't speak for two whole minutes. 'Are you *sure*?'

'Not a hundred per cent,' I said wryly, 'but on a scale of one to ten, I'm a nine.'

'I told you I thought I could smell garlic,' Mum said. 'But, goodness, to go to so much trouble! What if I'd died?'

'Fortunately, you didn't and neither did Delia.'

'Fancy Harriet thinking Delia was Krystalle Storm!' Mum scoffed. 'The notion!'

We both laughed but it wasn't really that funny because, unless Mallory discovered something incriminating about Harriet's husband, my mother was still the prime suspect – and even more so with this latest discovery.

I had an awful thought. 'You say you still have Harriet's manuscripts.'

'I don't know what to do with them.'

'Couldn't you have sent them back to the publisher?'

'I'd opened the envelopes,' Mum said. 'And since you said I could be sued for plagiarism, I'm glad I didn't.'

'You need to get rid of them straight away,' I said. 'When the police search your writing house—'

'What?' Mum turned ashen. 'Why?'

'They'll search everywhere, Mum,' I said. 'Harriet was murdered. When the truth comes out about who you really are, of course they will.'

'Burn them,' Mum declared. 'That's what we'll do. We'll burn them!'

'Or just tell Mallory everything,' I said quietly. 'That's the best thing to do. It really is.'

But my mother wasn't listening. 'No! I have a better idea. We're going to shred them. Delia says Marion shreds everything.'

'There is no we. You'll do that,' I said. 'I'm not getting involved. Now, is there any other reason why you popped in? I have a lot to do.'

I picked up the empty cups and took them into the galley kitchen. Mum was hot on my heels.

'There is,' Mum said. 'Delia and I spotted the luscious Ryan last night in *Gladiator*. I must say he looked good. All oiled up and buff.'

'Honestly, the pair of you should really act your age,' I scolded.

'We are acting our age. That's what ladies of our age do. We like to window-shop, but we don't want to buy the goods.' Mum grinned. 'He was killed very early on. Delia is convinced she saw Marion as a handmaiden in Lucilla's entourage. She towered above everyone else, but her name didn't come up in the credits. We Googled Ryan Cartwright and he had a few little roles in films that no one has heard of. Isn't it sad? From Hollywood to Little Dipperton.'

A Land Rover flashed past the window and stopped. A door slammed, and moments later, Lavinia was standing in the showroom in her tattered Barbour coat, wellies and a woolly hat. She seemed agitated. 'Looking for Edith,' she said, and peered around the room. 'Is she here?'

'No,' I said.

'Not even in the kitchen?' Lavinia asked.

'Not even in a cupboard,' Mum shot back.

'Is everything okay?' I asked.

'She's gone,' Lavinia said.

Lavinia pronounced 'gone' as *gawn*. The UK might have moved on with its love of regional accents, but Lavinia clung to her cut-glass Queen's English for grim death, along with her short sentences, which were often hard to follow.

'Not down for breakfast,' Lavinia continued. 'Not at the stables. Alfred not seen her.'

'And her Land Rover?' I asked.

'Still at stables. Horses all there.'

'Perhaps she just wanted to go for a walk,' Mum said. 'Where's Mr Chips?'

'Dog's gone.'

'There you are, then,' said Mum. 'She's just taken him for a walk.'

Lavinia looked hopeful. 'Do you think so?' But then her face fell. 'The thing is, Edith's not been well. Dizzy spells and whatnot.'

I thought of Edith's recent confusion in the stableyard and at the staff party on Sunday evening. 'Does she have them when she's riding?'

'Or driving?' Mum put in.

Lavinia hesitated, then nodded.

'Eric's searching grotto.' Lavinia retrieved the two-way radio from inside her coat. 'Jolly good things, these are.' She raised a finger presumably for us to wait. There was a click. 'Eric, Lav here. Over.'

There was a crackle, and then we heard Eric say, 'Have you found her ladyship, milady?'

'No. Over. Where are you?'

'Grotto. Over.'

'Keep looking. Over and out.'

'Do you want me to help you find her?' I said.

Lavinia nodded again.

Leaving Mum behind as the point person, I went to get my coat.

Five minutes later I was sitting in the front of Lavinia's Land Rover, which was filled with the usual equestrian detritus – a discarded snaffle bit, dandy brushes, a lot of mud, a few leading reins and a woven halter. What had started out as a sunny if cold day now sported a low grey sky that promised more snow.

Lavinia set off, turning out of the gates and up Cavalier Lane to circle the far side of the vast estate. I was having doubts that Edith would have walked so far and voiced them.

'But I'm sure we'll find her,' I added, more to reassure Lavinia than myself.

The Land Rover skidded slightly and clipped part of a stone wall. Riding shotgun was rather like being on Mr Toad's wild ride.

'I think this gala is a mistake,' Lavinia burst out.

'Oh, so do I!' I agreed. 'With everything going on, we should cancel it.'

'But we can't,' Lavinia wailed. 'Too late. Vendors not paid. Edith furious. Furious about Frith.'

'Frith?'

'Painting Rupert sold,' Lavinia said miserably. 'Got twenty thousand. Had to pay Cartwrights somehow. Should have stuck with Pansy's Jamborees.'

I remembered Lavinia's dotty friend Pansy from Pansy's Jamborees. In fact, I'd been surprised that the gala had not been put into Pansy's capable hands but perhaps it was because she didn't have access to all the big names.

'I suppose the Cartwrights are better connected than Pansy,' I ventured.

'That's what Piers said when I asked him how we could raise enough money to repair the guttering,' Lavinia said. 'Hire the Cartwrights! They know everyone, all the big families in Europe and loads of celebrities. All his chums have used them. And then one thing led to another. Rupert and Ryan got on like a house on fire, and Rupert persuaded

Ryan to stay on for a few months as a consultant. You know, get the estate back on track. Make some decent moolah.'

'And, of course, Marion's mother lives close by,' I said, thinking that the Cartwrights' arrival now made sense.

'She sees her nearly every day,' said Lavinia. 'Marion told me she's so grateful for being here during her mother's last months.'

Lavinia stopped the Land Rover next to a five-bar gate that bordered a dense forest.

'The Black Forest,' I mused.

'Yes. The Black Forest,' Lavinia whispered. 'Darling Harry. I so miss his Biggles days.' She gulped and I could have sworn she wiped away a tear. 'Got something in my eye.'

When I'd first moved to Devon, it was one of the first places on the estate that seven-year-old Harry had taken me as his alter-ego Squadron Leader James Bigglesworth, the legendary, if fictional, First and Second World War fighter pilot. We'd played a game of make-believe in which I was his co-pilot: we flew a dangerous mission over enemy territory and, in this case, the Black Forest. It seemed a lifetime ago. Harry had packed away his Bigglesworth uniform of goggles and white scarf, his books and memorabilia, and was now an active Sea Scout under the command of Simon Payne.

Lavinia pointed her two-way radio in the direction of a grassy bridleway. 'Do you know where you're going?'

'I think so,' I said. 'The path comes out at the edge of the grounds.' I thought for a moment. 'Would Edith have walked so far?'

'Eric coming from east,' said Lavinia. 'You from north. Rupert south, blah blah blah.'

I jumped out and watched Lavinia's Land Rover execute another awful three-point turn and drive away, noting a lot of foliage in her rear bumper.

I was completely alone.

I stepped into the semi-darkness of the woods and started trudging along a snowy path dotted with animal footprints. The quiet of the forest felt creepy. I moved as quickly as I could.

Fifteen minutes later the trees petered out and ended at a magnificent yew hedge that ran along the boundary of the estate's formal gardens. In another time, it would have been perfectly clipped and manicured. Now it was unruly but still beautiful. I skirted the hedge until I came to an archway and stepped into the topiary garden. Shapes that, in another time, would have been perfect pyramids flanked grassy walks for ladies in long dresses to perambulate with their parasols. They still looked magical covered with snow.

The ground rose gently to the ha-ha, then fell steeply away into a deep grass-filled ditch. Originally used to keep cattle and sheep out of the formal gardens, a ha-ha could vary in depth from two feet to nine. I looked along the ditch, which stretched the length of the snow-covered lawns and stopped at another area of dense woodland.

I could see a splodge of colour and heard a dog barking.

Thank God! It was Edith and Mr Chips.

I called, expecting Edith to return my greeting but she didn't. In fact, Edith didn't move.

I called again and Mr Chips tore over, tail wagging and wanting attention, but I was gripped by the most terrible fear that Edith was dead.

I half ran, half stumbled across the snowy lawn, shouting, 'Edith! Edith!'

At first, I thought she had collapsed until I realised she was sitting on the edge of the ha-ha, her feet dangling over the side. She looked up, but her eyes didn't seem to recognise me.

'Oh, Edith,' I said breathlessly, as I joined her. 'Everyone is so worried about you. What are you doing out here? It's . . . Oh, no,' I whispered.

There, half submerged in the snow, was a body in a fake-fur coat.

It was Pam Price.

Chapter Twenty-four

'And with another snowfall,' Delia chattered on cheerfully, 'Pam wouldn't have been found until the thaw. No one goes near the ha-ha.'

Mum and I were sitting in the kitchen at the Hall, waiting for Mallory to come.

I was on my third cup of coffee laced with brandy.

An hour had passed since I'd found Edith, who refused to speak to anyone. She had gone straight to her room with instructions not to be disturbed.

'What I can't wrap my head around is what Pam was doing lurking in the grounds in the first place,' Delia mused. 'Doesn't she live miles away?'

I let Mum and Delia chatter on with their theories. Pam Price was drunk. Pam Price was having a tryst with Eric. Pam Price had come to steal the family silver. But none of us could understand how she had come to be dead in the ha-ha.

'I just feel sorry for Lance,' Mum said. 'Poor boy. Or

perhaps he's relieved. Perhaps he can do what he really wants now. What do you think, Kat? You've hardly spoken a word.'

'She's in shock, I expect,' said Delia. 'Although, judging by the number of bodies your daughter manages to find, this should be old hat for her.'

'I am sitting here, you know,' I said. 'And speaking of old hat . . .' I gave Mum a knowing look and a surreptitious nod at Delia's green gloves and scarf. Of course we couldn't tell Delia our suspicions but we both knew we'd have to get them back.

'I think we've had enough of the gossiping,' Marion said, as she breezed into the kitchen. She looked paler than ever. Dark circles bloomed under her blue eyes. 'Mallory wants to set up a mobile incident room in the courtyard. It's all so dreadful. Honestly, I've lived in some of the most dangerous cities in the world, but nothing compared to this place.'

'Did Mallory offer any theories about what Pam was doing in the ha-ha?' Mum asked. 'Her car must be some-where. Have they found her mobile phone? According to Kat, Lance said his mother got a phone call late last night, went out and didn't come back.'

'I really don't know, Iris.' Marion's tone was sharp.

'You'll have to cancel the gala now,' Mum said.

From your mouth to God's ears, I said to myself.

'Ryan's already talked to his lordship and he insists it go on,' said Marion.

'His lordship does?' Mum sounded surprised. 'We've had two deaths—'

'And everyone knows that accidents – or, in this case, bodies – come in threes,' Delia interrupted.

'That's just superstitious nonsense,' Marion said. 'Too much money has been spent already. Refunding the tickets at this late stage would be complicated, to say nothing of losing deposits on the catering and live band.'

'Really?' I was surprised that Rupert had been so adamant and said so.

'If you want to try to persuade them both,' said Marion, 'be my guest.'

'We all know how determined men can be.' Delia shot my mother a knowing look. 'My husband was a bit of a bully, too.'

I half expected Marion to deny the accusation, but she just said, 'We were hired to make this gala a success. Ryan's determined, that's all. Yes, determined.'

'Was your husband a bully, Iris?' Delia persisted.

'No,' Mum said. 'But he was determined all right. Especially when he was on a case.'

Marion spun round. 'A case? What kind of case? Was he an investigator?'

'Yes,' Mum said. 'And very good at it too.'

'Where is your husband now?' Marion said.

'He's dead,' said Mum, bluntly.

'Oh, I'm sorry, I didn't know.' Marion's hands fluttered to her throat. She seemed very rattled this morning and had none of her usual poise. 'There's a lot going on at the moment.'

'And you're also having to deal with your own mother,' Mum reminded her gently. 'How is she?'

Marion gave a sad smile. 'Hanging in there. Just hanging in. There's not much anyone can do really.'

'You're a good daughter,' Mum said. 'I suppose you see her every day?'

'I try to and that includes today,' said Marion, suddenly all business. 'Excuse me. This has been a very upsetting morning.'

My phone rang. I glanced down at the unfamiliar number. It was Margery, who had just picked up my message to call her.

Unfortunately, she wasn't much help. Margery had no idea who had posted the advertisement for the peppermint-green Ford Fiesta and she didn't have any resident going by the name of Arthur Matthews either. She would, however, check the visitors' book.

'Was that Margery from Sunny Hill Lodge?' Mum asked. 'Any luck with that green car?'

'What car?' Delia demanded.

'No, everything's fine,' I said quickly. Even though Marion knew about the emerald switch, Delia didn't.

Mum must have sensed my reticence because she said, 'Can I use your shredder, Marion? Delia told me you had one.'

Marion seemed surprised. 'Why, yes. Help yourself. It's in the back porch.'

'Just a few documents that I don't want to leave lying about,' Mum added, although she didn't have to explain.

'The front door is unlocked. But please remove your shoes,' Marion said. 'There are guest slippers on the rack.'

Mum stood up. 'Well, I don't know about anyone else, but we could be waiting for Mallory for hours. I'm off. You know where you can find me.' She turned to me. 'Are you coming, Katherine?'

I followed Mum into the freezing cold corridor, with its flagstone floor, that connected the servants' wing to the outside courtyard. This part of the Hall felt as if it were in a time warp, with the range of larders, still bearing their original plaques, lining the corridor.

Outside, it was just as Marion had said. The mobile police unit had arrived. Mallory was talking on the phone but ended the call and waved us over.

Mum gave me a nudge. 'He's such a handsome man. Where's our Shawn? I would have thought he'd have been round here in a flash to see if you were all right. Still, as we said earlier, finding dead bodies is the norm for you, these days.'

'He's busy, Mum,' I said, more sharply than I intended to. 'And, besides, I didn't find the body. I found Edith. It was Edith who found the body.'

'Are you feeling okay, Kat?' Mallory searched my eyes. 'Two bodies in less than twenty-four hours . . .'

'Kat's used to it,' Mum said, but added hastily, 'not that she isn't upset, of course.'

'I spoke to Margery Rook about the Ford Fiesta,' I said. 'She told me she couldn't recall a visitor or a resident called Arthur Matthews.'

'Ah. Yes. I was going to talk to you about him,' said Mallory. 'The car was sold last week to a young woman called Yasmin Fletcher.'

'O-kay,' I said slowly.

'Ms Fletcher is going to pick it up after Christmas,' said Mallory. 'And this is where it gets interesting. Arthur Matthews died years ago. The car has been sitting in a garage on a housing estate ever since. And since Arthur Matthews is dead, who sold Ms Fletcher the car?'

'The same man who has been driving it to the Emporium,' I realised. 'The mysterious Oliver.'

'Ms Fletcher said she didn't meet the seller. Everything was done on email. No phone number. One set of keys were sent by registered post to her home address – which is in Harrogate by the way – along with the documents and instructions of where to collect the vehicle on the day after Boxing Day. Ms Fletcher paid the money into a PayPal account. We're tracking down the identity of the account owner right now.'

'But how did this Yasmin Fletcher find out about the car if she lives in Harrogate?' I was bewildered. 'Was it through Sunny Hill Lodge?'

'No,' said Mallory. 'The car was also advertised online. Someone is going to a lot of trouble to cover their tracks. I'm realistically optimistic that it's connected to the theft of your emerald.'

'And I'm realistic that we won't see the emerald again,' I said gloomily.

'Did you talk to your friend in art fraud?'

I filled Mallory in on my discussion with David. 'But he doesn't have much hope either.'

'Speaking of cars,' said Mallory, 'an hour ago, we found Pam's silver Polo in the Morrisons car park in Totnes.'

'Morrisons? How weird,' I said.

'So it's likely that whoever killed her must have had an accomplice,' Mum declared.

Mallory raised an eyebrow. 'I'm interested in your theories.'

'I think Pam was lured to the grounds of the estate. There's a green lane that runs along the boundary line. Pam's body was dumped in the ha-ha and then her car was driven to Morrisons where it was abandoned. The killer was then scooped up by his or her accomplice.'

Mallory went very quiet. 'Would you step into the mobile unit for a moment?'

'I'm afraid I've got important things to do this morning,' said Mum. 'Can't it—?'

'No, it can't. I'd like to speak to both of you.' Mallory used a tone I had never heard before. 'Right now.'

Chapter Twenty-five

With three people inside, the mobile unit felt claustrophobic. There was a space heater keeping the place warm, but it was stuffy. Condensation dripped down the windows. A narrow counter housed a handful of mismatched mugs, a kettle, some instant coffee, tea, and an open bottle of milk.

Mallory didn't offer either of us refreshments. There was no gentle smile. He gestured for us to take a seat on the hard bench next to the drop-down table. My mother spread herself out. I had one cheek on the edge. Mallory must have noticed my discomfort, but he didn't say anything.

Mum seemed calm. I, however, felt nauseous. Was this about Harriet Bone or Pam Price or both?

Mallory took out his notebook. 'Kat, why don't you tell me how you knew both women?'

I told him, he listened and made notes, then bombarded me with questions, which were easy for me to answer because I had nothing to hide.

I could feel my mother's leg jiggling against mine. She was getting nervous. He then asked Mum the same questions and, by some miracle, the subject of Krystalle Storm didn't come up.

'Both women bore a puncture wound behind the ear,' Mallory said. 'Both women fell and broke their necks.'

'But Pam fell into the ha-ha,' I said. 'Wouldn't the snow have cushioned her fall?'

'Pam Price was killed elsewhere,' said Mallory. 'But as yet we don't know where.'

'And we're only too happy to do some brainstorming if you need our help,' Mum suggested. 'Aren't we, Kat?'

'Oh, I think you can definitely do that, Mrs Stanford,' said Mallory. 'You see, we've found a connection between Harriet Bone and Pam Price.'

'How?' I thought back to the staff party. 'As far as I know, the two women had never even met.'

'Perhaps they were Facebook friends?' Mum suggested.

Mallory ignored her. 'What Harriet Bone and Pam Price have in common is Honeychurch Hall.'

Mum and I exchanged puzzled looks.

'And you.'

'Me?' Mum's jaw dropped. 'But I never even met Pam Price and I only—'

'No, not you, Mrs Stanford,' said Mallory, quietly. 'Katherine.'

I was stunned. 'I don't understand.'

'Pam Price knew the emerald was fake,' said Mallory. 'You told me she threatened to blackmail you.'

I looked at Mallory in astonishment. 'You can't be serious. She just asked me to get her son a job.'

'Ah, yes, a job,' said Mallory. 'Or that's what you told me.'

'But it's the truth!' I exclaimed.

'And believe me,' Mum said, 'Katherine is an appalling liar.'

'Your reputation is very important to you,' Mallory ran on. 'There is a lot at stake to ensure this gala is a success. Not just financially, but for you too.'

'Yes, but I told you I refused to auction off a fake,' I retorted.

Mallory turned to my mother. 'Mrs Stanford, you are the family historian.'

'That is correct.'

'You're very familiar with not just the family tree but you have intimate knowledge of the grounds.'

'That is correct,' Mum said again.

'You shared your theory of how Pam Price ended up in the ha-ha.'

'I was just being logical,' Mum told him.

It slowly dawned on me that, to an outsider, Mum and I could look guilty.

Mallory studied us both. 'You share a very close bond, don't you?'

'Of course we do,' Mum answered. 'We're mother and daughter.'

'And you look out for each other—'

'Where's the crime in that?' Mum's voice was rising. 'Kat promised my late husband that she would always be there for me. That's why she moved from London. It sounds like you're accusing us of murdering two women we barely knew!' Mum was indignant.

'Everyone is a suspect until they're ruled out,' said Mallory.

'You sound just like a policeman,' Mum said, with disgust.

'That's because I am a policeman,' he said coldly. 'Everyone is capable of murder. Perhaps it wasn't intentional. Perhaps things got out of hand, and someone panicked and tried to cover it up, and they called for help. It happens. But that doesn't take away the fact that it's still a crime and someone has to pay for it.'

I couldn't speak. My hands were clenched so tightly under the table that my nails left marks in my skin.

'What aren't you telling me?' he said quietly. 'I've been a police officer for a very long time, and I can tell when someone is holding something back.'

I nudged Mum's leg in a desperate hint for her to speak up. She moved it away.

No one spoke. The silence between us grew.

'Is that it?' Mum said. 'Can we go?'

Mallory's eyes were hard. 'Yes. But, as the old saying goes, don't leave the country.'

As we walked back to Mum's Mini, she gave a huge sigh of relief. I was desperately upset. I liked Mallory and didn't want him to think badly of me.

'Well, that was a little too close for comfort,' said Mum. 'But I think we put on a united front. Let's go and shred those manuscripts.'

I regarded my mother with dismay. 'You just don't seem to understand how serious this is. You should have told him who you are! Why can't you tell him?'

'For obvious reasons, Katherine,' Mum said. 'And it's my business, not yours. Why do you worry so much? It's me who'll be going to prison. Mallory knows we had nothing to do with Harriet's or Pam's death. He's just playing detective. He knows we're innocent. He's all puff.'

'Yes, we are innocent,' I said. 'But don't you see? Since it's not you and it's not me, who is the killer?'

Chapter Twenty-six

Fifteen minutes later Mum pushed open the front door to the Cartwrights' cottage with a plastic carrier bag full of brown envelopes. I recognised them the moment she showed me. It had been some months ago when they'd begun to trickle into my PO box.

I hadn't been inside this cottage since Peggy Cropper had moved out.

We took off our outdoor shoes and left them on the mat. In a small cubbyhole there were pairs of the white cloth mules that were offered in spas or upmarket hotel rooms. Mum slid her feet into a pair, but I followed her in my socks.

The Cartwrights had redecorated, and it was immaculate. The wooden beams had been painted white, the furniture was pale grey and cream, and a new carpet in a nondescript beige had been laid. I noticed that the cushions on the two-seater sofa had been placed on their sides, just as Marion had ordered, and were perfectly spaced apart.

The Christmas tree in the corner was an expensive fake, decorated with translucent glass ornaments. Only the hideous cottage-cheese-type ceiling had escaped Marion's paintbrush but that was white anyway. There wasn't a splash of colour anywhere. A framed photograph on a pale grey side table was in tones of dark grey and white.

The Cartwrights had certainly gone to a lot of trouble if they weren't planning on staying.

On the dining table Marion's art supplies were laid out in a neat row – a calligraphy set, a compass divider, rulers and erasers – with paper of varying sizes. I noticed an empty wastepaper basket under the table.

Delia had said how tidy everything was and she was right.

We walked into the kitchen, which, again, was immaculate and painted white. There were only two items to mar the kitchen counter and those were a Smeg kettle in white and a matching toaster.

A glass-paned kitchen door opened into the back porch where a new washing-machine and tumble-dryer were stacked beside the shredder. A key rack hung above a light switch. I only noticed it because a bright green key fob jumped out with the numbers 175 and 174. The two keys were small. They looked like the kind I had for my storage unit in Exeter and for which I was paying a fortune. I kept meaning to downsize but just never got around to it. I'd guessed that the Cartwrights had a place to store their personal possessions. They certainly weren't in the cottage.

Mum handed me several large envelopes. 'You open those and I'll shred them.'

'I don't want to do your dirty work,' I said, but did it all the same.

Mum flipped the switch on the shredder and started feeding the papers through the slit. 'If you want to know what to buy me for Christmas, I'd like one of these.'

'Bad luck,' I said. 'I've already bought your present.'

The shredder buzzed happily away.

'You do know that the original manuscripts still exist, don't you?' I reminded her. 'They'll be on her computer.'

'As long as they aren't anywhere near me, I don't care.'

A whirr and a click signalled that another of Harriet's masterpieces had been destroyed. I felt oddly guilty.

Neither of us spoke over the sound of the machine until Mum had finished.

'I was thinking,' Mum said. 'Why would anyone want those women dead? I mean, yes, Krystalle Storm has a lot to lose but since Krystalle Storm didn't do it, who did?'

'We've gone through this already,' I said, with a sigh.

'Why steal a necklace that wasn't even made of real pearls or real diamonds?' Mum mused. 'And then we have the real emerald being switched for a fake.'

'What did you just—'

'Did the shredder work okay?' Marion appeared in the doorway.

'You've made the cottage so lovely,' Mum said quickly.

I caught Mum's eye and saw the alarm that I was sure was reflected in my own. Had Marion heard us mention Krystalle Storm?

I hastily pointed to the key rack. 'Are those keys for a storage unit?'

Marion looked startled. 'Yes, why?'

'I have a unit in Exeter and need something much closer,' I said. 'Where's yours?'

Marion gave her flight-attendant smile. 'Not too far from here.'

'Is it thermostat controlled?' I blabbered on. 'I have some paintings. I can't use the outdoor container things. They can get damp.'

Marion frowned. 'Outdoor containers?'

'You know,' Mum added helpfully. 'The ones they use on container ships. Kat's right. It must be thermostat-controlled. Clothing can smell so musty.'

'We just have boxes. There's no storage in this cottage and the cellar is a little damp.' She thought for a moment. 'Oh, and the cases of Veuve Clicquot champagne, our emergency glasses, and a few things for the raffle.'

'Well, we'd better not take up more of your time,' said Mum. 'Thank you for allowing me to use your shredder.'

Marion stepped aside for us to pass. As we walked through the sitting room, Mum paused at the side table and pointed to the framed black-and-white photograph of Marion and Ryan standing arm in arm. In the background was a cruise ship.

'I've never been on a cruise. What a beautiful couple you make,' said Mum. 'You've led such a colourful life, dear. It makes all of us so boring.'

I looked, too, but then I stopped in my tracks. The name of the ship was the *Octavia Royale*. I distinctly remembered

Harriet asking Marion if she had been on it and Marion had said no.

'Now, if you don't mind, I need to get on,' said Marion. 'I'm hoping to see Mum today and it's already getting late.'

'I hope Kat is as good a daughter to me as you are to your mother,' said Mum.

'It depends if you behave yourself,' I teased.

We set off down the drive. As usual, Mum grumbled about the circuitous route we always had to take to get from one side of the estate to the other. As we turned back into the main gates once more, Mum groaned.

'Oh!' she cried. 'And I thought we'd seen the last of him.'

Shawn's car was parked behind my own. I felt a flutter of butterflies coupled with a feeling of dread. Mum let me out. 'Why do you have to be so unkind about Shawn?' I demanded.

'Because he's too weak for you!' Mum said lightly. 'Always dithering about. I'd rather you'd stayed with Dylan.'

'His name was David!' I retorted.

'At least David had a bit of oomph about him.'

I didn't answer. I got out and slammed the door.

Mum drove off with three chirpy toots on the horn.

'I was just about to give up,' said Shawn. 'This is a professional visit unless,' he pointed vaguely in the direction of Mum's red Mini, 'you've talked to your mother.'

I unlocked the door and dashed to disconnect the alarm. I was nervous and hit the wrong code twice.

'It's your date of birth,' said Shawn, who was standing right behind me. He gently pushed me aside and tapped in the code.

We both moved at the same time and got stuck in the door. Stepping back, he gestured for me to go ahead. 'I'm sorry,' he said.

'No, I'm sorry,' I whispered.

We stood apart in silence, and then he opened his arms and I just tumbled into them. Shawn held me close. Tears stung my eyes.

'Please don't let my mother come between us,' I said.

'You know how I feel about you,' he said. 'And you know my conditions.'

Conditions? There were conditions? I pushed him away. 'Presumably sending my mother to prison is one of the conditions.'

'And who is to blame for that?' Shawn responded. 'I can't keep protecting your mother.'

'She can look after herself,' I snapped.

Shawn took off his outdoor coat and boots. I noticed his socks had a steam-train pattern on them. He headed for the kitchen. I trailed after him.

Shawn switched the kettle on. We didn't speak again until we were seated on the sofa in the living room.

'You said this was a professional visit,' I said tightly.

'I had a long chat with Timothy Bone this morning,' Shawn began.

'You did?' I was surprised. 'What about the case you're working on?'

He scowled. 'Hit a dead end.' His eyes met mine. 'I know I've been distracted and I apologise. It's a new role and I must make a good impression.'

I felt a burst of affection and relief. 'It's just a setback, surely,' I said. 'And I understand. I really do.'

'I offered Mallory my assistance,' said Shawn. 'And now, with the second murder, he needs all the help he can get.'

'I'm so glad you're here,' I said.

Shawn's jaw hardened. 'You won't be when I tell you why.'

Chapter Twenty-seven

'It seems that Harriet stalked another romance author a few years ago,' said Shawn. 'Timothy Bone told me she sent fanfiction manuscripts to Salome Steel along with gifts that were laced with—'

'Arsenic. Oh dear.'

'Timothy Bone worked for the post office,' Shawn went on. 'He was able to use his contacts to locate Salome Steel's PO box just like he tracked down your mother's.'

'It's actually my PO box,' I pointed out.

'Don't split hairs! Mr Bone wasn't going to admit it because it put his pension in jeopardy, but when he was informed that his wife had been murdered, he was only too happy to talk to us.'

I felt sick. 'What else did he say?'

'Harriet unmasked Salome Steel and it turned out that she was a he, and a very proper, decorated, retired military gentleman at that,' Shawn went on. '*Paparazzi Razzle* offered a reward to anyone who could uncover – and prove – his true identity.'

I told Shawn that Harriet had boasted about having connections with *Paparazzi Razzle* and that she had won a cruise on a ship called the *Octavia Royale*.

'And you didn't think to tell me?'

'Because you kept reminding me that it was Mallory's investigation!' I pointed out.

'Look up Salome Steel and you'll see what damage that woman did to his life,' said Shawn. 'And what damage she could have done to your mother's.'

I didn't know what to say but then the most awful suspicion started to creep into my mind. What if Mum had done it, after all? She didn't have an alibi. She was an excellent liar and an expert at embellishing the truth. For the first time since Harriet's death, I felt a tiny bit of doubt.

'Kat?' Shawn prompted. 'You have to tell Mallory.'

I looked at Shawn with a heavy heart. 'I'm sorry. I just can't. Mum made me promise.'

Shawn flushed. He opened his mouth to say something, then thought better of it. Grabbing his coat, he pulled it on and stomped to the front door, shoving his feet viciously into his outdoor boots. Without a word, he left and slammed the door hard behind him. I heard his car start up and roar away.

And then the tears just came.

My mobile rang. I rummaged through my tote bag, searching for it and desperately hoping it was Shawn, but it was Margery Rook again. 'Have I caught you at a bad time?' she asked. 'You sound breathless.'

'I had to run to the phone,' I lied, suppressing a sob.

'I found the name of the person who was responsible for posting the advertisement about that car on the notice board.'

'Thank you,' I said, thinking I couldn't really care less.

'Marni M. No surname, I'm afraid,' said Margery. 'She visited one of our residents called Rose Matthews just the once. Rose passed away, let me see, about two months ago. I'm afraid Belle must have forgotten to take the card down.'

Mallory had said that Arthur Matthews had died years before but I had an idea. 'What about someone called Oliver? Did he ever visit Rose?'

'No,' said Margery. 'The only person who ever visited Rose was Marni M and, as I mentioned, it was just once.'

'Thank you anyway,' I said.

'My husband and I are really looking forward to the gala on Friday. We're hosting a table. The tickets are a little pricey but it's for such a good cause. And, of course, we're intrigued by the mystery guest. Would you happen to know who it is?'

'I don't,' I said. 'Sorry.'

We exchanged a few more pleasantries before I hung up, then called Di. Perhaps the name Rose Matthews was familiar to her.

She answered immediately. I could hear Christmas music in the background and the hum of voices.

Suddenly I remembered that she and Pam had been friends. I would have to tell her what had happened. Unfortunately, it came out more bluntly than I'd intended.

Di gave a cry of shock. 'Dead? How? A car accident? When?'

I hesitated. Now was not the time to tell Di that Edith had found Pam's body in the ha-ha in the grounds of the estate. 'No one knows at the moment,' I said carefully. 'I'm so sorry.'

'Poor Lance. Oh dear. Is someone with him? Wait, hold on. I can't hear properly. Too noisy.'

I waited for a few moments until Di came back on the line.

'Is that why the police were here this morning closeted with Fiona in her office?' she said. 'And why the toilets haven't been touched today? What's going on? What aren't you telling me?'

'Steady on, slow down,' I said. 'I told you, I don't know.'

'So why are you calling me?'

'Are you familiar with a resident called Rose at Sunny Hill Lodge?' I asked.

'There are at least forty residents, Kat.' Di sounded annoyed. 'Maybe. Why?'

'She had a visitor called Marni?'

'The name doesn't ring a bell. Why?'

'It was this Marni who posted the ad for the Ford Fiesta.'

'Do you want me to check the visitors' book?'

'No. It's okay,' I said, and explained that Margery already had. I'd hit a dead end.

'Do you want me to bring Emerald Barbie to the gatehouse tonight?' she said.

'I thought you didn't have a car,' I said. 'And, besides, it's out of your way.'

'I'm happy to, honestly,' said Di, and I knew she meant it. 'I'll see you later.'

I went to my desk, pulled out my laptop and started it up. I had to know who this Salome Steel person was.

She – or should I say he? – had no social media presence and, just like Krystalle Storm, no website. But the shocking affair had certainly got enough media coverage. *Paparazzi Razzle* had offered a prize for whoever could uncover the identity of the author of *Voodoo Vixens* (Heat Level 5).

Salome Steel had turned out to be Admiral Charles Gunn (Retired), who had enjoyed an impeccable forty-year career and had received the St John's Bravery Award from the Queen.

Thanks to Harriet's sleuthing, the admiral's flawless reputation lay in tatters and the internet was full of memes of him in corsets and holding whips. Even his English bulldog Horatio hadn't escaped public ridicule.

No wonder Shawn had reacted as he had.

Harriet was on the front page of *Paparazzi Razzle* accepting a giant cheque from the editor for ten thousand pounds, with two tickets for a Mediterranean cruise on the *Octavia Royale*.

My heart skipped a beat. There it was. Confirmation that it was the same ship I'd seen in the photograph in the Cartwrights' cottage. Being on the same ship didn't necessarily mean they were travelling at the same time, but I didn't believe in coincidences.

I Googled the *Octavia Royale*. She was an old liner that mostly cruised the Mediterranean.

And then an article jumped out involving a crew member's accidental fall from the ship. I remembered Timothy Bone telling me that someone had gone overboard and that their holiday was cancelled mid-cruise. The verdict was death by misadventure and, since the body was never found and the man – who turned out to have been the head of security – had health issues, it was assumed to have been a heart attack.

It was no good. I had to talk to Mallory. As I started to dial, a call came in.

It was Lavinia and she sounded distraught.

'Edith's missing again,' she said. 'Dark in half an hour. Need your help. Meet in stableyard?'

I told her I was on my way.

In the end I didn't get very far. As I headed up the drive, I spied Edith's Land Rover parked outside the wrought-iron entrance to her beloved equine cemetery.

Chapter Twenty-eight

The equine cemetery was set on a gentle slope and enclosed on three sides by a thick, ancient yew hedge. The fourth side overlooked the River Dart. It was beautiful.

In the fading light, I followed Edith's footprints in the snow, weaving through the headstones that marked the graves of much-loved horses, like April Showers, Sky Bird, Nuthatch, Braveheart and Mr Manners, the horse that Edith had mistakenly believed she was to ride only yesterday.

It was going to be another freezing night. Lavinia was right to be worried. Edith wasn't well.

I found her sitting on the wooden bench that had been built in memory of her brother following his tragic death, which had become immortalised in *Gypsy Temptress*, the first in my mother's Star-Crossed Lovers series. It told my mother's own story when she'd lived on the road and had come to Honeychurch Hall in her childhood. It was there that she had witnessed the torrid affair between a young unmarried Edith and the gamekeeper.

I thought of the fallout that Mum's exposure would have on this family. It wasn't just *Gypsy Temptress* that was based on the Honeychurch dynasty. Her official appointment as the Honeychurch historian had given her access to many Honeychurch scandals over the centuries, from one ancestor running a Turkish harem in London to another who'd lived in the desert with a sheikh. My mother often said she'd never be able to write all their stories before she died. Naturally, Mum's gift as a storyteller meant that much had been embellished but who would stop to question what was fact or fiction? Seeing Edith's small figure sitting there made me realise that perhaps it was Edith Mum wanted to protect and now I knew I wanted to protect her too.

Thank God I hadn't called Mallory. I had made my decision. There would be no conditions. If Shawn truly loved me, he would have to wait.

I called to Edith, but she didn't look around. When I joined her on the bench, she passed me her silver hip flask. 'Cherry brandy,' she said. 'Used to drink this stuff all day out hunting.'

I took a deep draught. After everything that had happened that day, the fiery warmth certainly hit the spot.

'Of course, there wouldn't be hunting today,' Edith went on. 'The ground is too hard.'

'When was the last time you went out?' I asked.

'Five years ago,' said Edith. 'Rupert put his foot down. Told me it was too dangerous.'

Since Edith rode side-saddle, he had made a good point.

'Rupert says no to everything,' Edith moaned. 'I'm

trapped. A prisoner. Not just in this old body but in everything I do. Riding and driving are all I have left.'

I felt for her. 'It must be very difficult.'

Edith turned on me. She was angry. 'How would you know?' She tapped her forehead. 'It's all still working up here. It's the body that's slow!'

'Lavinia's worried about you,' I said. 'She mentioned you'd been having dizzy spells.'

'It's nothing,' Edith said dismissively. 'I get up too quickly, that's all.'

'Is that why you were parked at Bridge Cottage on Sunday afternoon?'

Edith looked blank.

'The . . . er . . . altercation with Harriet Bone,' I reminded her.

'I pulled over to take a nap,' said Edith. 'Good heavens! Can't I have a nap? Everyone thinks I'm going senile but of course I'm not. Let them think it. I hear everything that's going on with those frightful Cartwrights. The morning room is next to the gladiator's office.'

I smiled at Edith's nickname for Ryan. 'I don't think he likes the English weather,' I said. 'Maybe things will change once Marion's mother dies.'

Edith seemed surprised. 'Marion's mother died the week after they arrived, pet.'

I knew for a fact that Marion's mother was still very much alive. 'I must have misunderstood.'

'I hear everything,' Edith said again, 'and I can tell you that there was no love lost between mother and daughter. She was just bundled into a nursing home and forgotten.'

'I thought she was living at home and had carers,' I said.

'Rupert wants to put me into Sunny Hill Lodge too,' Edith continued. 'Over my dead body.'

'Wait,' I said. 'Marion's mother was at Sunny Hill Lodge? Are you sure?'

'Of course I am,' Edith asserted. 'My son has been encouraging me to spend a week or so there in respite. According to the dictionary, respite is a rest from something *unpleasant*. Unpleasant!'

'I'm sure he doesn't mean it in that way,' I said.

'He thinks it will break me in, get me used to the idea.' Edith's voice trembled. 'The only way I'm going to leave Honeychurch Hall is feet first.' She shook her head and muttered, 'I'd rather die than go into a nursing home.'

I could see that Edith was getting upset and I couldn't say I blamed her. When Mum and I first moved to Honeychurch Hall, Rupert had been scheming to get Edith into Sunny Hill Lodge and he had failed.

'I caught Marion coming out of Lavinia's bedroom last week,' Edith said suddenly. 'She claimed to be dusting but Mrs Evans is the housekeeper. I don't trust her. I don't trust the Cartwrights either. Why couldn't they have stuck with Pansy? We all know that Lavinia's brother is an irresponsible buffoon. And then Lavinia goes ahead and hires Mrs Price's son to film it all. The apple doesn't fall far from the tree. Mark my words.'

'Lance is very talented,' I protested but I also wondered

how Edith could be so insensitive. Had she already forgotten that only a few hours earlier she'd found Pam's body?

'It sounds like Pam hadn't had an easy life,' I said tactfully.

Edith gave a snort of disgust. 'Naturally when Piers inherited the title from his father, he wanted to make changes to the running of the estate. Yes, the Carew shoot was discontinued, but Mrs Price was given the option to stay on. *Naturally* they had to move out of their cottage but there was nothing wrong with the studio flat over one of the garages. I didn't understand all the fuss.'

A studio flat for three people?

'Mr Price was already a known drunk,' Edith said. 'It came as no surprise that he drove into a tree. But that was hardly Piers's fault.' She passed me the hip flask again. 'Many years ago, I went to wait for Aubrey in the drawing room at Carew Court and when I opened the door, I saw Mrs Price slip a silver snuff box into her pocket. Of course I demanded she empty them.'

'Oh.' Was this the theft that Di had alluded to and of which Pam was innocent?

'But the snuff box wasn't there,' Edith said. 'I'm certain she had a hidden pocket under her overall. I insisted on calling the police but they never found it. Fortunately Aubrey believed me and Mrs Price was fired.'

This certainly explained Edith's distrust and dislike of Pam but it gave no reason to kill her. If anything, it would have been the other way around.

I took a deep breath. 'Have you any thoughts on what Pam was doing in the grounds in the middle of the night?'

Edith turned to me, her eyes sharp and cold. 'Why don't you come out with it and ask me if I killed her? Detective Inspector Mallory has.'

Edith was intimidating at the best of times and I felt myself shrink before her gaze.

'I thought no such thing,' I protested.

'I went to the chapel,' Edith said simply.

'The chapel?' I frowned. 'Is there a chapel?' My mother had never mentioned one to me.

'It's in the woods beyond the ha-ha,' said Edith. 'The bell tower is still standing and a few walls, but the roof has gone and the trees have done the rest. A stray bomb caught it when the Germans were bombing Plymouth during the war.'

'Where exactly is this chapel?'

'A quarter of a mile past the ornamental lake,' said Edith. 'It's not easy to find. The path is overgrown unless you take the green lane from the village. It dead-ends at the wood.'

'Have we ever ridden that way?' I didn't think so.

'It's not a loop and I'm not fond of there-and-back rides,' said Edith. 'They can be so dreary.' She reached into her coat pocket and pulled out a mobile phone with a leopard-spot case.

I gasped. 'Where did you find it?'

'It was in the font,' said Edith. 'I forgot to give it to Mallory.'

Mallory had been desperate to get his hands on Pam's phone. Now we would find out who had called her that fateful night. I tried to power it up but the battery was flat. 'How many people know about the chapel?'

'Good heavens, pet,' said Edith. 'It was built in 1340 so I

would say quite a few. Now, it's been lovely talking to you but I'm tired now.'

Edith stood up, our conversation clearly over.

'Mallory will be pleased with this,' I said, holding the mobile. 'Thank you.'

Edith rolled her eyes. 'Why can't we have Shawn back?' She stared straight into my eyes. 'Are you getting wed?'

My stomach turned over. 'To Shawn?'

Edith nodded. 'I've known Shawn since he was born,' she said. 'I think I know you too, Katherine. Love is a strange thing. You don't have to have shared interests to make a success of marriage, and passion soon fades, but you need four very important things. To be best friends, to laugh together, to be able to take your partner anywhere without feeling embarrassed and . . .' she paused, then lowered her voice '. . . and have fun in bed.'

'Edith!' I feigned shock.

'Goodness!' Edith chuckled. 'We were all young once.'

'Is that what you had with your husband?'

She thought for a moment. 'Three out of the four, and I won't tell you which of the four was missing.'

She offered me her arm. We made our way back up the hill before parting ways.

I didn't say a word as she got into the Land Rover and started the engine. Nor was I surprised when she didn't drive back to the Hall but in the opposite direction.

I stood there for a moment with Pam's mobile phone in my hand. Pam might have been killed in the chapel, but that didn't explain how she'd got to the ha-ha.

I slipped the phone into my pocket and returned to my Golf. Quickly, I called Lavinia to tell her that I'd found Edith and she was safe.

When I got to the gatehouse a Speedy Cab taxi was parked outside and Di was in the driver's seat.

She joined me at the front door, carrier bag in hand, but she wasn't smiling.

'Thank you for bringing Barbie,' I said. 'I see you have wheels.'

'Perk of the new job.' Di looked serious. 'Can I talk to you for a moment?'

I unlocked the door, the alarm beeped and I dashed on ahead to turn it off.

I took off my coat. 'Drink?'

'No, thanks.'

'Is everything okay?'

'No,' said Di. 'I don't know how to say this, so I'll just say it.'

My heart started to thump. 'What's wrong?'

Di's eyes searched mine. 'I took a closer look at Barbie, Kat.' She hesitated. 'I'm obviously not the expert here but I do know a little bit about jewellery.' She hesitated again. 'That emerald is a fake.'

Chapter Twenty-nine

Di was furious. 'You knew all the time!'

'It wasn't like that—'

'Jesus, Kat,' Di fumed. 'I felt accused of everything under the sun. Fiona Reynolds has been on my back. Someone's been shoplifting and, apparently, they think it's me. You made me feel like crap. I can't believe you didn't tell me. I thought we were friends.'

'We are friends,' I insisted. 'I didn't tell you because I kept hoping the original stone would turn up.'

Her face was flushed.

'Well, obviously it hasn't, has it?' Di exclaimed. 'Maybe there never was a real emerald.'

'Of course there was,' I replied. 'The stone was switched when the doll was stolen.' Whatever suspicions I'd had about my friend's involvement had vanished. I felt wretched. 'I'm truly sorry, Di. I never suspected you. Ever.'

Di regarded me with disappointment. It was a lie, and she knew it.

'And you're not cancelling the gala?' She was incredulous. 'You're seriously auctioning a fake?'

'No,' I said. 'I've already decided I'm going to donate one of my own dolls. It's just not common knowledge yet.'

There was a knock on the door and Marion stepped inside. Di and I had been so caught up in our argument that neither of us had heard her car arrive. Right now, Marion was the last person I wanted to see. With a superhuman effort, I made the introductions.

'I'm sure we've met before,' said Di, suddenly.

'Everyone says that, don't they, Kat?' Marion smiled. 'And as I tell everyone who asks, it's usually my husband they recognise rather than me.'

Recalling Edith's comment about Marion's mother, I said, 'Perhaps you saw each other at Sunny Hill Lodge.' It was a long shot but I was curious to see what Marion would say.

Di frowned. 'No, I don't think so.'

'That's the expensive nursing home, isn't it?' said Marion. 'Beautiful Georgian house?'

'Expensive, yes, that's the one,' Di muttered.

Marion shook her head. 'Ryan and I found it was cheaper to pay for carers to come in three times a day.' She gestured outside the gatehouse. 'I only stopped by because I wanted to talk to Speedy Cabs about this Friday's gala. Do you know where the driver is?'

'It's me,' said Di. 'I'm the driver.'

Marion's eyes widened. 'Didn't you just say you worked at the Emporium?'

'I'm doing a bit of moonlighting,' said Di.

'Will you be driving on Friday evening?' Marion said.

'I don't know yet,' Di replied. 'A lot of regulars want the work. They expect big tips! Speaking of work, I need to go. I don't want to get fired during my first week.'

As Di left the gatehouse, she turned to me with a hand gesture to call her and mouthed, 'Important.'

I gave a nod.

Marion picked up the doll. 'Ryan's right,' she said. 'Only an expert would know this stone was fake.'

'Marion, I know this isn't what you want but I've got the perfect solution.' I marched over to a shelf and brought down one of my favourite dolls. 'This is a rare Émile Jumeau. She's French and was made in 1880.'

I waited for the fallout, but Marion didn't say a word.

'I know my mother can make an elaborate green ballgown for her,' I went on. 'She's brilliant with a needle.'

When Marion still didn't speak, I said, 'I thought this would be a good solution.'

She bit her lip. 'Ryan won't agree to that. I'm completely on your side, Kat. I just don't know what to do.'

Her eyes brimmed with tears. I let her run on about how difficult it was living with Ryan. 'It was a huge mistake to come back here. Never go back, that's what they say, don't they? But I had to see Mum. I wanted to spend these last few months with her. I thought working for his lordship and organising this gala would give Ryan something to do, make him happy but . . .'

'I'm sorry.'

'I'm afraid . . . I'm afraid we'll be moving on after this. Ryan hates England. He complains of the cold all the time.

And the rain. I don't think . . .' she gulped '. . . I don't think our marriage will stand this and you seem to be the only person I can talk to.'

I felt uncomfortable and struggled for something to say. 'Do you want a cup of tea?'

'I don't have time. Sorry. Please forget I said any of that. How unprofessional of me!' Marion straightened her shoulders. 'But the show must go on, mustn't it?'

'Yes,' I said. 'But with a different doll.'

Marion gave a heavy sigh. 'All right. I'll try to make Ryan agree.'

'Thank you.' I felt an overwhelming sense of relief.

'In return, can I ask you a favour? I promise it'll only take half an hour.'

'It depends on what it is,' I said cautiously.

'Ryan wants me to go to the storage unit to pick up the champagne this evening. Six cases of Veuve Clicquot. He wants it all in place for the morning. I also need to collect our emergency coupes and flutes.' She smiled. 'There are always breakages. What do you prefer when you drink champagne? A coupe or a flute?'

'I haven't really thought about it,' I said.

'Did you know that the coupe was modelled after Marie Antoinette's breasts?'

I laughed. 'No. But I'll definitely remember.'

I also remembered that Marion had said the storage unit was quite far away, but when I reminded her she rolled her eyes. 'You forget. We lived in LA. Anything further than five miles was considered far because it took an hour to get there in traffic. You mentioned that you were looking for a new storage unit. You can see what you think. I swear we'll be back within the hour.'

'Okay,' I said. 'Just let me get my coat, send off a couple of texts and quickly use the loo.'

I left Marion admiring the Jumeau doll and heard her say, 'Maybe she *is* classier. I always thought Barbie was a bit over the top.'

I took Pam's mobile out of my pocket and plugged it into my charger in the kitchen, then sent Mallory a text from my own phone to say that Edith had found Pam's mobile and to ask her for details.

Marion was waiting for me at the door. I set the alarm and we left.

She seemed to have cheered up as we drove away in her Land Cruiser and regaled me with stories about Ryan's failed Hollywood career and how his one big scene in *Troy* with Brad Pitt had ended in disaster when Ryan got food poisoning. 'As the cameras were rolling!' She laughed. 'I've never seen anyone run off a set so fast.'

I found Marion easy to talk to. I could see why she was so successful at her job. But the more I listened, the more I sensed cracks in their marriage. Neither of us brought up the subject of Harriet Bone or Pam Price and for that I was glad. I was also relieved that she seemed to have accepted the Jumeau solution. Even though I still had to break the awful news to Cathy White, I felt marginally better, and at least she wouldn't be out of pocket, thanks to my insurance policy. I was positive she'd have one of her own, too.

We turned off the A38 and entered the outskirts of North Brent. I didn't know the village well. In the 1930s the Great Western Railway criss-crossed Devon and Cornwall with a gazillion little single-track lines. It stopped at places with names like Staverton Halt, Garra Bridge and Hope Cove. Some stations were nothing more than a plank of wood serving as the platform and a tiny signal box surrounded by miles of farmland. Now the former ticket offices had been turned into second homes or Airbnbs and the tracks left as grassy rides or cycle paths.

Marion drove along the old high street, which was lined with cottages very similar to those in Little Dipperton. We entered a housing estate, and she wove through a maze of residential streets decorated with lights, inflatable reindeer and life-size Father Christmases anchored to roofs with ropes. It all seemed very cheerful in the dark. I wondered how it would look in daylight.

At the end of the estate, the road went downhill in more ways than one. It was full of potholes the size of craters. The streetlights that hadn't been vandalised flickered with yellow lights and all but one fizzled out as we came to the end of the road and stopped in front of two opposing banks of up-and-over garages.

If one of those garages was the Cartwrights' storage unit, no wonder it was cheap.

Our headlights picked out a rusted barbed-wire fence and litter, and a steep railway embankment that stretched into the darkness above. The old single tracks might have vanished, but I knew those would be the mainline tracks from Penzance to London's Paddington station.

Marion switched off the engine but made no move to get out of the car.

I felt an irrational twinge of anxiety.

'I may as well tell you everything,' said Marion. 'This used to be a council estate and it's where I grew up.' She pointed to a just visible terrace of boarded-up houses covered with graffiti, and even though snow lay on the ground, it couldn't hide abandoned crates, oil drums and rubble.

I looked at the desolate wasteland in the eerie, yellow-lit darkness.

'They're going to be demolished,' said Marion. 'There are talks of building an industrial estate or putting up new houses, but who would want to live so close to the Inter-City railway line? I had to, and every night it sounded like a tank was going to break into my bedroom. Even the walls used to shake.'

'My London flat is next to the Putney tube station,' I said, trying to quell a rising sense that something was off. 'I know what you mean.'

Marion stared at her childhood home. She seemed lost in a memory. 'My mother was first in line to sell the house. She wanted the cash. Not that there was much left after paying off all her debts. Slot machines were her favourite way of spending what money she got from her unemployment benefit. Her brother, my uncle, lived next door. He gave her his garage and told her to keep them both,' Marion went on. 'They can't develop the land without buying them out. They're mine now. I'll wait for the right price and sell. It's not as if Ryan and I need the money.' She gave a heavy sigh. 'I didn't like my mother very much.'

'Mothers can be a challenge sometimes,' I said, hoping to lighten the conversation. Marion's mood was worrying me. 'I can understand how you must have felt.'

Marion turned to me. 'I don't think so,' she said quietly. 'My mother doesn't remember which man was my father. And, frankly, I haven't got a clue. I couldn't wait to get out. I envy your relationship with Iris. Mine just didn't care about me. When I was eighteen, I ran away to make my fortune in Hollywood. And the rest, as they say, is history.'

'That must have been tough,' was all I managed.

Marion sat back in her seat and pulled a face. 'I can't believe I just told you my life story. I'm glad I met you, Kat Stanford. Come on. Let's get this over and done with so we can go home. Maybe we should open a bottle of champagne!' She grinned. 'But let's not tell Ryan.'

Marion left her handbag on the driver's seat and got out. I put my tote over my shoulder and followed her.

She pulled out the green key fob that I'd seen hanging in the back porch and unlocked the padlock to one of the garages. I couldn't see a number. The door creaked and made an ear-splitting screech as she pulled it up and over and turned on the overhead fluorescent light. Puddles dotted the concrete floor.

Inside were dozens of cardboard boxes, all labelled. Some had 'VHS' and 'LPs' on the sides. More boxes sat on an orange crate and were covered with a removal blanket. I saw the Veuve Clicquot boxes and others marked 'Champagne coupes and flutes' and felt a weird sense of relief. A stupid part of me had wondered if she had lured me there for some sinister reason but I must have been imagining it.

Marion pointed to the boxes. 'Mum's junk. Not worth much now unless you know of anyone who deals in records.'

'I might.'

'Auction stuff under the blankets – old lamps, useless pictures, you know,' she said, with a laugh. 'The kind you'd never hang on the wall but feel guilty for throwing away.'

At the back there was a pine chest of drawers, a toy chest and an old wardrobe. The furniture was stencilled with Beatrix Potter characters.

Marion saw me look. 'Those were mine. I'd hoped to give them to my kids but it wasn't to be.'

'As my mother says, what you've never had, you'll never miss,' I said lightly.

'She's right,' said Marion. 'Let's get cracking.'

After several trips back and forth to Marion's Land Cruiser, I had to part with my tote bag, which kept falling down my arm. I left it on the front seat of her car. Finally, we had finished.

'Oh, one more thing. The extension cords.' Marion pointed to a box in the corner where a mass of cables was spilling over the edge. 'The ballroom just doesn't have enough sockets.'

'You think of everything.'

'We've been doing this a very long time.' A mobile pinged with a text. I knew it wasn't mine. 'Oh, damn.' She pulled hers out of a pocket. 'I've got to take this. Can you get that last box?'

I headed to the back of the garage but the moment I picked up the box, there was a roar of metal and a clang followed by a click.

'Hey!' I shrieked, and ran to the door. 'Marion! Hello?' I screamed her name again but then, to my horror, I heard her car engine start and pull away.

I had left my tote bag and my mobile in Marion's car. No one knew I was there. Di was working tonight. My mother wasn't expecting me and Shawn wanted to take a break in our relationship.

I was trapped.

Chapter Thirty

It took a few moments for everything to sink in. Surely Marion wasn't going to leave me here. No, there had to have been a misunderstanding. A mistake. Was this to do with the gala and, if so, how would Marion explain a missing MC and auctioneer?

Unless she and Ryan weren't planning to be at the gala.

I had to find a way out.

Rattling the garage door was useless. It was shut and locked. But not all the garages, especially those that were warped, had appeared locked to me.

I looked up.

The breeze-block divider wall did not reach the apex of the roof. There was a space in between. I felt certain I could squeeze through it and drop down into the adjacent bay.

I dragged the chest of drawers to the wall and clambered on top but the opening was still out of reach. Jumping down, I searched for one of the boxes that could hold my weight. Most proved to contain old saucepans, plastic kitchen utensils and stuffed toys. In the end I found a child's nursery chair behind a stack of lampshades. I set it on the chest of drawers.

It worked.

I hoisted myself up onto the wall and was able to peer into the neighbouring bay. It was surprisingly neat. There was a car under a tarpaulin and a spotlessly clean workbench with three side drawers standing against the rear wall. An array of lights and magnifying glasses sat on top. A portable space heater and a high stool nested underneath the bench.

For a moment I tried to make sense of what I could see. My heart skipped a beat. At the edge of the tarpaulin, I could see peppermint-green paintwork. It was the Ford Fiesta.

There had been two keys hanging from the green fob in Marion's kitchen, which must have belonged to these two garages.

I didn't hesitate. I heaved myself over and dropped down onto the concrete floor.

The mysterious Oliver had been described as tall, with wavy grey hair, a moustache and heavy-rimmed glasses. I was an idiot. It must have been Marion all the time. She must have been wearing a disguise.

'Oliver' had been watching the Emporium for weeks. But how would 'he' have known when I wouldn't be there? I was certain now that the phone call asking me to meet Shawn in the car park had come from Marion. I just hadn't recognised her voice, and why would I have done? She was an actress.

I stared at the workbench, my mind in overdrive.

I opened the first drawer and went very still.

It was full of professional jewellers' tools.

The pieces of the puzzle were starting to fall into place.

Marion had stolen Emerald Barbie and switched the stone.

A small fridge stood in the corner. I opened the door, not surprised to find a hidden safe with a high-tech locking system. I felt a surge of hope. Perhaps the emerald was still here.

An Inter-City 125 sounded its horn and thundered by, shaking the foundations. Marion hadn't lied about that.

Emerald Barbie had been returned the following morning, early enough for Pam to have disabled the alarm and for someone to have slipped in unobserved.

The UPS man. That was it! And I bet it was Ryan in the driver's seat. Pam had said she'd sent him away but he must have come back, waited for the right moment, and returned the doll.

But then I took in the full meaning of my discovery. The Cartwrights' enterprise was a serious and highly skilled operation. Switching the emerald was not a one-off affair.

I thought of Harriet's necklace and the *Octavia Royale*. Marion must have been on that same cruise in the Mediterranean. She'd even had the gall to show her own pearl and diamond necklace to Mallory! Timothy Bone had mentioned that they'd had the necklace authenticated onboard ship. It was a stretch, but what if the Cartwrights had offered that service? Marion had told me that she and Ryan had both worked as crew but I'd assumed in the capacity of stewards. How else could Marion have switched the diamonds for zircons?

Harriet had said she'd recognised Marion and Marion had panicked, but I still couldn't work out how Harriet had ended up in the stumpery.

My heart began to thunder in my chest. Two deaths and now I knew everything. I knew far too much.

There wasn't a moment to lose. I had to escape.

In the corner of the garage was a tyre iron. I set to work on the old up-and-over door. It didn't take long to buckle and, although I couldn't pull it all the way up, I was able to lie flat and squeeze through the gap at the bottom.

Free, I rolled out onto the concrete apron. The place seemed more desolate than ever. I was completely alone.

And then I saw the headlights of an approaching car.

Marion was coming back.

Terrified, I started to run towards the terrace of derelict houses, but a barbed-wire fence stopped me at the boundary. I was caught in the car's headlights. I turned, defeated.

But it wasn't Marion. It was a Shogun, Ryan's Shogun, and he was alone.

He cut the engine and jumped out.

'Kat? Kat? Is that you?' Ryan's obvious surprise swiftly changed to concern. 'What's going on? Are you all right?'

I hesitated. Under the yellowing glare of the one working streetlight Ryan seemed confused. Surely he knew that Marion had locked me in the garage. Why else would I be here? Why was he here without her?

A brief flash of pure fear passed through me. What if Ryan had come to finish off what Marion had started?

But then I had an idea. Ryan didn't know I'd discovered

the Ford Fiesta, the jewellers' tools and, most incriminating of all, the hidden safe.

'Where's Marion?' I demanded.

Ryan didn't answer.

'What are you doing here?'

Still no answer. Ryan seemed frozen to the spot. He looked over his shoulder. He seemed nervous. And then I saw the Land Cruiser returning. Marion was driving very fast. I looked at Ryan, who seemed even more jittery, which made me scared. Why had they come in two cars?

The Land Cruiser skidded to a halt just feet away from where I stood. Marion flung open the door and jumped out. She was livid.

They say that attack is the best form of defence.

'What the hell is going on, Marion?' I shouted. 'Why did you lock me in the garage?'

'Lock you in the garage?' Marion glared at her husband. 'Nonsense. Isn't that nonsense, Ryan? It was a misunderstanding.'

'Yes,' Ryan echoed. 'A misunderstanding. The door has a faulty mechanism, right, babe? But it looks like . . .' He paused. I could almost see his brain trying to work out the obvious that not only had I been locked in but that I'd got out. 'You managed to get out anyway.'

Maybe Ryan *hadn't* known, and if he hadn't, then why had he come out here alone?

'Yes,' Marion said slowly. 'You sure did.' I followed her gaze to where the yellowing light seemed to spotlight the garage door where I'd made my escape.

'Go back to your car, Ryan,' said Marion, calmly. 'I'll deal with this.'

Ryan didn't answer but he also didn't move.

'She knows,' Marion said. 'She knows everything, you idiot. Look.' She jabbed a finger at the buckled garage door and the gap beneath.

I tried to keep my head. 'That's how I got out.'

'That's how she got out,' Ryan echoed.

'I know that. But she wasn't in that garage!' In that split second I could tell it was Marion who was in charge and that Ryan wasn't the high-maintenance husband she had made him out to be. Not only that, he seemed afraid of her.

'I honestly don't know what's going on,' I lied.

'You might be clever but you're a terrible actress,' said Marion. 'You left your mobile in my car. Your friend Di sent you a text.'

'Okay,' I said. 'She's my friend. We work together. We often exchange text messages.' I thought of Di as she left the gatehouse, gesturing for me to call her. What had she been going to say?

'Let's all just go home,' said Ryan.

'Oh, my God, Ryan!' Marion said, exasperated. 'Get back in the car. I'll handle it. As usual.' She thought for a moment. 'Why didn't you tell me you were picking up the champagne this evening?'

'I thought I mentioned it,' Ryan stammered.

A flicker of suspicion crossed Marion's features. Her eyes narrowed, then grew hard. 'We'll talk later.'

Still Ryan didn't move. 'If you do this, it's over between us.'

'I doubt it,' Marion sneered. 'You'll never leave me.'

What was happening here? Was Ryan Marion's partner in crime or not? And then I saw it, shielded by the hem of his Barbour jacket: Ryan's mobile phone. He was recording everything.

Marion withdrew a hand-sized metal object from her coat pocket. I couldn't see what it was, but from the look on Ryan's face, it wasn't good.

'Marion, don't,' Ryan pleaded. 'I told you I never wanted anyone to get hurt.'

Ryan looked me straight in the eye and gave an imperceptible nod towards his phone that was out of Marion's line of sight. Yes, it looked like he was recording the conversation. Was he encouraging me to ask questions?

'The woman in the shepherd's hut,' Ryan said. 'And then Pam—'

'Shut up,' snapped Marion.

'You killed Harriet Bone,' I blurted out. 'I saw her necklace, Marion. You replaced the diamonds with zircons.'

Ryan gave me an encouraging nod. But what if I was wrong? Maybe Ryan was just finding out how much I knew – in which case I'd walked straight into a trap. Two against one. I didn't stand a chance.

Marion gave a heavy sigh. 'Ryan and I had a nice little thing going onboard ship.'

'You did, not me,' Ryan said. 'It was your idea.'

'We offered a lovely authentication service for tourists,' Marion said. 'It was an easy switch. But then Glenn – he was the head of security – got suspicious.'

It was my turn to be confused until I remembered the article about the head of security falling overboard and that Timothy and Harriet had been on that very same cruise.

'Harriet was on deck that night,' said Marion, as if reading my mind. 'She was the one who saw it happen.'

'I wasn't there,' Ryan added quickly. 'I was serving at the captain's table.'

'I know you weren't there, Ryan,' Marion said wearily. 'You're never there. You're such a loser that I bet you won't even turn up to your own funeral.'

I needed to throw doubt into the mix. Harriet hadn't been too concerned about the necklace: she had just wanted to prove her mother-in-law wrong. I was also pretty sure that she hadn't seen Marion on deck that night or she would have said something to her husband, let alone the authorities. I might still be able to get out of this. The more Marion believed I didn't know anything, the higher the chance she'd let me go.

'How could you be certain that Harriet had seen you on deck that night?' I said suddenly. 'I spoke to her husband, and he didn't mention anything about foul play being suspected on that cruise. He was upset because Harriet had won the cruise in a contest, and they weren't eligible for a refund and had to pay their way home. Nothing more.'

'I told you she hadn't seen you, babe,' Ryan put in.

Marion hesitated, then shook her head. 'No. She saw me. She recognised me. Why else would she stand outside my window on Sunday night and scream that she knew who I was?'

'Harriet must have recognised you in *Gladiator*,' I said. 'My mother and Delia watched the movie and saw you too, only your name didn't come up in the credits.'

'That's because her stage name was Marni Matthews,' said Ryan, helpfully.

'Ah.' I nodded. 'Your mother was called Rose, wasn't she?'

But Marion wasn't listening. 'No. You're wrong. Harriet knew who I was. I know she was trying to blackmail me.'

It was just as Mum and I had suspected. Harriet had been looking for Delia, believing that she was Krystalle Storm.

Ryan looked at me again and, yet again, held tightly on to his mobile phone.

'Why am I wrong, Marion?' I said. 'Help me understand.'

'After the yelling outside my bedroom window, I got dressed—'

'I was fast asleep and—'

'And went to pay her a call.' Marion made a weird gulping sound, half gasp half laugh. 'At first she seemed confused to see me. When I asked her why she was standing outside my window, shouting, she just burst out laughing.' Marion frowned. 'Then she said something about me trying to throw her off the scent by giving some clothes to Delia. I had no idea what she was talking about.'

Of course! Harriet must have been very confused. She would never have thought Marion was Krystalle Storm because it had been Delia who had been wearing the arsenic-laced gloves and scarf.

'Then she gave me a hard time about fanfiction,' Marion went on, 'whatever that is, and flew into a rage when I wouldn't admit I was that romance writer, Krystalle Storm.'

I seized on this extraordinary turn of events. 'But don't you see? Harriet really *did* think you were Krystalle Storm. It's got nothing to do with the pearl necklace and the *Octavia Royale.*'

Marion made that weird noise again. 'I thought, okay. If she wants me to be Krystalle Storm, then that's who I'll be.'

'But how did you lure her to the stumpery?' I asked.

'I wasn't there,' Ryan said yet again.

'Once I admitted I was Krystalle Storm, Harriet changed. She became very excited. It was quite sweet, really.' Marion sounded incredulous. 'She believed me when I blamed my agent for everything. She couldn't stop apologising for her rudeness.'

Poor Harriet.

'When Harriet wanted to prove just how much she loved my books and mentioned the stumpery, well,' Marion shrugged, 'the rest, as they say, is history.'

The irony wasn't lost on me. No wonder Marion had freaked out when Mum had accused her of being Krystalle Storm during the police investigation.

'And Harriet just fell from the lookout,' I said firmly. 'I think we can all agree that it was a terrible accident. We can go home and forget this ever happened.' I deliberately avoided the topic of Pam, and when I remembered that Mallory had said the puncture wounds in both victims weren't common knowledge, I added, 'I don't know why the police suspect foul play. But, as we all know, the police aren't perfect. They can make mistakes.'

Marion gave another heavy sigh. 'We could have done, but thanks to Ryan's *mistake* with Pam, I'm afraid it's too late for that.'

'I just carried her, that's all. I didn't kill her,' Ryan whined.

'But who dumps a body in a ditch?' Marion sneered. 'You didn't even try to bury her.'

All hope vanished that I could have talked my way out of this.

'It was you who pushed her off the bell tower.' Ryan was still whining.

'And she couldn't climb up there quick enough,' said Marion. 'It's funny how an envelope filled with the promise of oodles of cash can make even the laziest of people get moving. And I didn't touch her – not really.'

Marion stepped so close to me I could smell coffee on her breath. 'I had no idea she was Lance's mother. How could I have connected him with that awful woman? Let me tell you, I did Lance a favour. Now he can be free to follow his dream.'

'I still don't understand what Pam has to do with any of this,' I said.

Marion rolled her eyes. 'Seriously? I'd been watching your area ever since Emerald Barbie appeared on the scene. I will say that she was a challenge to snatch but, luckily, with a little help from poor Annie, the carol singers and a quick call to your friend Di, it worked out perfectly.'

I had to keep her talking for Ryan's recording.

'I already know that you're Oliver,' I said. 'And I'm impressed with how you pulled it all off.'

Marion smirked. 'Nanny-cams are amazing, aren't they?

I popped a little camera in a sprig of holly and wedged it on the wall light opposite your space. It was fun watching the comings and goings from the café, enjoying a leisurely cappuccino. You're a creature of habit, Kat. I just had to wait for the perfect moment. Your friend certainly takes a lot of phone calls, and when she does, she always leaves her post. Silly girl.'

'But why hurt Pam?' I said. 'She wasn't even there when you stole Emerald Barbie. She was cleaning the Gents.'

'Pam was there when Ryan put our Barbie back,' said Marion.

'Ah.' I nodded. 'Ryan was the UPS delivery guy. You knew that Pam got to work early and that Nigel wasn't there until eight thirty. The alarm had already been disabled so it was easy to sneak in. Although he got the colour of the van wrong. It should have been brown.'

'That's my husband for you.' Marion shot Ryan a look of contempt. 'He thought Pam saw him put the doll back.'

'She didn't,' I said. 'She would have told me.'

'Unfortunately Ryan also put Barbie on the wrong shelf and I had to go and fix yet another of his mistakes.' She gave yet another heavy sigh. 'I don't think Pam saw me but I couldn't take that risk. Oh, and by the way, she's been filching bits and pieces for weeks. She hides them in her box of tissues on the cleaning trolley. So, to be honest, she's no great loss.'

I pulled my coat closer. I was starting to shiver from a mixture of cold and nerves.

'You're getting cold.' Marion checked her watch. 'It's time to go anyway. I wouldn't want you to miss your train to London.'

'Marion! Stop!' Ryan's voice sounded different. Scared.

Pure fear coursed through my body again.

Marion pointed to the steep embankment. 'Shall we go?'

I had to think of something. 'Mallory has Pam's mobile.' It was a lie. Pam's mobile was being charged in my gatehouse.

'What?' Marion was furious.

'I'm afraid Ryan left it in the font,' I said. 'Your call to ask her to meet you at the old chapel will be on there.'

Marion laughed. 'You think I'd use my own phone?' Her mood switched to one of annoyance. 'I thought you told me you'd thrown it in the river.'

'Sorry,' Ryan mumbled.

'You drove Pam's Polo to Morrisons,' I said. 'It was caught on CCTV.' And then I guessed: 'You took a taxi home and it was Di who picked you up, wasn't it? I'm surprised you didn't recognise her.'

'I'll have to deal with her later,' said Marion. 'I can't take any chances, dear. She knew my mother was at Sunny Hill Lodge and that I was selling the Ford Fiesta. That's enough for me. I'm always very careful, never sloppy.'

'But Di didn't know your mother was there,' I insisted. 'I asked her.'

'What does it matter now?' Marion pointed to the steep railway embankment. 'Come along, Kat. I don't want you to miss your train.'

Chapter Thirty-one

I dug my heels in. 'I'm not going anywhere.'

Quick as a flash, I felt a piercing pain shoot through my arm. I jumped back and cried out. Marion was holding a compass divider in her hand. My heart dropped. So this was her weapon of choice. She'd pushed Harriet off the lookout and Pam off the bell tower – and, most likely, a man off a cruise ship. And now it was my turn.

'You used that on Harriet and Pam,' I whispered.

'I was bullied at school, you know,' said Marion. 'Taunted because I lived in a rough neighbourhood and my mum entertained gentleman callers. That's what she liked to call them. I had to protect myself, you understand.' She brandished the compass divider.

'Marion. You don't have to do this.' I cried out in pain again as she darted in and stabbed my thigh.

'Do you want Ryan to carry you up there? Because he will,' said Marion, adding, with malice, 'He works out, don't you, darling?'

Ryan stood there, doing nothing.

Marion jabbed the needle into my arm again. For something so small, it really hurt.

I started to climb the embankment. My legs felt like lead. I was so terrified that with every step I stumbled. Adrenalin coursed through my veins but, rather than fight or flee, I felt numb. Marion was so much taller and stronger than me.

I stopped to catch my breath and play for time. Mallory must have got my text. Wouldn't he be trying to call me? Wouldn't he wonder where I was? I looked down and saw that Ryan was heading back to his car. Hope surged. Maybe he'd go and get help.

'Ryan's recorded everything. You know that, don't you?' I said. 'He's going to betray you.'

'He'll never leave me,' said Marion, simply. 'He doesn't have the guts.'

'The gala,' I said desperately. 'How are you going to explain my disappearance?'

'Oh, that's easy,' said Marion. 'You and Shawn have broken up and you're heartbroken. Oh, yes, I know about that. I have my eyes and ears everywhere. Delia really has a bigger mouth than me.' She laughed. 'But then came the humiliating discovery that the emerald was a fake and the damage to your reputation was too much for you to bear.'

'You still have the emerald, don't you?' I said. 'It's in the safe.'

'You're not just a pretty face,' said Marion. 'And some other stones besides and, of course, the cash. The problem with the über-rich is that they get caught up in acquiring stuff. So much greed it makes you puke. They have safe-loads of jewellery that they rarely wear. It was all so easy to switch the stones. Ryan moved them along to his contacts and, hey, no one knew until it was too late.'

Marion was right. I'd seen it myself. It was the acquisition and prestige that went with bidding on high-end jewellery that, after being worn for a special occasion, was rarely looked at closely a second time. Diamonds were the easiest to switch, but a true emerald needed flaws to be authentic and that was Marion's mistake.

'I must admit there was nothing worth switching at Honeychurch Hall, which was very disappointing,' Marion went on. 'Family heirlooms are difficult. The stones have unique settings, and I don't have the time or the inclination to fiddle with all that detail. No. We're going to cut our losses and get out.' She looked at her watch. 'Quite soon, actually.'

'Please don't do this,' I begged.

'You brought it on yourself.' She looked at me with sadness in her eyes. 'I think we could have been good friends.'

'We still can be!'

'I'm sorry, Kat,' said Marion. 'Truly I am.'

'And the celebrity guest?' I said. 'What about that?'

Marion laughed. 'You're so gullible!'

It was exactly as I had feared. 'You never intended to be here for the gala, did you?'

'Fifty grand in cash from ticket sales and an emerald worth thousands and thousands of pounds? What do you think?' Marion studied me with curiosity. 'Although, in fairness, the emerald wasn't in the original plan. But when you told us about it, how could we resist it?'

I knew Marion would never let me go now.

I had to think of something. Think, Kat, think!

'So why did Ryan come back here on his own?' I said urgently.

Marion faltered. 'He just came to pick up the champagne. He didn't know I'd already got it. That's all. Yes. He came for the champagne.'

I heard a car start. It was the Shogun.

'Look!' I cried. 'Ryan is leaving!'

Marion glanced over her shoulder. Sure enough, Ryan sped away.

When her eyes met mine again, I saw something I'd never seen before, a flash of disbelief, then despair, and then it was gone.

We'd reached the top of the embankment and I looked down into the cutting at the train tracks so far below. There was the click and whistle of electricity that heralded an approaching train. I was rigid with terror.

'Next one,' Marion said, in my ear. I felt the needle press against my neck. 'Wrong direction.'

'Why are you doing this?'

'Because I can,' she said. 'The thing is, I really love Ryan despite his flaws. Have you ever loved someone and known they were a total loser, but you kept hoping that they'd shape up one day? I've been with him for almost thirty years so you could say I'm invested. No kids. No real home, although the villa in the Med is quite nice but we're rarely there. Just chasing dreams and then, *pouf*, you wake up and you're fifty years old – oh, yes, I know. I don't look fifty, do I?'

And then we both heard them. Police sirens. Marion froze.

We looked back and saw a series of flashing blue lights snaking through the housing estate below. A horn blasted twice to herald an approaching train.

And then, to my horror, Marion took three big strides and threw herself off the embankment.

Chapter Thirty-two

'Two shattered legs, broken ribs and a punctured lung,' said Mallory the next morning, as we sat in Mum's kitchen with Di. 'But Marion will live.'

It turned out that it had been Di who had raised the alarm when I hadn't replied to her text, which said she had picked Marion up from the Morrisons car park and taken her to North Brent. Ryan was waiting there in an empty pub car park.

Worried, Di had gone back to the gatehouse where my car was parked outside but I wasn't there. Mallory had received my text about Pam's mobile being found in the font, and when Mum and Shawn said they hadn't seen me and couldn't reach me on the phone, they all knew something was wrong.

Calls to the Hall proved futile until Delia mentioned Marion had said she was going to fetch some cases of champagne from her storage unit.

Mallory took up the story. Yasmin Fletcher had been given the address of where she would pick up the Ford Fiesta after Christmas. 'I guessed that the garage and the storage unit were one and the same.'

When the police broke into both garages, they found the safe full of cash – presumably from the ticket sales – a pouch of zircons, Harriet's pearl necklace, and the emerald. There was also a list of buyers in Amsterdam that David Wynn was working through, a burner phone and two disguises – Oliver's outfit and a UPS uniform.

Di revealed that the taxi company had a 5 a.m. pick-up booked for the morning of the gala to Bristol airport. It was just as Marion had said. They were going to make a run for it.

'I know you recognised Marion that night in the Morrisons car park,' I said to Di. 'But why didn't she recognise you?'

'I was wearing a beanie and a scarf,' said Di. 'It was so cold. She didn't want to make conversation and neither did I.'

I frowned. 'One thing I find hard to believe is that you never saw her at Sunny Hill Lodge.'

Di shrugged. 'My mother's bed bound. I only visit her in her room.'

'And Marion, a.k.a. Marni Matthews, visited her mother just once,' I said. 'I wonder why?'

'I'll tell you why,' said Mallory. 'Marion admitted that she had hoped for a reconciliation of sorts with her mother but instead she was told the brutal truth that she'd never been wanted.'

'I always wanted you, darling,' Mum interjected.

'Thanks, Mum,' I said grimly. 'Something's been puzzling me. Why was Ryan recording our conversation on his mobile if they were both planning on doing a runner before the gala? He was practically feeding me the questions.'

Mallory grinned. 'Ryan wanted a divorce.'

Mum hooted with laughter. 'But . . . he always said he was never going to leave Marion.'

'He wanted to but it was too complicated,' said Mallory. 'He was born in California and they were married in California, where the divorce laws are legendary. Given their financial track record, it would have been messy to say the least. They had joint accounts. Everything was shared. He was looking for a way out.'

'I'd wondered why Ryan had come to the garages alone,' I said. 'He hadn't come to pick up the champagne. He'd come to get the emerald!'

'No wonder Marion attempted to take her own life,' Mum said. 'Maybe she really did love him after all.'

'Marion's original plan had been for them to pick up the emerald the night before the gala,' said Mallory. 'But Ryan was booked on the ferry from Plymouth to St Malo *tonight*.'

'I wondered why he was so flustered when he found me wandering around the forecourt but I couldn't be sure,' I said. 'He really hadn't known that Marion had locked me in. But then . . .' I swallowed hard '. . . if they had stuck to the original plan, they would have come back for the emerald together and . . . what would have happened to me?'

'And what about the Ford Fiesta?' Mum chipped in. 'Wasn't the buyer going there to collect it?'

Mallory looked into my eyes. 'I asked Marion that very question. She said that had Ryan not turned up and you had stayed trapped in the garage, she would have burned the garages down.'

'Fire.' I felt sick.

'But that didn't happen,' Mum said briskly, and changed the subject. 'So it sounds like Ryan really was trying to distance himself from Marion by recording your conversation.'

'He'd hoped it would give him a lighter sentence but . . .' Mallory began to chuckle '. . . unfortunately, he forgot to hit the record button.'

'Didn't I tell you Ryan Cartwright is all trousers and no mouth – or should I say brain?' Mum laughed.

As for Annie, when Mallory finally tracked her down she seemed frightened and, at first, pretended she didn't know what he was talking about. When Mallory commented on Annie's new clothes and pointed out that she still had the price tags attached, which could look bad for her, Annie admitted that a 'nice gentleman with a moustache' gave her fifty pounds in cash. All she had to do was walk in with the carol singers and pretend to faint when they sang 'God Rest Ye Merry, Gentlemen'.

'And that was when Marion called Di,' I said. 'Just as she tricked me with Shawn's bogus message to meet him outside.'

'She got Di's number from one of her business cards,' said Mallory. 'It was all perfectly timed.'

Mum raised her hand. 'Since Marion's mother died within a week of the pair of them starting work at the Hall, why did she keep up the pretence?'

'Ryan says they were hoping for a haul of Honeychurch heirlooms but the dowager countess kept following them around,' said Mallory. 'When Kat was given the Emerald Barbie for the gala, they changed their plan and went for a more ambitious prize.'

'So what happens to them now?' I asked.

'We have enough evidence to charge them both,' said Mallory. 'David Wynn is on the case and working closely with numerous international police entities to take a look at the Cartwrights' employment history and see what other gems they've switched.'

'So much for Hollywood dreams,' Mum said. 'Ryan was very good in *Gladiator*. Were they aspiring actors or was it all a big ruse?'

'Their acting aspirations were all true,' said Mallory. 'The Cartwrights hoped to find fame and fortune in Hollywood. They had a few walk-on roles but nothing ever seemed to pan out. As actors they knew how to play the part and they did it well. In Hollywood it's all about networking and who you know. By taking employment in celebrity homes, it gave them the chance to get closer to the fire. Let's face it, there are a lot of talented people out there. Getting noticed is often down to luck and being in the right place at the right time.'

'But where did the cruise ship fit in?' I asked.

'After the Cartwrights' stint in Hollywood, they started working on super-yachts and cruise ships,' said Mallory. 'That's how they gained access to Lady Lavinia's brother's jet-setting world.'

'Marion mentioned something about issuing authentication certificates,' I said.

'That's right,' said Mallory. 'They ran a pop-up luxury jewellery store on board the *Octavia Royale* where they offered the authentication service.'

'When Harriet asked me to value her necklace on the night of the staff party, Marion was there,' I said. 'She knew I'd identify the stones as zircons. She would have known that the authentication certificate would eventually be traced back to her.'

'But what happened with the head of security?' Mum asked. 'Did Marion cop to pushing him overboard?'

'She didn't,' Mallory said. 'But Ryan told us she'd done it. He told us that Marion was becoming increasingly paranoid and it was another reason he wanted out.'

'That's true,' I agreed. 'Marion was convinced that Harriet had seen her that night onboard ship. She was also positive that Pam had noticed her return the Barbie doll.'

'Ah, Pam Price.' Mallory nodded. 'Ironically, thanks to Marion, I can confirm that Pam was the shoplifter at the Emporium. We found hidden objects at the bottom of the boxes of tissues on her trolley and in her home.'

Di looked sheepish. 'I feel such a fool. I believed Pam's story about her innocence. I'm so gullible. So stupid.' She bit her lip and looked away. I knew she wasn't just talking about Pam, and it would seem Mallory did too.

'You did what you did because you wanted the best for your mother,' he said. 'I'm afraid there is little legally we can do about these loan sharks at the moment because you signed a contract. But I can confirm that they are now under surveillance.'

'Maybe I'll win the lottery,' Di whispered.

'And Lance?' I said. 'How's he holding up?'

'Obviously he's upset,' said Mallory, 'but at the same time, I think he feels he can finally do what he wants. We were able to match the burner-phone number with Pam's mobile that night. Marion did call Pam and she asked to meet at the abandoned chapel—'

'Which I didn't know existed,' I pointed out. 'Did you, Mum?'

Mum shook her head. 'I can't believe I didn't.'

'Marion discovered it when she was creating the maps for the guests,' said Mallory.

'But why would Pam go there in the first place?' Mum sounded puzzled. 'How silly.'

'Money,' I said.

Mum's eyes widened. 'You mean *blackmail*?'

I nodded. 'I think Pam saw through Oliver's disguise. She recognised Marion.'

Mallory gave a mischievous grin. 'Well, Marion does have a distinctive face . . .'

'Mouth, you mean,' Mum said, somewhat unkindly. 'Why did she pick a moustache? If she'd picked a beard her mouth would have been hidden behind all that fur.'

'Despite everything,' I said, 'I feel sorry for her.'

'Don't. She would have killed you, too,' Mallory said bluntly. 'The use of the compass divider was a little unusual. But it certainly had the desired effect. All it took was a little prick.'

'Speaking of which,' said Mum, all wide-eyed innocence, 'where's Shawn?'

I glared at her. 'He's working, Mum.'

'Shawn got a new lead on that case,' Mallory said, evidently sensing this must be a sensitive issue. 'It's a big break.'

'Well. Good,' Mum said. 'A big break is exactly what Kat needs.'

In many ways I was relieved that Shawn had gone away. As Harriet Bone had said, I needed to get my head straight. True, the Krystalle Storm identity crisis had, once again, been avoided but Shawn hadn't budged on his position with regard to our relationship.

'Well, it looks like the show will go on.' Mallory broke into my thoughts. 'But without the mystery guest.'

I was struck by a brilliant idea. 'Not necessarily,' I said slowly. 'Leave it with me.'

Chapter Thirty-three

The Christmas gala and silent auction were a huge success. The only no-shows were the Cartwrights, who were currently awaiting arraignment in cold cells.

The gourmet food and wine were incredible, the waiting staff top class, the live band magnificent and the ambience second to none. Lance did an excellent job and enjoyed himself so much that he admitted his mother had perhaps been right all along and maybe he might want to go to film school. It turned out that Pam had been squirrelling money away for that very purpose for some years. 'It would honour her memory,' he said, and confided that he was riddled with guilt. 'I understand now that she only wanted the best for me.'

Lavinia's friend Pansy from Pansy's Jamborees stepped in at the last minute to help with logistics, and we all pulled our weight to make the gala a success. Even Edith graced us with her presence, dressed in her finery and sparkling with Honeychurch heirlooms.

We learned that Edith's dizziness had been largely caused by an inner-ear problem and was easily treated. The diagnosis had been such a relief that she was back to her usual defiant self and had already applied for a new driving licence. However, her bouts of confusion still gave cause for alarm even though she insisted she'd been putting it on.

Delia's 'skin condition' was clearing up. Mum had finagled a way to grab the scarf and gloves when Delia wasn't looking and 'accidentally' spilled red wine on both. The beret, she destroyed.

I felt a pang of what I could only describe as jealousy when Di turned up with Mallory, who looked devastatingly attractive in black tie. Shawn was unable to come because of work 'pressure' and had given him his ticket. But when I went to greet them at the door, I noticed that Di was dressed in her beanie and scarf. Mallory had come by taxi and it so happened that Di had been his driver.

'I feel like Cinderella,' said Di, as she scanned the room, which was packed with revellers. 'But don't feel sorry for me. I brought it all on myself. You were right. Mum doesn't know where she is or even who I am. I've found her a lovely place overlooking the sea and, guess what, it's free! I threw myself on the mercy of the NHS and they were so nice. I wish I'd done it sooner. She'll be moving there after Christmas.'

Harry approached, looking so grown-up in black tie. He was already as tall as Lavinia even though he wasn't yet ten. He pointed to a set of double-doors at the far end of the room, his eyes alive with mischief. 'The reindeer are getting restless.'

I grinned. 'It's time.'

As I made my way to the podium, I struggled to control my nerves. This could either make or break the gala.

Mum and Delia hurried to the front, peering eagerly in the direction of the closed double-doors – framed with garlands of holly – which would shortly open to reveal our mystery guest.

I looked up to the minstrels' gallery and gave a thumbs-up to Lance to start rolling the camera and to the band to begin their welcoming drumroll.

A fanfare of trumpets prompted Rupert to do his bit and throw open the double-doors with great panache.

'May I introduce our mystery guest,' I said. 'He's come all the way from the North Pole.'

Eight donkeys wearing antlers, their harnesses covered with bells and tinsel, meandered in half-heartedly pulling a sleigh on runners. At the reins was Eric Pugsley, dressed in full Father Christmas gear, shouting, 'Ho, ho, ho.' Unfortunately, Eric had attempted to dye his jet-black eyebrows white and they were now a startling orange. Also, unfortunately, Eric seemed to have little control over his 'reindeer' who seemed far more interested in feasting on the table arrangements.

There was a moment of stunned silence and my heart dropped. These people had paid a fortune for a mystery guest and then my mother yelled, 'This is how we do things in the countryside! Merry Christmas!'

The whole room exploded with laughter, especially when Alfred, dressed as an elf, walked in with a bucket and shovel to clear up the odd donkey deposit.

Cameras flashed, the room erupted into a frenzy of applause and whistles. The donkeys got a standing ovation. When the noise died down I introduced Cathy White and thanked her for the generous donation of Emerald Barbie. Although we'd lost our after-dinner speaker, Lady Lavinia stepped in and gave a surprisingly good presentation on the plight of these lovable creatures throughout the world. She also announced the winners of the silent auction and the raffle, and seemed to enjoy herself.

It was only much later in the evening that I could finally relax and enjoy myself. Mallory appeared at my side holding two glasses of Veuve Clicquot champagne. 'For you,' he said, with a smile. 'Congratulations. You did an amazing job.' He leaned in and gave a low chuckle. 'What happened to Father Christmas's eyebrows? They're bright orange.'

Mum and Delia joined us but I noticed that Delia didn't look so happy. 'Eric Pugsley?' she said, with disgust. 'What kind of mystery guest do you call that?'

She scanned the room and waved her empty champagne glass. 'And who are these celebrities? I don't recognise any-one famous. Where's Kim Kardashian?'

'Oh, I don't know,' said Mallory, casually. 'I'm quite certain that Krystalle Storm is here somewhere among us.'

My stomach flipped.

'What? Where?' Delia gasped, and scanned the room again, which, despite the late hour, was still full of couples on the dance floor. 'Who? How do you know?'

Mum grabbed my arm to steady herself. Her nails dug into my flesh.

'I think Mallory's teasing,' I said quickly, as I remembered Shawn saying that Mallory was an excellent policeman. I tried to stay calm. I thought back to the uncomfortable scene in the mobile police unit when Mallory knew we were hiding something.

'Oh, please!' Delia wailed. 'Tell us, please!'

Mallory's twinkling eyes met mine. He grinned. 'To quote an oft-used line, I'm afraid I'm not at liberty to say.'

I felt a rush of gratitude. It was all I could do not to hug him.

'But she's here?' Delia persisted, scanning the room a third time. 'Iris? Who do you think it is?'

'Oh, who cares?' Mum said cheerfully. 'Let's all raise our glasses in a toast. Merry Christmas.'

'Merry Christmas,' we chorused.

'Yes,' said Mum. She added quietly, 'A *very* Merry Christmas to me.'

Acknowledgements

When people ask me where I find my ideas, I always reply that they are everywhere. They could come from a chance conversation overheard in a pub, a line read in a newspaper or some dastardly local in a nearby village who needs to be dealt with – figuratively speaking.

The seed for *A Killer Christmas at Honeychurch Hall* began when I found my original Sindy doll (1963, dressed in denim jeans, striped top, white sneakers and sporting a Jackie O hairstyle) in my storage unit and wondered how much she would be worth to a collector. Not much, as it turned out. But what about Sindy's rival, the buxom Barbie? Au contraire! In fact, in 2016, an original Barbie doll in mint condition (1959) was sold at auction for $27,450. And so the Barbie seed was sown. Full disclosure: as far as I know, Emerald Barbie only exists in the pages of this book and, for that matter, North Brent does not exist at all either.

However, the Christmas card with a photograph of a white hare in the snowy Monadhliath Mountains of Scotland does exist. It is one of many stunning images captured by the supremely talented wildlife photographer Heidi Crundwell. I hope she won't mind me using her beautiful image as my fictional videographer's calling card.

I'd like to thank my neighbour Cathy White for opening her beautiful woods for me and my dogs to roam. The bluebells this year were spectacular. As a gesture of my gratitude, Cathy has a cameo appearance in this latest adventure and, true to my word, she is neither victim nor villain.

For anyone astute enough to notice that the donkey in the story is named after me, thanks go to my friend Faustina Gilbey for gifting me Hannah, a delightful white donkey from the Donkey Sanctuary in Sidmouth, Devon. One of the fun things about modern technology is being able to watch Hannah on a webcam. I can tell you that she leads a far more interesting life than her namesake.

My heartfelt thanks also go to:

Major Crime Detective Inspector Steve Davies for sharing his vast knowledge of tactical weapons (along with a few links to video demonstrations). Although I opted for a gentler murder method, I feel I can now speak with authority on the pros and cons of a taser vs electric cow prod.

My wonderful boss of twenty-three years, Mark Davis, Chairman and CEO of Davis Elen Advertising in Los Angeles. I'm not sure what happened to my promise to only give you six months of my working life but here we are, all these years and books later. Thank you for your never-ending support and enthusiasm.

My wonderful agents, Dominick Abel and David Grossman. Thank you for taking such good care of me on both sides of the Atlantic. I can't believe I was finally able to meet Dominick in New York this summer for a much-belated gin and tonic. Covid-19 has a lot to answer for.

My incredible publishing team at Constable, with a special thank you to Krystyna Green, fellow canine enthusiast and dream editor, and the fabulous, sharp-eyed Hazel Orme.

My multi-talented VA, Krissy Lilljedhal, who keeps me on track. Did anyone seriously believe it was me doing all those amazing graphics on social media?

My family, who have always encouraged me to follow my dreams, with special thanks to my mum (who is a little like Iris Stanford) and much-missed dad for passing on his sense of humour, to my daughter, Sarah, who keeps me organised, and to my muses: the Hungarian Vizslas, Draco and Athena. Long may we roam the Devonshire countryside together.

No acknowledgement would be complete without thanking my kindred spirits in the writing community lifeboat: Rhys Bowen, Kate Carlisle, Elizabeth Duncan, Mark Durel, Carolyn Hart, Jenn McKinlay, Clare Langley-Hawthorne, Andra St. Ivanyi, Julian Unthank, Marty Wingate and Daryl Wood Gerber. I'm forever indebted to Claire Carmichael, my writing instructor at the UCLA Extension Writers' Program, from where my writing journey really began.

And now for a bittersweet nod to my dearest friend, Barbara Ballard aka Scout, who sadly passed away this summer. It was Barbara who penned my very first fan letter. As an insecure, debut author, I was chuffed to bits. Our email exchanges grew into a cherished friendship. I miss you.

Finally, I want to thank the libraries and bookstores for carrying my books and my wonderful readers for borrowing and buying them. Without you . . . my stories would still be in a drawer.